THIN
AIR

THIN AIR

A JESSICA SHAW THRILLER

LISA GRAY

Published by Thomas & Mercer, Seattle
www.apub.com

Amazon, the Amazon logo, and Thomas & Mercer are trademarks of Amazon.com, Inc., or its affiliates.

ISBN-13: 9781542093644 (hardcover)
ISBN-10: 1542093643 (hardcover)
ISBN-13: 9781477818305 (paperback)
ISBN-10: 1477818308 (paperback)

Cover design by Ghost Design

Printed in the United States of America

To my mum, for always believing in me

PROLOGUE

I park the car four streets away and walk the rest of the way. The house is conveniently situated at the end of the block, hidden in shadows, out of sight of prying eyes.

It's dark now, but I know in daylight the wood siding is the color of dried mud, and the paint hasn't been refreshed in years. At least, not since she moved in. I'm surprised to see the porch has been swept clean of fallen leaves and is empty save for a metal bucket with two pairs of outdoor boots—one adult size, one toddler size—next to the front door.

I pass the sign hammered into the front yard's overgrown lawn, warning the house is protected by Smith & Wesson, and I laugh quietly to myself in the darkness.

I know a gun isn't going to save her tonight.

I walk silently up the porch steps and see the curtains are drawn across the big front window, a flickering yellow glow escaping from a tiny gap where the material doesn't quite meet in the middle. As I approach the front door, I hear music playing softly inside. It's late, but I know she won't be asleep. I raise a gloved hand and knock on the door, the sound muffled under the soft leather.

She opens the door, and I have to admit she looks beautiful, backlit by the candles burning in the room behind her. The music is louder now, one of those depressing Seattle bands everyone listens to these days. Her eyes are glassy, as though she's drunk or high, and she looks at me, confused for a second.

Then she says, "I wondered when you'd show up. I guess you'd better come in."

I follow her into the living room, and she asks if I want a drink. I say nothing. She walks over to the bar cart anyway and fills a glass with red wine. She tops up her own glass, which is sitting on the coffee table on top of a tattered cardboard coaster from a local bar. I assume it's not her first bottle of the night.

She says, "Hey, what's with the gloves? Is it cold out tonight?"

I still say nothing.

She holds out the wineglass, but I make no move to take it from her.

"Suit yourself," she says and shrugs.

As she turns to put the glass next to her own on the table, I catch her full on the face with a powerful punch. She is stunned. She drops the glass. The red liquid soaks into the cream carpet. Blood streams from her nose, and she staggers. I deliver another blow, and this time, she goes down.

I'm on top of her quickly, knees pressing into her chest, the knife in my hand. I'm aware that my breathing has accelerated, but my hands are steady, and the cut to her throat is clean and precise. Her blood mixes with the merlot on the carpet, and I know she'll bleed out in minutes, that the job is done.

But I'm unprepared for the rage that follows, the furious pumping of my own blood through my veins, as I watch the life drain slowly from her. I lift the knife above my head, and I plunge it deep into her heart. And then I do it again and again, until finally the rage is gone and I'm slumped on top of her, exhausted. Then there is a new sensation flooding my insides, and it takes a few seconds before I figure out what it is.

Elation.

It's my first kill, but in that moment, I know it won't be my last.

I stand and put the knife back in the pocket of my pants. I walk to the hallway and listen at the foot of the stairs for any movement from the rooms above. I hear nothing.

I return to the living room. The music is still playing. The flames from the candles cast strange shadows on the walls. I walk over to the cream leather couch. I look at the lifeless body on the floor, and I smile.

Then I sit. And wait.

1

JESSICA

Jessica Shaw stared at the faces in front of her, thinking most of them were probably dead. Dead or didn't want to be found. Squinting against the late-afternoon California sunshine pouring in through the window, she leaned closer to the MacBook screen for a better look at the photos.

There was the missing mom who'd vanished from her home in the middle of the day. The middle-aged guy who'd left for work one morning and never arrived at the office. The teenage girl who'd failed to return home after school. There were thousands of other similarly tragic stories, all of the people apparently disappearing into thin air.

Dead or didn't want to be found.

The way Jessica saw it, most missing adults fell into these two distinct categories, like a gambler in a Vegas casino deciding whether to nudge his pile of chips onto black or red. Red, they were probably dead. Black, they might just come back. After seven years as a private investigator, five in New York and the last two on the road, she usually had a pretty good idea from the get-go which of those scenarios she was dealing with.

Jessica was mentally sorting the faces on screen into blacks and reds when the waitress's voice broke into her thoughts. She quickly closed the laptop. A diner wasn't the ideal place for this kind of work, but she liked to think of shopping malls, motel rooms, gas station restaurants—hell, anywhere with a decent Wi-Fi connection—as her office. It made her feel like she was really working and not just running away.

Today's office was a small diner in Simi Valley, a pleasant medium-size city tucked into the southeast corner of Ventura County. Thirty miles from downtown Los Angeles, it was best known as the venue for the Rodney King trial in '92 and then as the final resting place of Ronald Reagan twelve years later.

Jessica didn't know it just yet, but it was also the place where her life was about to change forever.

She'd never visited this particular diner before, but she had been to diners just like this one a million times. A low-budget, low-expectation establishment. High stools in front of a sticky counter. Day-old doughnuts displayed in a glass case dotted with eager fingerprint smudges. Waitresses wearing powder-blue uniforms and white tennis shoes and forced smiles while handing out coffee refills.

One of those waitresses was hovering over her now. "What're you having?" The waitress tapped a crimson acrylic nail impatiently against her notepad as though she had someplace more important to be.

Jessica had looked at the menu, with its gaudy, hand-drawn cartoons of pizzas and burgers and wipe-clean laminated plastic, just long enough to locate the Wi-Fi code and fire up the laptop. Glancing at it again now, she saw a hardened eggy glop covered the appetizers. So much for wipe clean. It was a late lunch, the best part of the day having been spent packing up her things, ready to move on again. Maybe LA this time. Or San Francisco or San Diego.

She ordered a grilled cheese sandwich and black coffee, hoping the sandwich was on the menu despite not having its own cartoon. She didn't want to have to ask the waitress for a few more minutes to decide. This was Donny's Diner, not the goddamn Ritz.

"Five minutes for the sandwich," the waitress said. "I'll go get the coffee now."

Jessica flipped the laptop screen back up and peered over it at the woman while she busied herself making the drink. She was a straight-from-a-bottle redhead in her late forties whose name was Nancy, according to the plastic tag that hung at a lopsided angle and seemed to deliberately point at her heaving bosom. Nancy's breasts looked real, despite the close proximity to Tinseltown and its plastic surgeons, but still managed to look porny as they strained to escape from the one-size-too-small uniform.

Turning her attention back to the laptop, Jessica tucked a stray strand of short blonde hair behind her ear and checked her emails. There were no new additions to the inbox since she'd last looked this morning.

No inquiries from frantic parents or concerned spouses wanting help in tracking down missing loved ones. No surveillance work tailing a member of the staff on behalf of a suspicious employer. Not even a request for one of those honeytrap jobs that basically involved encouraging men to hit on her in hotel bars before confirming to distraught wives that they were, indeed, married to lying, cheating douchebags.

She almost always turned those ones down unless she was really broke. And Jessica hadn't been broke for a while. Not since the insurance money had cleared and the house sale had gone through. These days, she usually advised the honeytrap clients to spend their hard-earned cash on a good divorce lawyer instead.

With nothing that might push her in the direction of her next move, Jessica went back to the missing persons websites and ate the grilled cheese sandwich once it arrived. She was idly contemplating having one of the stale doughnuts when a breaking news alert popped up on the screen with a muted ding. The sentence was brief and to the point. She sat back heavily against the booth's hard vinyl seat and sighed, all thoughts of dessert now forgotten.

She turned to Nancy. "You might want to take that down now."

The waitress looked up from behind the counter, where she had been emptying loose change into the cash register. "Sorry, hon—did you say something?"

Jessica nodded to a poster taped to the wall behind the older woman. It was a sheet of paper with the word *MISSING* in big bloodred capital letters across the top. Underneath, in a smaller black font, were the words "Have you seen this person?" The paper was glossy, the printout good quality. The same as others Jessica had seen around town the last couple of days hanging in bars and restaurants, stuck on shop front windows, pasted to streetlight poles.

A color photograph showed an unsmiling young Asian woman with ebony hair that shone like wet tar and eyes that were every bit as dark. She looked pissed with whoever was behind the camera taking the photo.

A twenty-year-old college student, Amy Ong had been reported missing by her roommate after failing to return home from a Saturday-night date. Young, beautiful, and smart: the holy trinity that guaranteed her image had been splashed across every news channel and newspaper in LA and the surrounding areas for the last few days. Not like the girls with average looks from the wrong side of the tracks, who barely merited a mention in the inside pages.

Jessica repeated, "You might want to take that down now."

"Oh, have they found her?" Nancy's drawn-on eyebrows shot up in a hopeful expression as far as the Botox would allow. "I bet she's been with some boy, and her cell phone ran out of juice. Happens all the time. I should know—my kid's the same age."

"She's dead."

The older woman's face crumpled under her heavy foundation.

Jessica went on. "They haven't officially confirmed the identity yet, but it sounds like it's Amy Ong. Cops are treating it as murder, according to the news."

Nancy's hand flew to her mouth, and her mascara-rimmed eyes widened. "Murder? Good Lord. That poor girl." Then she shook her head sadly and turned away. She began peeling the Scotch tape that held the poster in place, careful not to snap her crimson acrylic nails.

Dead or didn't want to be found.

Amy Ong was now one of the former. A life with so much promise apparently snuffed out in an instant. Jessica had wondered if the young woman's disappearance might lead to some work coming her way, but that was clearly a dead end now. Literally. She preferred her cases much colder anyway, like a bottle of Bud Light straight from a cooler, and this one had never gotten to be anything other than lukewarm.

It was time to move on. Either the toss of a dime—heads for north, tails for south—or pick a new case from a missing persons website and show up in town and pitch for business.

Jessica signaled to Nancy to refill her cup, then continued skimming through the gallery of images on the screen, waiting for a face to pique her interest. Like a horny bachelor trawling dating sites in search of a Friday-night hookup.

> Janine Solomon. Seventeen. White. Female. Missing for two months. Missing from Albany, New York.

No way was Jessica going back to New York State. She kept on scrolling.

> John Preston. Fifty-nine. White. Male. Missing for six weeks. Missing from Richmond, Virginia.

Too far to drive to from here. Pass. She kept on scrolling.

> Shondra Williams. Thirty-nine. Black. Female. Missing for eighteen months. Missing from Coolidge, Arizona.

That one was a maybe.

Jessica checked her emails again. There was a new message in the inbox. The subject read, "Your next case?" The sender was "John Doe."

Opening the message, she expected to see a query from a potential client with an outline of the case they wanted her to take on. Instead, there was only a website link. Jessica was wary of opening links or attachments from unknown senders, but she could see from its address that this one was for a missing persons website she was familiar with.

She clicked on it.

The page loaded to show a missing person listing with a photo of a little kid of about two or three years old. She had mousy brown hair and big blue eyes and was clutching a Barbie doll in grubby, chubby fingers.

Jessica felt a hot flush hit her cheeks hard and fast, like sudden exposure to a tanning bed with new tubes.

It couldn't be.

She looked again.

Holy shit.

The coffee she'd just sipped turned bitter in her mouth. The scrape of metal cutlery on plates at the next table suddenly seemed far too loud. The smell of fried onions from the kitchen out back made her want to throw up all over the wipe-clean laminated tabletop.

Dead or didn't want to be found.

Jessica Shaw now knew there was a third category she had never even considered.

Those who didn't know they were missing.

2

AMY

Amy Ong ran her fingers softly along the clothes hanging in the closet as she tried to decide which outfit to choose. She pulled out a red satin dress, held it in front of her, and stared at her reflection in the full-length mirror on the inside of the closet door.

The dress had been a gift from her parents. Her mom and dad had wanted her to have something special to wear to the celebratory dinner they'd organized when she had been accepted to study criminal justice at Cal State LA after winning two coveted scholarships. Amy was the oldest of three girls born into a working-class Chinese family and was the first Ong to go to college. All of her relatives were proud of her success, but none of them were surprised. Amy had always been the smart girl. The good girl.

A wave of sadness washed over her as she thought of her family back in Ohio, and she shook her head as though the action would help rid her of the negative emotion. She turned her attention back to the task at hand. The dress was relatively modest, sitting just below the knee and without even a hint of cleavage on show, but the shimmering red material contrasted perfectly with her pale skin and long dark hair. Just right for date night. It was Saturday evening, she was heading to a cool bar in Hollywood to meet a guy, and she had to look like she'd made an effort.

She shoved the dress back in the closet between two sweaters.

But not *too* much of an effort.

"I really wish you wouldn't go."

Amy jumped at the sound of the voice behind her. She spun around to see her roommate, Kasey Taylor, sitting on the edge of one of the two single beds that took up most of the space in their small bedroom. She was pulling agitatedly at a loose thread on the bedcover. It was Kasey's tell, fidgeting with stuff when she was anxious.

"Shit." Amy laughed. She held a hand to her chest, where her heart pumped furiously beneath her trembling fingers. "I didn't hear you come into the room. You almost scared me half to death."

Kasey didn't return the smile. She looked at Amy with a worried expression. "It's not too late to cancel."

A pretty blonde with girl-next-door looks, Kasey was studying theatre and dance and had already appeared in a couple of commercials for a well-known tampon brand, but Amy knew her best friend's concern wasn't an act.

She turned back to the closet. "You know I can't do that."

"Sure you can," Kasey said. "All you have to do is pick up your cell and send a text. You know, something along the lines of 'Not going to make it tonight. Or ever. Don't contact me again, loser.'"

"I don't have his cell phone number."

"So stand him up."

"I can't."

Amy picked out tight blue jeans and a white tank top and threw them onto her own bed. Then she bent down and fished out a pair of gold strappy sandals from the bottom of the closet. She dropped her bathrobe to the floor, wriggled into the jeans, and pulled the tank top over her head, combing her fingers through her hair. As she sat on her bed to fasten the sandals, she could feel Kasey's gaze on her.

Eventually her friend spoke. "Look, I've got another commercial in a few weeks. The pet food one. I could—"

"No," Amy snapped, then instantly felt bad about using such a sharp tone with her best friend. "I appreciate what you're trying to do, sweetie, but the answer is no." She stood, did a little twirl. "Now, how do I look?"

"Amazing," Kasey said glumly.

Amy lifted the bottle of Chanel Chance she shared with Kasey from the dresser and spritzed the scent onto her neck and wrists. She unplugged her cell phone from where it was charging next to the perfume bottle and slipped it into her faux-leather purse alongside her wallet, driver's license, hairbrush, cosmetics, breath mints, car keys, and a single condom.

"Wait," Kasey said. She opened the bottom drawer of the dresser, rummaged inside among bras and panties, and then produced a can of pepper spray. "At least take this with you."

Amy held up her bulging purse. "No space." She gave Kasey a quick hug. "Don't worry—I'll be fine. I always am. Don't wait up."

She left the bedroom before Kasey could persuade her to change her mind.

Outside, the early-evening air was still warm, but goose bumps dappled the skin on Amy's arms as she emerged from the housing complex's stairwell onto the street. The sun was dropping rapidly into the horizon, the brightness of the day giving way to a starless dusk.

Her heels clacked loudly on the asphalt as she made her way across the student parking lot to her beat-up old Mini. She climbed inside and turned the key in the ignition, praying silently the car would start the first time. She was already running late, and a cab all the way out to Hollywood was out of the question.

The engine sputtered and coughed and finally caught, and Amy breathed a sigh of relief as it rumbled softly beneath her. The radio burst into life, playing a sad song about lost love on one of her favorite country music stations. She felt the knot of anxiety in her belly loosening just a little. The clock on the dash glowed bright green. She'd probably be a few minutes late, but she knew he would wait for her.

Amy shuddered. She thought about having a couple of glasses of wine tonight, just enough to settle the nerves, but she knew it wouldn't be worth the risk.

The car's interior was illuminated by the amber glow of a nearby streetlight, and Amy caught a glimpse of sad eyes in the rearview mirror. She sighed. She had no idea who the girl staring back at her was anymore. She released the hand brake and edged slowly out of the parking space.

Amy Ong.

The smart girl.

The good girl.

If only they knew.

3

JESSICA

The listing on the Lost Angelenos website didn't offer much information beyond the basics.

The name of the kid in the photo was Alicia Lavelle, and she was three years old when she disappeared. She was last seen with her mom on a fall day at the grocery store, then the post office, then nothing. She officially became a missing person the next day after what was described only as "a serious incident" at the family home.

That was almost twenty-five years ago.

There had been no concrete leads regarding her whereabouts in the years that had passed since. Jessica read the listing again. Then she studied the photo until the little girl's features were seared onto her brain. But she didn't have to. It was a face she already knew well.

The face in the photo was her own.

Jessica had seen enough pictures of herself as a kid in old family albums to know what she'd looked like at that age. But she'd never set eyes on this particular photo before.

She tapped out a rapid response to the email.

Who is this? Do I know you?

Jessica hit send and waited. A few seconds later, there was a new message. An automatically generated email advising that her message could not be delivered. She shut down the laptop.

She tucked a ten-dollar bill under the coffee cup, then slipped the laptop into her oversize shoulder bag and slid out of the booth. As she stood, Jessica's legs turned to rubber, as though the coffee had been spiked with a generous measure of liquor. Ignoring the strange looks from Nancy, she made her way unsteadily toward the exit.

Outside in the parking lot, the temperature had hit the high eighties, and the heat from the steaming blacktop burned through the soles of her sneakers. Her armpits felt damp under the light cotton T-shirt she wore. She wiped sweaty hands on the back of her gray skinny jeans and walked over to a black Chevy Silverado languishing in the shade of a giant oak tree. The truck's covered bed was large enough to hold two medium-size suitcases and a cardboard carton filled with the rest of her personal belongings. Everything she owned was stored in the back of a truck.

Jessica pointed the Silverado in the direction of the parking lot exit and punched letters and numbers into the car's GPS system. There would be no interstate travel this time, no long days and longer nights spent on never-ending, identical-looking freeways. No need to toss a dime to decide which direction she was headed next. Her destination was a neighborhood in northeast LA, about forty miles away. Depending on traffic, it was a journey that should take no more than an hour.

She steered the truck onto East Los Angeles Avenue and passed shopping plazas and fast food outlets and a health center and a Wells Fargo. Amy Ong stared out sullenly from yet another poster attached to a tree trunk with plastic cable ties. Jessica hooked a right onto First Street and followed the signs for the 118 freeway.

Simi Valley and its perky bungalows and clipped lawns and double garages disappeared behind her and were soon replaced by the impressive, sprawling peaks of the Santa Susana Mountains. Pockmarked with shale and sandstone and shrubs in sunbaked camouflage shades of green, khaki, and brown, the wide-open spaces were so different from the narrow gray New York streets where Jessica had grown up.

Her childhood memories stretched back only as far as those various cramped apartments she'd shared with her father in noisy, low-income neighborhoods in Queens, before Tony had finally scraped together enough cash for the house in Blissville.

He had died two years ago, leaving her with a mother she couldn't remember and a father she'd never forget and no one to call right now who could tell her the missing persons listing was nothing more than a crazy, stupid mistake. She bit her lip until she tasted blood and floored the gas, the City of Angels in her sights.

Eagle Rock sat in the San Rafael Hills, sandwiched between Glendale to the west and Pasadena to the east and named after a huge rock outcropping that cast a shadow resembling an eagle with outspread wings at certain times of the day.

Jessica remembered reading an online *LA Weekly* article describing the place as one of America's "hottest neighborhoods," which meant young urban professionals had moved in, house prices had rocketed, and trendy bars and restaurants had sprung up all along Colorado and Eagle Rock Boulevards.

The last known sighting of Alicia Lavelle had taken place on York Boulevard, another of Eagle Rock's main thoroughfares.

Jessica exited the Glendale Freeway directly onto York, where candy-colored homes in Craftsman and mission revival styles flashed by on either side, and drove until she came to a crossroads. There was a bunch of restaurants to the left, a Presbyterian church to the right, and an ARCO station straight ahead. Jessica didn't need food, salvation, or gas, so she drove straight through the intersection and passed a late-night pharmacy and a drive-through Starbucks before spotting a small motel just off the main street.

The gentrification sweeping the rest of Eagle Rock clearly hadn't filtered on down to the Blue Moon Inn just yet. It was a tired single-story building the color of old bones, with a flat roof edged with blue neon lights. A row of ten rooms stretched out behind the office. A blinking red-and-blue neon sign advertising vacancies and low rates stood sentry by the entrance to the lot. By *low rates*, the proprietors meant twenty-five bucks a night, and that was just fine by Jessica. All she wanted was a soft bed and some hard liquor.

Stepping inside the motel's lobby, she found an unmanned varnished wood counter taking up most of the east wall. A small, chipped table next to the front entrance held an ancient Mr. Coffee machine, some paper cups, and a tidy pile of glossy brochures. By the big picture window was a seating area with a round, glass-topped coffee table flanked by two small wicker couches. The type that always creaked loudly when you sat on them, no matter how plump the cushioned seat covers were.

The door behind the desk opened, and she could hear an old Stones tune playing low on an unseen radio in the office beyond. A round belly appeared in the doorway. The man attached to the gut had a white beard and a matching cloud of hair and looked old enough to remember the song when it was first riding high on the Billboard Hot 100. His smile was wide and warm, as though he was surprised to find a guest waiting.

"What can I do you for?" he asked.

"I need a room for a week," Jessica said. "Maybe longer."

She handed over an ID and an Amex card. The deskman glanced at the driver's license and swiped the card in a new pay machine that looked out of place in the dated surroundings. He used his trigger finger to stab some details onto a keyboard hooked up to a chunky computer monitor. Then he reached into a cubbyhole unit with ten slots and pulled out a key attached to a white plastic fob with the number five stamped in gold foil that was starting to flake off.

"The name's Jeff Hopper, but folks call me Hopper or Hopp," he said. "Never Jeff. You need anything while you're staying here, just buzz the office. You'll find the number on the room telephone."

"Sure, no problem."

Hopper gestured to the flyers on the table. "If you're after someplace nice to eat or information on local hiking trails or any other tourist stuff, you should find what you're looking for among that lot. Or I can give you some personal recommendations, if you'd prefer?"

"Thanks," Jessica said. "But I'm here for business, not pleasure."

Hopper smiled again and shrugged.

She looked at him more closely. He was at least sixty. Unless he was a relative newcomer to Eagle Rock, he would remember the Lavelle case, might even have known Alicia and her mother. He would certainly have been aware of the rumors flying around at the time. She had come across enough motel and hotel owners in the last couple of years to know they fed on local gossip. What they didn't know wasn't worth knowing.

"I'm a private investigator," she said. "Looking into the Lavelle case."

Hopper raised an eyebrow. "Now, there's a blast from the past. Why now?"

"The anniversary is coming up."

He scratched his beard. "It's not a special anniversary, is it? Surely it's not been twenty-five years already?"

"Yes, it has. But I figure when someone is still missing, every year that passes is special."

Hopper frowned. "I guess. But if you're a private investigator, someone must've hired you to come to Eagle Rock and look into the case."

Jessica smiled tightly. "Let's just say I'm here on behalf of an interested party."

Hopper looked disappointed but said nothing.

"You lived in Eagle Rock long?" she asked.

"All my life. Baby, boy, man."

"Did you know the Lavelles?"

"The kid I never met, but I'd see the two of them around the neighborhood often."

"What about the mother? Did you know her?"

"Most folks around here knew Eleanor when she worked at Ace's Bar. She was hard to forget."

"In what way?"

"Oh, she was pretty, for sure. One of the reasons Ace Freeman was so quick to give her a job. But she had something else going for her. In a man, I guess you'd call it charisma. A certain kind of charm that can't be faked—you know what I mean?"

Jessica nodded, but Hopper's eyes were fixed someplace over her shoulder and almost thirty years in the past. "Where is Eleanor now?" she asked.

Hopper's eyes refocused, and his bushy white eyebrows bunched together in confusion. "She's dead."

Jessica blinked. "Of course."

They both stood in awkward silence for a couple of seconds.

Then Jessica said, "One more question."

"Shoot."

"Where can I find Ace's Bar?"

Inside, the bar was comfortingly gloomy. The main light source was a dull lamp hanging low over a pool table in the rear of the room and some neon signs advertising domestic beers.

Four booths butted each wall on either side of a U-shaped bar. Fewer than half of the eight booths were occupied. A couple sipping beers and snacking on a basket of fries and chicken wings. An older man with a deck of cards laid out in front of him. A table full of outdoor workers who'd just clocked out for the evening, judging by the eye-watering yellow safety vests and dirty boots they were all wearing.

Like the Blue Moon Inn, Ace's did not look like an Eagle Rock hotspot regularly frequented by twentysomething hipsters. It was a spit-and-sawdust dive, probably kept in business by customers who lived or worked nearby and who had been drinking here forever.

Three high stools faced the smaller curved end of the bar. From a gash in the maroon leatherette seating, the middle one spewed nicotine-colored foam that brought to mind a freshly popped pimple. Jessica climbed onto the stool to the right and glanced up at a small television screen mounted above the bar. It was tuned to a news channel with the volume on mute.

A blonde reporter with big hair and too much makeup was doing a piece to camera with a motel sign glowing softly in the background. The scrolling text along the bottom of the screen read, "Latest: Amy Ong murder hunt." Jessica figured the grubby building was where the body had been found.

The blonde was replaced by a good-looking black man who was speaking to a bunch of reporters. He was probably in his late forties or early fifties but wore the years well. He had a couple of days' worth of stubble, closely cropped dark hair smudged with gray at the temples, and a physique that suggested he worked out daily. His charcoal dress pants and black open-necked shirt looked both smart and expensive. The shirtsleeves were rolled up, exposing well-defined arms. On his wrist was a big gold watch. On his belt was a big gold cop's badge. The name across the bottom of the screen identified the man as LAPD detective Jason Pryce.

Jessica didn't know the name, but she knew the face. She'd seen him once before, just before quitting New York for good, on a day she'd spent the last two years trying to forget.

She'd never been to a funeral before. Hadn't known any dead people well enough to bother before Tony had prematurely met his maker. Even if she had, she would have made her excuses and sent a nice sympathy card instead, picked out one with a thoughtful verse. Funerals just weren't her thing. But when your own father was the deceased, it was a hell of a lot harder to get out of.

On that day, she'd felt like an actress thrust into the starring role of a movie she hadn't auditioned for, for a part she didn't want. All those eyes on her, looking for a performance, and she couldn't get into character, didn't know her lines.

The church had been busier than expected, despite the bad weather, with lots of people Jessica had never met before crammed into the pews. A surprising turnout, given how much Tony had kept to himself.

There were smug couples holding hands, their new platinum and diamond rings glinting under the light from the stained glass windows. Young moms bouncing babies on knees, pacifiers jammed into their tiny mouths so they wouldn't embarrass their parents in front of God. Tony had made a pretty good living shooting weddings and family portraits, and Jessica had thought those who'd made the effort to show up must have really liked his photos.

At the back of the church had sat a man on his own. He'd worn a well-cut navy suit and a crisp white shirt and a silver tie. Raindrops had glistened on his shoulders like crystals. His face had been wet, but it had been difficult to tell if the source was tears or rainfall. He'd been gone by the time everyone else had moved on to the wake. Thinking back to the mourners in the church, Jessica now had a name for the unknown man in the navy suit.

His name was Detective Jason Pryce.

4

PRYCE

It was after ten p.m. by the time Jason Pryce left his desk at Hollywood Division and another twenty minutes before he turned the key in the lock of his Los Feliz condo. His muscles ached with exhaustion, but his brain felt like it had been hot-wired.

He slipped off his shoes and padded along the polished parquet floor to the master bedroom and peeked inside. His wife, Angie, was already asleep in bed. He quietly pulled the door shut and tapped his knuckles gently on the one directly across the hallway. Dim light escaped from the gap where it had been left open a few inches. When there was no answer, Pryce stuck his head around the door, and his daughter looked up at him and grinned.

Dionne sat cross-legged on the bed with a laptop perched on her knees and a pair of giant red headphones propped on top of her dark curls. They had been a present for her sixteenth birthday last month and had been an almost permanent fixture on her head ever since. She pulled the headphones off, unleashing the sound of canned Justin Bieber into the bedroom.

"Hey, Daddy," she said. "I saw you on TV."

"Oh yeah?" Pryce moved a couple of stuffed toys out of the way and sat on the edge of the bed next to her. "How'd I do?" He hated media interviews and tried to avoid them whenever possible. But with his boss, Lieutenant Sarah Grayling, on an anniversary break in San Luis

Obispo more than three hours away, it had been left to Pryce to feed the reporters the standard lines.

"Not too bad," Dionne teased. "You're definitely getting better."

Her smile vanished suddenly and was replaced by a deep frown. She looked up at him, her serious expression bathed in the soft-pink glow from the fairy lights wrapped around the bed frame. She said, "You're gonna catch the guy who hurt that girl, right?"

"You bet I am, sweetheart." Pryce ruffled her hair, and Dionne made a face. He said, "Ten more minutes of Facebook and that terrible music, then bed. Okay?"

"It's not Facebook," she protested. "I'm finishing this month's book club for the paper. Deadline is tomorrow." She pointed to a teetering pile of paperbacks on her desk.

Dionne was the reviews editor of the school newspaper and had her heart set on a place at Berkeley studying journalism once she graduated. The thought of his little girl leaving home to go to school near San Francisco—or anywhere else, for that matter—in just a couple of years' time made Pryce's stomach sink like a stone thrown into a lake. Not for the first time, his thoughts turned to Amy Ong's parents and the hell they must be going through right now.

The Ongs had been given the death notice by local cops in Ohio, where the family lived. Pryce had then spoken to Mr. Ong on the telephone himself and assured the girl's devastated father he would do everything in his power to bring her killer to justice. And he fully intended to keep that promise.

"What's the verdict?" he asked Dionne. "Anything worth reading?"

"Mixed bag," Dionne said. "The postapocalyptic one was very cool. The romance ones, not so much." She pretended to stick two fingers down her throat. "I don't think any of them would be your kind of thing, Daddy. No car chases or buildings being blown up."

Pryce wasn't a big reader, unlike Dionne and her mother. He preferred watching movies. Usually ones with car chases and buildings being blown up. It was probably Charles Bronson's fault he had ended up being a cop. He stood up with a groan.

"Ten minutes, young lady." He gave Dionne a mock-stern look. "I'm going to take a shower, and these lights had better be out by the time I'm done."

She stuck out her tongue, and he laughed despite himself.

In the bathroom, Pryce peeled off his shirt, pants, and underwear and dumped them in the laundry basket. He turned the heat of the shower as high as he could stand it, relishing the near pain of the hot needles of water stabbing his back and shoulders. He soaped himself from head to toe and tried to scrub the stench of the crime scene from his skin. Rid himself of that all-too-familiar copper tang of blood, the unmistakable scent of death. If only he could wash away the memories along with the stink, he thought. Watch as the fragmented images swirled away down the drain along with the soap and shampoo.

What had happened to Amy Ong was bad, but it wasn't the worst Pryce had seen in almost thirty years on the job. He knew what was really bothering him wasn't just what had happened to her; it was *where* it had happened.

The Dreamz Motel was a place he'd sworn he would never set foot in again. He had been there once before, one night a long time ago, and he had spent more than half his life trying to forget about it.

It had been a night much like this one. Warm and sticky, with the curtains flapping gently in the barely there breeze from the open window of his tiny apartment. Angie, his new girlfriend, lying in bed next to him. He remembered being woken sometime before dawn by the shrill ringing of the telephone on the nightstand and the panicked whispered conversation that had followed. He had somehow managed to convince Angie to go back to sleep, that there was nothing to worry about, even though his hands were shaking so badly he'd struggled to fasten his belt.

He had stopped at a pay phone outside an all-night liquor store on Sunset on the way to the motel and made a call of his own. One that he couldn't risk Angie overhearing. At that hour, the only other people around were transients bundled under flattened cardboard and sleeping bags in doorways or early-morning cleaners making their way to silent, empty office blocks. No one had taken any notice of Pryce.

His short, tense conversation had been punctuated by the occasional scream of a siren in the distance, and he'd kept his back to the traffic for fear of being recognized by a colleague in a passing cruiser. After hanging up, he'd quickly gotten back into his Ford Taurus, grateful the car was dark and anonymous, and headed toward La Brea and the Dreamz Motel.

He had paced for a while under the motel's big vertical sign, its red letters and white background glowing soft and hazy and dreamlike under the thick smog. He had asked himself over and over again what the hell he was doing. Every instinct Pryce had had screamed at him to jump straight back into his car and drive as fast as he could back to his apartment and climb into bed with Angie. No harm done.

But he had known turning his back on the situation was never really an option. That was why he had agreed to the meeting at the motel in the first place, even though he'd known he was risking everything—his career, his freedom, Angie. So he had walked into the motel room and sat on a bed that felt like it was filled with rocks, and he had waited for the knock on the door.

Today, it had been another phone call that had brought him back to the Dreamz Motel.

The place was a two-story dive just off Hollywood Boulevard and within spitting distance of the Walk of Fame, although the thousands of famous names immortalized in five-pointed terrazzo-and-brass stars were the closest its guests ever came to rubbing shoulders with the A-list.

The building had been a vibrant pink when Pryce had last been there, but the paint was now bleached the color of cotton candy after years of exposure to the merciless LA sun and a general lack of upkeep. Tiles were missing from the stucco roof, and white paint flaked off the metal railings of the upper level like dandruff. The big vertical sign was still there, advertising vacancies, HBO, and refrigerators in every room. These days, there was also a communal hot tub, if you weren't too fussy about stripping down to your bathing suit with the couple having an affair in the room next door.

This time, there had been no deserted parking lot, no milky dawn light and lazily blinking neon.

Instead, he had been met by chaos.

A media chopper had circled noisily overhead, and a bunch of reporters and cameramen and photographers had congregated behind the yellow crime scene tape like a skulk of starving foxes desperately trying to sniff out a tidbit or two. He had ignored their shouted questions as he'd ducked under the tape. By the end of the day, he would have enough of his own.

His partner, Vic Medina, met him outside the motel room and handed him a pair of latex gloves and some shoe protectors. Pryce snapped on the gloves and pulled the shoe protectors over his loafers and took a deep breath before crossing the threshold.

Inside, an ancient AC unit rattled loudly, spewing out freezing-cold air. A police photographer was hunched over a queen bed, initially blocking Pryce's view of the victim. At first, all he could see was a pair of bare feet with red-painted toenails resting on a dated floral bedcover exactly like the one he had sat on himself years earlier.

As the photographer snapped the body from various angles, Pryce looked around the room. The cream shade covering the small window was faded and stained. A film of dust coated a desk scarred with cigarette burns. Two plastic cups sat on a table along with an empty fifth of whiskey. Beneath his shoe protectors, the maroon carpet felt sticky with years' worth of other guests' spilled liquor and body fluids. A couple of crime scene investigators hovered around the table, dusting for prints and dropping items into plastic evidence bags.

Pryce wrinkled his nose in distaste. "What the hell was a smart kid like her doing in a dump like this?"

"Who knows?" Medina shrugged. "But I don't think the management has to worry about her leaving a negative review on TripAdvisor any time soon."

Amy Ong had suffered heavy blows to the face and multiple stab wounds and slash marks to the neck and torso. Defense wounds on the palms of her hands indicated she had tried to put up a fight against her attacker without success. The pinky on her right hand had been severed completely. A couple of flies buzzed around the gaping holes in her chest. The girl's left arm hung over the side of the bed, once limp but now stiff with rigor mortis.

She wore a white terry cloth bathrobe smeared with dried carmine streaks. It lay open, exposing black lace panties and small pale breasts. Pryce had to fight the urge to cover her up with the robe, to try to preserve some sort of dignity for her in death. He noticed her clothes were folded in a neat pile on an easy chair under a floor lamp, illuminated like a display in a department store window, never to be worn again.

Next to the clothing was a cheap faux-leather purse filled with cosmetics, a hairbrush, breath mints, and a wallet with $200 in crisp twenties. Car keys for a Mini that wasn't parked in the lot outside. A driver's license provided a preliminary ID. Even in the DMV's digitally printed photo, Amy Ong was beautiful.

Pryce crossed the room to the tiny bathroom and looked inside. It was stark and empty. No toiletries. No bath or hand towels, although he guessed the ruined terry cloth bathrobe belonged to the motel rather than the girl.

He returned to the main room as the body movers carefully lifted Amy Ong from the bed onto the gurney. The sound of the zipper was loud in the small room as the body bag was shut with a sense of finality. Pryce watched as the gurney was wheeled from the room to the coroner's van waiting outside, sparking a sudden burst of commotion as reporters barked at cameramen to start rolling while flashbulbs popped on photographers' cameras. Another story to fill a few column inches or a couple of minutes of airtime, he thought angrily.

Pryce turned off the shower now. He toweled dry and pulled on a pair of shorts and a T-shirt. As he passed Dionne's room, he saw the door was still ajar, and the room was in darkness. He crossed the living room, pulled back the sliding door, and stepped out onto the balcony.

This high up, the night air felt cool against his skin, which still tingled from the hot shower. He plucked a bottle of MGD from an ice chest stored between two lawn chairs and looked out over the city. Ten stories below, the traffic was light, the sidewalks almost empty. Beyond the vast black expanse of Griffith Park, the lights of Glendale and Burbank twinkled like a million stars under an eggplant sky.

He knew the Hollywood sign stood off to the west, a symbol of hopes and dreams and the gateway to the studios that lay beyond the hills to the north. Warner Bros. Disney. Universal. Places that had the power to make those hopes and dreams a reality or turn them to dust.

Pryce knew the LAPD investigated as many as three hundred missing persons reports each month. Most of those who were reported missing were found or returned voluntarily within forty-eight to seventy-two hours. Of the 30 percent who weren't found in that time frame, Pryce wondered how many were native Angelenos and how many had come to Tinseltown chasing a dream. Kids just like Amy Ong. Chewed up and spat out by a town where your future could flip from stardust to shit in a heartbeat.

He drank his beer and thought about his own life. About all the things he still had to lose. His badge, his freedom, his home, Angie, Dionne. The feeling of dread that had been sitting heavy in his gut since he'd first taken the call about Amy Ong spread through his insides like a cancer.

Pryce finished the bottle and walked to the other end of the balcony to the sliding door for the master bedroom. He slipped into bed beside Angie. He listened to his wife snoring softly. He stared at the spot on the ceiling where he knew there was a crack he had never gotten around to fixing. The red digits on the alarm clock told him it was almost one a.m.

It was more than an hour later before he finally began to drift off to sleep. The last thing he remembered thinking was that something was coming. It wasn't here yet, but it was on the way. Like bad news in the mail.

It was coming, and Pryce couldn't do a damn thing to stop it.

5

JESSICA

A voice hauled Jessica back from the memory of Tony's funeral in Blissville two years earlier to where she was sitting now in a dive bar in LA.

She pulled her eyes away from the television screen and Jason Pryce's face. Looked at the acne-scarred, limp-bearded one belonging to the bartender. He was staring at her with an expression someplace between concern and impatience.

"Sorry, did you say something?" she asked.

The guy wore black flesh tunnels in his ears that had stretched the lobes to the size of quarters, and she realized she was talking to the gaping holes instead of his face.

"I asked if you were okay?" he said. "You look like you've seen a ghost."

"Just a bit freaked out by that business in Hollywood, I guess." She gestured to the television above the bar. The blonde with the big hair was back on screen. "Not exactly what you want to hear when you're staying in a motel yourself tonight."

"Ten bucks says she was a hooker. What can I getcha?"

The bartender was tall and skinny and didn't look old enough to buy alcohol, never mind sell it. Definitely not Ace Freeman, the bar's owner, who had given Eleanor Lavelle a job. This kid wouldn't even have been born when Alicia Lavelle had disappeared. In other words, less than useless when it came to getting pumped for information.

"I'll have a Scotch. And a beer."

"What kind of Scotch?"

"Decent."

"What kind of beer?"

"Cold."

He shrugged, his bony shoulders bobbing up and down beneath a T-shirt with the name of a band she'd never heard of emblazoned across the front and faded patches under the armpits. He sloshed two fingers of Royal Emblem into a glass. Then he popped the top on a bottle of Busch and placed it on the counter in front of her. Beads of condensation rolled down the dark glass. Jessica picked up the bottle and drank a third in one go.

As she gazed around the room, one of the outdoor workers caught her eye. He smiled and tipped his Dodgers baseball cap in her direction in a greeting that was supposed to be genteel but was just plain sleazy. He looked like he'd been wearing the cap since the team's last World Series win back in '88. He also looked old enough to be her father. Jessica gave him a disapproving look and turned away.

"Does Ace Freeman still work here?" she asked the bartender.

"Yes, he does."

"He around just now?"

"Night off. Anything I can help you with?"

"I doubt it."

He bristled slightly, then nodded at the two drinks in front of her. "Anything else?"

She shook her head and dropped some bills on the counter and told him to keep the change.

Jessica could feel the eyes of the hat guy following her as she made her way to an empty booth on the other side of the room and set the Scotch and beer down on a table sticky with overlapping drinks rings.

Flopping onto the seat, she pulled the laptop, a yellow legal pad, and a pen from her bag.

She turned to a fresh page in the pad and wrote *Jason Pryce* with a big question mark next to the name and underlined it three times. Jessica wanted to know what a cop from LA had been doing at her father's funeral on the other side of the country. But first of all, she needed to know as much as possible about the Lavelles.

She plucked a food and drinks menu from between a matching set of salt and pepper shakers and studied it to see if there was a customer Wi-Fi code printed on it. There was. It read, *iheartacesbar*.

She rolled her eyes and tapped in the pass code.

There was no need for fancy age-progression technology to tell Jessica the kid in the photo she'd seen in the diner had grown up to be her. But what she did need to establish was whether the image had been uploaded to the missing persons website by mistake. Human error maybe. Or just someone's idea of a sick joke. Most likely the person who'd sent her the email, the mysterious "John Doe."

The name John Doe was used to refer to a male whose identity was unknown, especially corpses in crimes where the victim was unidentified. Had the website link he'd emailed to her been about any other missing person, Jessica would have assumed the sender was likely a true crime nut with a particular enthusiasm for the case. Someone who had probably emailed a number of private eyes in an attempt to spark some interest in finding out what had happened, especially if it was a long-forgotten cold case.

Was it simply a coincidence that she might actually have a personal connection to this one? Jessica wasn't a big believer in coincidences.

She had an excellent contact in New York, an IT geek whom she could ask to examine the email for her and try to track the sender through their IP address. But that kind of work would take time and money. And if John Doe had figured out the link between Jessica and Alicia Lavelle, he was clearly smart. Certainly not dumb enough to be sitting in his bedroom, firing off emails on a laptop, and waiting for a knock on his door. Even so, she forwarded the email to her IT contact and asked him to try to shed some light on the sender. Then Jessica turned her focus to the Lavelles.

She opened Google and noticed her fingers were shaking as she typed the words *Alicia Lavelle* into the search bar. Taking a deep breath, Jessica clicked the button to search for images. Most of the results were irrelevant, hits for famous Alicias instead—Alicia Keys in concert, Alicia Silverstone in *Clueless*.

The first ten results *were* relevant. Six were of the photo she was now familiar with, in varying sizes and quality. The other four were of another different photo.

Different outfit, different backdrop, same little girl.

Alicia Lavelle.

Jessica Shaw.

Shit.

Next, she searched for newspaper reports from the time of the disappearance but found nothing from the early '90s. Too long ago to have been uploaded online. The photos of Alicia Lavelle produced by the image search were either from missing persons sites, including Lost Angelenos, or from anniversary pieces written in the last fifteen years or so when it had become more common for newspapers to post print articles on their websites.

Had she still been alive, Eleanor Lavelle would have been fifty. Her death could have happened at any time over the last twenty-five years and for any number of reasons. Run over by a truck. An incurable illness. Maybe even took her own life after failing to come to terms with the loss of her daughter.

Or none of the above, as it turned out.

According to the anniversary pieces, the cops in charge of the investigation at the time didn't just wind up with one cold case festering away in their open-unsolved files.

They had two.

The disappearance of a three-year-old girl.

And the murder of the child's mother the same night.

The first photo Jessica had seen of Alicia Lavelle, while drinking coffee in the diner in Simi Valley, was clearly a cropped version of the original. She was looking at the original now. Little Alicia, with the brown hair and the blue eyes, holding on to the Barbie doll. Its hair had been hacked off, just like the one Jessica had taken everywhere with her until she was about ten years old. In this picture, Eleanor Lavelle was crouching down next to her daughter.

Jessica stared at her.

She had red hair and blue eyes, like Jessica's mom, but they were clearly not the same person. Her mother was a woman called Pamela Arnold, who had died in an automobile accident when Jessica was just a baby.

Tony had told her the full story once years ago. The accident had happened on a Friday evening. They'd been out of milk and coffee and bagels, and Pamela had been in the mood for a nice bottle of pinot noir. So she'd grabbed the keys to her VW Bug and headed out to buy some wine and groceries.

She'd never made it to the store.

The car had been found at the bottom of a hillside mottled with rocks and trees, about a hundred feet below a narrow bend in the road. It had been crushed like an accordion, and the police had told Tony that Pamela hadn't stood a chance. Death would have been instantaneous. They didn't know what had caused her to veer off the blacktop and hurtle straight through the flimsy crash barrier. Possibly a wild animal on the road or a drunk driver in the wrong lane. They could only speculate.

All Jessica had been left with was a single photo of her mother to remember her by.

She reached into her bag for her wallet and slid the picture out and studied it.

It had been taken in a park on a late fall day, which you could tell from the red, orange, and gold leaves on the trees in the background. Pamela wore an emerald-green crocheted beret and a long matching scarf, and in her arms was a baby of about six months old. On the back of the photo, in Tony's familiar block handwriting, were the words *Pamela and Jessica, October 1989.*

Jessica compared the faded picture with the image of Eleanor Lavelle on the laptop screen. Both women shared the same hair and eye color but otherwise were nothing alike.

The same couldn't be said for Eleanor and Jessica.

If Eleanor had been sitting next to her right now, here in Ace's Bar, most people would only notice the obvious differences between them at first glance.

Eleanor's red hair tumbled past her shoulders in thick, loose waves, whereas Jessica's was chin length and peroxide blonde, courtesy of a ten-dollar drugstore dye carton.

Eleanor's skin was pale and dusted lightly with freckles, while months spent traveling through some of the hottest states during the summer had given Jessica a deep golden tan.

They both had blue eyes, but Eleanor's were clear and bright like a desert sky at high noon, and Jessica's own were the blue gray of the ocean on a stormy day.

Eleanor had no visible piercings, tattoos, or birthmarks, in contrast to the permanent artwork stretching from the shoulder to the wrist of Jessica's right arm and the tiny diamond stud in the left side of her nose.

Look a little closer, though, and she thought she could see some similarities. The same long, straight nose. The same rosebud mouth. The same sharply defined jawline.

Jessica picked up the Scotch and downed the lot in one go, wincing as the whiskey burned her throat and the fire hit her belly. She closed her eyes and rubbed her temples, where a headache was starting to bloom.

She heard someone slip into the booth on the seat opposite, the old leather creaking and cracking under the person's weight, followed by the thunk of two glasses hitting the wooden tabletop. Jessica sighed heavily, fully expecting to see the middle-aged worker with the dirty ball cap sitting in front of her.

She opened her eyes. It wasn't the guy with the hat. It was a man who was completely and utterly gorgeous. Proper Hollywood looks, like he had just walked off the set of a movie on the other side of town and had somehow ended up in Ace's Bar instead of the Chateau Marmont.

He pushed one of the drinks, which looked and smelled like Royal Emblem, toward Jessica with the tip of his forefinger and grinned at her in a lopsided kind of way that probably got him laid often or into trouble a lot.

He was about forty, with green eyes and dark hair that curled at the nape of his neck. He wore a red-and-black plaid shirt. A battered tan leather messenger bag was slung over a broad chest and rested by his hip. His knees bumped against hers under the table, suggesting he had long legs. She guessed he was around six feet tall.

"You're the private investigator," he said.

It was a statement, not a question.

"Word sure travels fast around here," she said.

"Hopper told me. I'm staying at the motel too."

Jessica raised an eyebrow. "Is that so? I guess the twenty-five bucks a night doesn't stretch to some discretion when it comes to his guests."

The man took a sip of his whiskey and looked at her intently over the rim of the glass. "Don't be mad at Hopper," he said. "He's a good guy. He was only looking out for me. He knew I'd want to know that someone was in town asking about the Lavelles. I'm looking into the case too, what with the anniversary just around the corner."

"And you are?"

"Jack Holliday."

"You're a journalist."

It was a statement, not a question.

Holliday looked surprised, then impressed. "How did you know?"

"I'm a private investigator. It's my job to know stuff."

The byline of one of the articles she'd skimmed when she'd first sat down belonged to Jack Holliday, but he didn't need to know that.

"You're from New York, right?" he asked.

"Let me guess—Hopper told you that too?"

"Guilty as charged. But if you're from New York, why are you working the Lavelle case? Plenty of good PIs right here in LA."

Jessica gulped down a mouthful of whiskey, didn't answer him.

"Are you even allowed to work here?" he pressed. "Aren't there licensing laws about crossing states?"

Jessica set down the glass and looked at him coldly. "You asking to check my credentials? I'm a licensed PI with the state of New York. If a case takes me to another state, then I'm perfectly within my rights to continue my investigation outside of New York. Not that it's any of your business."

The truth was she had no jurisdiction to work this case in California—or any of the others she'd taken on while on the road—but staying in New York simply wasn't an option. Jessica figured as long as she got results, her clients didn't give a damn about paperwork and regulations either.

Holliday asked, "So can I assume this mystery client of yours is based in New York?"

"You can assume whatever the hell you like."

"But you just said you can work in different states if the case originated in New York."

"I was speaking in general terms. Not necessarily about this case. Yes, there are rules about this kind of stuff. No, I don't always play by the rules. Why are you so interested anyway?"

"I've been looking into the case myself on and off for a while now," Holliday said. "If I crack it, I figure there could be a Pulitzer with my name on it. Maybe even a publishing deal for one of those true crime books."

He grinned as though he was joking, but Jessica suspected he was deadly serious about the prize and the book deal.

"I wish you every success," she told him. "But if you don't mind, I have work of my own to do."

He nodded at the laptop. "You won't find much online. Believe me: I've looked. Some anniversary pieces, half of which I wrote. Plenty of crackpot theories on internet forums. That's about it."

He leaned across the table. He smelled good. A mixture of soap and spicy aftershave and whiskey. "You spoken to the cops?"

"Not yet."

"The detective in charge of the investigation was a guy called Bill Geersen. He retired a few years back. The others won't let you anywhere near the files. It's technically still a live case even though no one at the LAPD has taken any interest in years. And you're from out of state."

"I can ask."

"They'll say no."

"There's always bribery. Or theft."

Holliday smiled. "No need for any of that. A contact of mine works in Evidence Archives." He patted the messenger bag. "I have a copy of the files right here."

"And you're telling me this because . . . ?"

"I thought we could work together. I scratch your back; you scratch mine."

"I'm not sure we know each other well enough for such intimate physical contact."

He laughed. "What I meant was I share what I've got. You share what you've got."

"I just got here. I don't have anything. At least, not yet."

"Sure you do. Eleanor Lavelle's mother was a junkie who overdosed when she was a baby. She spent most of her childhood in care before leaving the system as soon as she turned eighteen. There's no record of any surviving family members anywhere."

"So?"

"So who's paying you to look into her murder after all this time? You give me the name of the person who sent you to Eagle Rock; I let you see the files."

Jessica shook her head. "No way."

He nodded, as though it was the response he had been expecting. "Think it over," he said. "I'm staying in room six. You know where to find me if you change your mind."

Holliday finished his drink and left, leaving her sitting on her own, staring at the faces of Eleanor and Alicia Lavelle.

Staring at her own face as a child.

6

ELEANOR

OCTOBER 2, 1992

Eleanor Lavelle dropped a couple of quarters into the slot and carefully punched in the telephone number scrawled on the crumpled piece of paper she held in her hand. She could barely hear the sound of the ringtone over the thumping of her pulse in her ears. She gripped the handset tightly, the plastic slick with sweat from her damp palm.

The phone rang and rang.

Eleanor was just about to hang up when there was a click as someone finally picked up.

A pause. Then, "Hello?"

"It's me," Eleanor said.

There was silence on the other end of the line. Eleanor stuck a finger in her ear, tried to block out the sound of traffic rumbling along York Boulevard.

"It's Eleanor," she said. "Eleanor Lavelle."

"I know who it is. How did you get this number?"

"It's listed."

"Are you fucking crazy? Phoning me like this? I told you I would be in touch with you, not the other way around."

"I, uh, hadn't heard from you," Eleanor mumbled. She heard the tremor in her voice and gave herself a mental kick up the ass. If she showed any sign of weakness now, any at all, it was over. She'd lose. And she couldn't let that happen.

Her eyes fell on a flyer stuck inside the phone booth. It showed a young woman whose large breasts were just about covered with a skimpy bra that matched equally skimpy red lace panties. Her legs were open, her finger in her mouth, a "come and get me" expression on her face. An ad for a strip bar in Hollywood.

Eleanor turned away.

"I ain't messing around," she said. "You've had more than enough time. I'm sick of waiting."

"I told you I'd take care of it."

"When? Time is running out. You know what will happen if you don't."

"Soon."

"How soon?"

"Real soon."

The line went dead.

"Shit!"

Eleanor slammed the handset into the cradle so hard it slipped and hung limply from its metal cord. She replaced the receiver more carefully, took a deep breath, and pushed open the phone booth door.

Her daughter was waiting patiently outside, watching the grocery store owner sweep leaves from the sidewalk outside the entrance to his premises. It was early fall but still warm, and Eleanor felt her Levi's and sweater cling to the sweat on her body. York was busy with Friday-afternoon shoppers, and she recognized a couple of regulars from Ace's from when she'd worked behind the bar there. They waved, and she smiled back.

"You said a curse, Mommy." Alicia's blue eyes were wide. "On the phone. I heard you."

"I know I did, sugar. I'm sorry. Mommy just got mad for a moment."

"Are you still mad?"

Eleanor smiled and crouched down so she was face to face with Alicia. "No, I'm not mad. In fact, Mommy is real happy. You wanna know why?"

Alicia giggled. "Why are you happy, Mommy?"

"Because we're going to be going on one of those big fancy airplanes soon. I bet you'd like that, huh?"

"Yeah! Where are we going?"

"Somewhere far away, where we can meet Mickey Mouse and go on lots of fun rides and do fun stuff together."

Alicia's eyes shone with excitement. "Can Barbie come too?"

The little girl held up her doll. Barbie's hair had been chopped off, and she was wearing a pair of Ken's slacks and one of his shirts. She looked more like GI Jane than Barbie. Eleanor hoped the replacement doll would be delivered soon.

"Sure, Barbie can come along."

"When are we going to meet Mickey?" Alicia asked.

"Real soon."

"Will Uncle Robbie be coming too?"

Eleanor's smile vanished. "No, he won't. It'll just be us two, sugar. And Barbie."

7

PRYCE

Pryce dropped a brown paper bag onto the desk in front of Medina and handed him a twenty-ounce takeout coffee. His partner took a sip and nodded approvingly.

"Two sugars, plenty of cream," Pryce said. "I know your order by now."

Medina unrolled the top of the bag, pulled out a warm bagel, and sniffed it. "Cream cheese." He smiled. "My favorite." He took a large bite and kept on talking while chewing. "You do know my birthday isn't until next month, right?"

Pryce slumped into the chair at his own workstation. He placed a plain bagel onto a napkin and cut it into four slices with a plastic knife. "No time for breakfast at home this morning." He held up his own coffee. Black, no sugar. "I'll be ninety percent caffeine by the end of the day."

"Rough night?"

Pryce nodded. "She was only a few years older than Dionne."

He didn't need to explain to Medina who *she* was. He popped a piece of bagel into his mouth and realized he wasn't even hungry. "Let's go over what we've got so far."

Medina scooted his chair around next to Pryce, who had a three-ring binder open in front of him. The murder book had replaced the missing person report filed by Amy Ong's roommate. Pryce flipped through the pages until he came to one of the witness statements.

"Okay, so we know from our chat with Tommy Getz, the motel's manager, Amy Ong checked into a room at the Dreamz sometime Saturday night. Getz doesn't remember the exact time, but he remembers the girl because she was, in his words, 'young and hot,' and the man she was with was 'old and fat.' According to Getz, the man paid for the room in cash. The security camera behind the counter is busted, so we have no visuals on either of them. Same goes for the parking lot camera."

Medina snorted. "Now there's a surprise. The shit that goes on in that place, I don't think their security cameras have ever *not* been busted."

"The body was found on Wednesday morning by the maid, a woman called Jackie Salvas," Pryce said. "She had been sick since Sunday, so she hadn't reported for work in the early part of the week. No one else checked out the room, so Amy Ong was left there, undiscovered, for more than three days."

"I spoke to Salvas myself," Medina said. "She was pretty upset. Place like that, she'd come across a couple of stiffs in her time, but those were crack addicts who had overdosed. First time seeing a young girl all cut up like that."

Pryce frowned. "Three days, though. They don't have a replacement maid if someone gets sick or takes a vacation?"

Medina shrugged. "I'm surprised they have a maid at all."

"Fair point. Sounds like our guy wasn't too clever at cleaning up either. Forensics have lifted some good prints from the whiskey bottle and both of the plastic cups. Hopefully we'll get a hit from the system. Anything from the autopsy yet?"

"Preliminary report came back this morning." Medina stretched over to his own desk, picked up a file, and handed it to Pryce. He finished his bagel and coffee while Pryce read through the report.

"Time of death was estimated between nine p.m. Saturday night and one a.m. Sunday morning," Pryce said. "Cause of death was cardiac tamponade, resulting from penetration of the pericardium." He noticed Medina's confused expression. "A stab wound to the heart," he explained. "That was the fatal one. She'd been stabbed eleven times in total. She had a broken nose and contusions to her left cheekbone. Severed finger defending herself. The report also says she had sex shortly before she died."

"You think he raped her?"

Pryce scanned the relevant paragraph and shook his head. "There were no signs of bruising or tearing around the vagina, indicating the sex was consensual. No traces of semen. They used a condom."

"Wasn't found at the scene," Medina said. "Probably flushed down the john."

Pryce let out a heavy sigh. "The report also says she was pregnant. Around three months."

"Aw, shit. But why bother with a condom?"

"Maybe she didn't know she was already pregnant. Or this guy wasn't the father. It's not just pregnancy young women need to protect themselves against these days."

"I guess."

"So what are we looking at here?" Pryce asked. "Amy Ong goes on a date, and things go better than expected; they decide to carry on the party at the Dreamz Motel, they have a few drinks, do the deed—and then what?"

"Could be this guy is into rough stuff?" Medina offered. "Slapped her around a bit while they were doing the business, she didn't like it, things got out of hand?"

"Maybe. But she was wearing underwear and a bathrobe when she was found, so she was most likely killed after they'd finished having sex."

"Okay. He wanted round two. She didn't. It turned ugly. Or maybe he was the baby's daddy and didn't take the news too good."

"Maybe," Pryce said again. He ran his hands down his face, rubbed his eyes. "Or maybe this was no ordinary date."

Medina looked confused. "What do you mean?"

"The roommate says she had no idea where Amy Ong was going or who she was meeting. Does that not strike you as weird?"

"I guess. But what do I know about what women talk to each other about?"

"Exactly." Pryce looked around the squad room. He spotted Silvia Rodriguez, a detective two, over by the filing cabinets. "Hey, Silvia," he called. "You got a minute?"

Rodriguez was a petite brunette, a couple of years younger than Pryce, who had gained her cop's badge in her midtwenties after finishing law school and having a change of heart over her choice of career.

"What's up, guys?" She perched on the edge of Medina's desk. "I hear you caught the Ong case? Sounds like a real nasty one."

"That's what I wanted to ask you about," Pryce said. "When was the last time you were on a hot date?"

Rodriguez raised an eyebrow, looked from Pryce to Medina and back to Pryce again. She held up her left hand and pointed to a slim gold band. "If that's your way of asking me out to dinner, Pryce, you're about fifteen years too late." She winked. "But if you're offering to take me to that fancy new Italian place on Melrose, I'll think about it."

Pryce laughed. "Yeah, and if Angie found out, it'd be my balls instead of meatballs they'd be serving up for the special."

"So what's all this about hot dates?" she asked.

"You went to college, right?"

"Sure did. Then I realized it was way more fun catching criminals than finding ways to let them walk."

"Cast your mind back to when you were a student. If you had a date on a Saturday night, you'd tell your roommate all about it, wouldn't you? Especially if you were close friends."

"Sure. We'd spend at least a couple of hours picking out the perfect outfit, doing hair and makeup, and figuring out if the guy was a keeper or not depending on where he was taking you."

"Huh?" Medina asked.

"You know, drinks in a bar, he probably just wants to get laid. Dinner in a nice restaurant, he might actually like you. A ride in his car with a six-pack in the back? Forget it."

"Who knew it was so complicated?" Medina said.

"With kids these days, it'd be much the same?" Pryce asked. "The stuff about knowing all the details, I mean."

"Probably even more intense now." Rodriguez laughed. "What with Facebook and Snapchat and Instagram, a guy's whole life is probably dissected before your girlfriends even let you agree to the date."

"Exactly," Pryce said. "Thanks, Silvia."

"Glad I could help."

Medina watched Rodriguez walk back to the filing cabinets, then turned to Pryce. "What now?"

"Now we pay a visit to Kasey Taylor and find out why she's been lying."

The midmorning traffic on the Hollywood Freeway was slow moving, and it was forty minutes later before Pryce turned his midnight-blue Dodge Charger onto Paseo Rancho Castilla in the east of the city. Up ahead stood a small cylindrical building painted in shades of beige and terra-cotta. The words *Cal State LA* were spelled out in sunshine-yellow letters above an LED screen welcoming visitors to campus.

Pryce pulled up next to an information window and waited until a woman with silver hair and a plump pink face appeared behind the glass. She pulled aside a small screen in the window and smiled at them. "How can I help you?"

Pryce reached through the open car window and showed the woman his badge. "Detective Pryce." He gestured to Medina. "This is my partner, Detective Medina. We're investigating the homicide of Amy Ong and were hoping to speak to her roommate, Kasey Taylor. Is Miss Taylor around this morning?"

The woman nodded grimly. "Your colleagues were here yesterday too. Such a tragedy. One moment, please."

She disappeared from view, and Pryce could hear tapping on a computer keyboard. A few moments later, she was back in front of the window. "As I thought, Kasey Taylor has been given compassionate leave from class at least until the end of the week. You should find her at her apartment on campus." She handed Pryce a parking permit and gave him directions to the housing complex.

They continued farther along Paseo Rancho Castilla. Passed by the student union building, which overlooked a busy sidewalk where bicycles were propped against trees and clusters of students sat on benches, drinking sodas and passing the time between classes. They took a right at the imposing redbrick affair that was the Luckman Theatre, onto Circle Drive, and parked in the lot in front of the music hall.

It was a gorgeous day, with clear blue skies overhead and a pleasant warmth in the air. They crossed the parking lot, weaving their way past students of all ages and cultures wearing tank tops and cutoffs and summer dresses and holding book bags and paper-filled binders.

Medina looked around him. "You know, I should've gone to college. Surrounded myself with all these beautiful, smart young women, instead of sweaty wannabe cops at the academy."

"Class of '55?" Pryce quipped, eyeing his partner's trademark outfit of blue Levi's jeans, tight white T-shirt, black leather jacket, and Ray-Bans.

Medina ignored the jibe and slicked back his long dark hair. "Maybe I'll become one of those mature students," he said. "Make something of myself."

"It's never too late, Fonzie. But you do know you need brains for college, right?"

They stopped in front of steep stone steps leading down through trees and shrubbery to the two- and three-story gray buildings of the phase I housing complex below them. From this vantage point, they could see the hills and rooftops of the western tip of the San Gabriel Valley stretching out for miles beyond the apartment buildings. They stood there for a moment, enjoying the view and the warmth of the sun on their faces, before making their way down the steps.

Kasey Taylor's apartment was on the second floor at the top of a dim stairwell. Medina rapped his knuckles on the door, and eventually they heard footsteps padding down the hallway before the peephole darkened. They both held up their badges.

"Miss Taylor?" Pryce said loudly. "Detectives Pryce and Medina from the LAPD. We'd like to ask you a few questions, if that's okay?"

They heard the scrape of a metal chain before the door opened to reveal a slim blonde woman wearing gray lounge pants and a loose pink T-shirt. Her hair hadn't been brushed, and dark circles stood out like smudges of purple paint on her pale, drawn face.

"Come on in."

They followed her down a short entrance hall into a compact living area, with a kitchenette off to the left and sliding patio doors leading to a balcony on the right.

"Can I get you anything?" she asked. "Tea? Coffee? Water?"

They both shook their heads, and she sank onto a blue two-seater couch that looked more functional than comfortable, like the kind usually found in office waiting areas. She tucked her legs underneath her and ran a hand through her unkempt hair.

"Sorry. I must look a mess," she said. "The doctor gave me sedatives to help me sleep, and I only woke up a half hour ago. I haven't had a chance to shower or dress yet."

Pryce sat on a bucket chair facing her. "No problem, Kasey. We won't take up much of your time."

"I already gave a statement to the officers who were here yesterday."

Pryce glanced at Medina, standing in the doorway. "We just wanted to ask a few more questions about Amy," he said.

At the mention of her friend's name, Kasey's brown eyes filled with tears. She blinked, and fat droplets spilled down her cheeks. She sniffed and wiped her face with the back of her hand. "What do you want to know?"

"How did you and Amy first meet?" Pryce asked. "Were you in the same class?"

"No, we became friends after being assigned to this apartment together. Amy is—*was*—majoring in criminal justice. I have no idea what that even means." She smiled sadly. "She was real smart."

"And you?"

"I'm studying theatre and dance. Totally different from Amy, although she was really good at helping me with my written assignments. I'm going to be an actress when I finish college. I've already done a couple of commercials."

Pryce didn't even have to look at Medina to know he was rolling his eyes. Everyone knew someone in this town who thought they were going to make it as an actress.

"The two of you were close, right?"

She nodded. "We roomed together for two years. She was my best friend." The last two words sparked a fresh wave of tears, and Kasey covered her face with her hands, her narrow shoulders shaking with each sob. "I'm sorry. I just miss her so much."

The girl appeared genuinely distraught, thought Pryce. If this was a demonstration of her acting skills, then Jennifer Lawrence had better watch out, because this kid clearly had Oscar glory in her future. He waited for her to compose herself, then leaned forward in his chair. "We want to catch the guy who did this to Amy," he said gently. "But we need your help, Kasey."

She looked up at Pryce and nodded. "Okay."

"When did Amy first mention to you that she had a date?"

"Um, I'm not sure. The day before, maybe."

"How did she know the guy?"

"I think they met online."

"You mean a dating website?"

"Yeah. Or maybe an app. Everybody on campus uses them to hook up."

Pryce thought of Tommy Getz's description of Amy Ong's companion at the Dreamz Motel. "Was he a student here at Cal State or someone older?"

She shrugged. "I don't know."

"Did she tell you his name? Where he's from?"

Kasey shook her head.

"These apps usually have profile pictures, right? Did Amy show you a photo of him?"

"No."

"What about the date itself? Did she say where she was meeting him? Where he was taking her? The name of a bar or restaurant?"

Kasey looked away, chewed on her fingernails. "I don't think she told me where she was going."

She was a terrible liar. Maybe Jennifer Lawrence had nothing to worry about after all.

"You know, I have a daughter myself," Pryce said. "She's a few years younger than you. Her name is Dionne, and she has a best friend called Shelley. They're inseparable."

Kasey stared at him, waiting for him to get to the point.

Pryce went on. "And what I know about teenage girls is they like to share stuff with their best friends. Dionne can spend hours chatting to Shelley about everything and anything. Boys, shopping, school, television shows, their latest celebrity crushes. You name it, I've overheard them talking about it. A lot of it involves Justin Bieber."

"So?"

"So my point is, Kasey, best friends tell each other things."

"I already told those other cops everything I know."

"I don't think you did."

Her eyes narrowed. "I don't know what you mean."

"Amy told you who she was meeting on Saturday night, didn't she?"

She looked away again. "No."

"Wake up, Kasey!" Pryce yelled, causing both Kasey and Medina to jump. "We're trying to catch the guy who killed your best friend. You seriously expect me to believe Amy had a date and didn't tell you a single detail about it?"

She pursed her lips. "I don't know anything."

"You're lying to me, and I want to know why. Who are you trying to protect? Amy? Him? Yourself?"

Kasey's head whipped around to face him. "I haven't done anything wrong," she snapped.

"What about Amy? Did she do something wrong?"

"No."

"So tell me who her date was with last Saturday night. So we can stop this guy before he does it again. Is that what you want? For him to hurt some other young girl? Do you really want that on your conscience?"

Kasey sighed and closed her eyes and slumped on the couch like a blow-up doll with all the air let out. More tears ran down her cheeks. "It wasn't a date," she finally mumbled.

"What?"

"I said it wasn't a date. Are you happy now?"

Pryce's cell phone buzzed in his pants pocket. He ignored it. "If it wasn't a date, what was it?"

She chewed on her bottom lip. "Amy called it a business arrangement."

"What kind of business arrangement?"

She glared at him. "Do I really have to spell it out to you?"

"Please do."

Medina's cell phone began to chirp. He stepped out into the hallway. Pryce could hear a muffled conversation taking place.

"Amy lost one of her main scholarships, okay?" Kasey threw her arm out, gesturing around the room they were sitting in. "This place might not exactly be the Four Seasons, but it isn't cheap either—and neither is tuition. She knew her folks didn't have the money, and she didn't want to go back to Ohio and give up on her career. She was desperate."

"She was having sex with men for money?"

"Look, she wasn't hanging around street corners. She didn't have a pimp. She wasn't on drugs. It was once or twice a month at most and with a handful of regular guys."

"And last Saturday?"

"She called him Frank. She'd met him maybe a half dozen times before. That's all I know. You have to believe me. I told her I didn't want to know anything about those men or what she did with them."

"Was this Frank guy the father of her baby?"

Kasey's mouth dropped open. "Baby? What baby?"

"Amy was pregnant. Three months."

"You're lying." She appeared genuinely shocked. "No way was Amy pregnant. I would have known."

"I'm not lying, and there's no mistake, Kasey. Amy was definitely pregnant, although it's possible she didn't even know herself."

Kasey nodded. Then her face changed as realization dawned on her. "No, she knew," she whispered, shaking her head. "She'd stopped drinking alcohol weeks ago. Said she'd put on a few pounds, wanted to lose some weight."

"Why didn't she tell you?" Pryce asked gently.

"Because she knew I'd convince her to have an abortion. Don't you see? She gave up the booze—that means she wanted to keep it."

Pryce nodded. "These men she was seeing—how did they find her?"

"Online. I don't know which sites."

"We have her laptop. Hopefully we'll find something in her browsing history."

"You won't. Her laptop was for college work only. She always used her cell phone for the . . . other stuff."

"Her cell phone is missing."

Kasey shrugged. "She always had it with her."

Medina reappeared in the doorway. He held up his own cell phone and pointed in the direction of the street.

Pryce stood up, pulled a business card from his back pocket, and handed it to Kasey. "Here are my numbers," he said. "If you think of anything else, call me. We'll see ourselves out."

Outside in the stairwell, Medina nodded toward the closed door. "I thought you said you needed brains to go to college?"

"Who was on the phone?" Pryce asked.

Medina broke into a grin. "Latents Unit. They have a hit on the prints."

8

JESSICA

Jessica woke with a dull ache behind her eyes and a sour taste in her mouth, her legs tangled in bedsheets as thin as cigarette papers. A two-inch gap in the curtains threw a narrow beam of light across a dusty hardwood floor.

It took a few seconds before she remembered which motel room she was in.

Which town.

Then everything came back to her in a rush.

After Holliday had left the bar, she'd had another whiskey. Then another. And then a double for the road, which was a walk of no more than ten minutes along York Boulevard from the bar to the motel.

Something jarred at the back of her brain now, the vaguest whisper of a booze-soaked memory dislodging itself. Jessica squeezed her eyes shut and tried to recall what was so important about that short journey. Then she remembered. The feeling of being watched every step of the way.

Every time she'd looked over her shoulder, all Jessica could see were dark shop fronts and empty parking lots, the sodium beam of car headlights occasionally sweeping across the empty street, emphasizing she was alone. Even so, she'd felt like someone's eyes were on her, following her. The kind of feeling that made the tiny hairs on your arms stand on end and your heart beat a little too fast.

Now, with the alcohol haze gone and in a locked room with a Glock 26 on the nightstand, Jessica should have been able to put her paranoia down to being drunk and on her own late at night in an unfamiliar town. But despite the locked door and a weapon within easy reach, she still couldn't completely shake off the feeling of unease.

Jessica threw back the sheets and walked gingerly to the bathroom. She had a cold shower to clear her head and scrubbed off last night's makeup with a rough washcloth. Gargled twice with mouthwash after brushing her teeth to get rid of the lingering whiskey aftertaste. Then she towel dried her hair; carefully applied eyeshadow, liner, and mascara; and dressed in slim black cropped pants, a striped T-shirt, and Converse sneakers. She needed coffee and carbs to get rid of what was left of the hangover.

The heat outside was as heavy as a wool coat, and the cloudless sky blazed bright turquoise and gold. Jessica glanced at the room to the right of her own, where a brass number six was nailed to the door. The curtains in the small, high window were open, and the parking space in front of the door was empty. She turned left, in the direction of the office.

There was no sign of Hopper or Holliday or anyone else in the lobby, but thankfully some doughnuts were still laid out on a tray on the counter. She piled a couple onto a paper plate, filled a takeout cup with strong black coffee from the Mr. Coffee machine, and took the breakfast back to her room.

She sat down at the desk, picked up a doughnut, and opened the laptop.

As a private investigator, Jessica regularly made use of various databases to carry out background checks for clients. The next hour was spent delving, as much as possible, into the past of Eleanor Lavelle. What she found was a woman whose short life seemed to have had more missing pieces than a yard sale jigsaw puzzle. No matter how hard she looked, Jessica couldn't quite see the full picture.

Holliday had been right about Eleanor Lavelle's early years. Eleanor's mother had been a known drug user and prostitute, with a long history of minor offenses: solicitation, possession, petty theft, drunk and disorderly behavior. An old police booking photo of Donna Lavelle showed a skinny twentysomething with a bad peroxide dye job sprouting two-inch roots, hard eyes, and cheeks like razor blades.

Eleanor Lavelle had come into the world in January 1967, and the woman who'd given birth to her had checked out just seven months later. It was the Summer of Love, when tens of thousands of hippies descended upon San Francisco's Haight-Ashbury neighborhood to make music and art and protest against 'Nam to a soundtrack provided by the Grateful Dead, Jefferson Airplane, and Quicksilver Messenger Service.

Around the same time, Donna Lavelle was pounding the backstreets of Hollywood, chasing johns, and scoring H. The flower children eventually grew up, got jobs, got old. Donna Lavelle never had.

It had been a Saturday in the middle of July when they'd found her. A feverishly hot day. The kind of day when the sun glinted off car windows, apartment blocks shimmered, and the blacktop began to melt beneath your feet. The kind of day when people lost their cool in the heat and tempers started to fray.

It wasn't a neighborhood where you'd expect the locals to call the cops, but that was exactly what Donna Lavelle's neighbor had done, complaining the baby next door wouldn't stop screaming. The noise had been going on all night and most of the day, and the woman had been convinced the child had been left on its own while its mother was out with one of her many male friends.

The two patrolmen who'd attended the call had found the place unlocked, the door slightly ajar, and Donna Lavelle sprawled on the couch, a cheap plastic belt still coiled around her arm and a dirty syringe lying on her belly. She'd been dead for a day, maybe two.

The baby, wearing a soiled diaper and a stained onesie, had been hot and hungry and suffering from malnutrition. She'd been taken straight to a nearby hospital before being turned over to child services a week later. There was no record of the baby's father or any other known relatives.

As she read through the words on the screen, it wasn't lost on Jessica just how much the intervention of a pissed neighbor might have impacted on her own life. That she might not even be sitting here today, sipping coffee and eating doughnuts, were it not for the actions of a woman who couldn't handle the sound of a screaming baby. Jessica took a deep breath and moved on to the next phase of Eleanor Lavelle's life.

Three years were spent in the care of a foster family with a view to an adoption that never happened. Jessica figured the circumstances of the foster carers had probably changed. Maybe they'd moved to another state or gotten pregnant and suddenly didn't have the room for someone else's kid. Either way, Eleanor had been one of the unlucky ones. A group home and two more foster families followed before she'd eventually aged out of the system at eighteen.

Then she'd disappeared. Vanished into thin air.

For the next three years in Eleanor's timeline, Jessica couldn't find a single record of employment, IRS payments, home ownership, or car purchases. Not even so much as a bank account in her name. She guessed Eleanor had made her living from cash-in-hand bar work, similar to the job at Ace's Bar, and had probably crashed at friends' places or moved from one short-term cash rental to another. But that was all it was, guesswork.

Eleanor Lavelle was a ghost until she suddenly reappeared as an apparently upstanding citizen of Eagle Rock in January 1988. She opened a bank account. She landed a job with a construction company. She paid taxes. She bought a car.

Her employment with Tav-Con lasted for ten months before she left, presumably to prepare for life as a stay-at-home mom. Following the birth of her daughter, Alicia, Eleanor had gone on welfare and lived at an address in Eagle Rock until her death in the fall of 1992.

Jessica had no idea whether those years spent under the radar had anything to do with Eleanor's violent end. If the things she did, the places she went, the people she knew were relevant in any way to her murder and the disappearance of her daughter.

A search for a current listing for Tav-Con in the Los Angeles area drew a blank. Five minutes later, Jessica had the reason why. The company had been sold in early 1993 to a rival construction firm, Premium Construction, for a not-too-shabby $6 million following the death of its owner, Lincoln Tavernier. The sale had been sanctioned by his daughter, Catherine, who had inherited Tav-Con after his passing. She'd later used some of the cash to set up her own advertising agency, according to various online profiles that all painted her as a successful, and formidable, businesswoman.

Jessica stood up and stretched and rolled her neck to relieve the knots of tension. She found a pack of Marlboro Lights and a BIC lighter at the bottom of her bag and walked over to the door with her cell phone.

She stood in the open doorway, lit a cigarette, and called the number for Catherine Tavernier's advertising agency. After a short conversation with her secretary and a sixty-second burst of Vivaldi's *Four Seasons* at an unnecessarily loud volume, Jessica was surprised to find she had an appointment with the woman at four p.m. that very afternoon at an address in Pasadena.

Next, she tried the main switchboard of the LAPD's Hollywood Station and was less surprised to discover that Detective Jason Pryce was unavailable, and they couldn't give out his cell phone number, no matter how important her call was. She left her name and her own digits before emphasizing again that she needed to speak to him as soon as possible.

Jessica took a final drag on the cigarette, dropped the butt on the ground, and crushed it beneath the sole of her sneaker. The cell phone screen in her hand told her it had just passed noon. She had time to kill before the meeting with Catherine Tavernier. She grabbed her bag and car keys, tucked her gun into her waistband under her T-shirt, and pulled the door shut behind her.

The offices of Eagle Rock's local newspaper were housed in a squat, single-story shop front squeezed between an artisan ice cream joint and a vinyl record store. Jessica had never felt any great desire to sample the kind of strange-sounding designer dairy products on display in the café's window. But the line for brown bread, burnt sugar, and red velvet Oreo ice cream had spilled out the front door and snaked along the sidewalk as folks sought a fun way to cool off on a sultry day.

She shook her head. *Only in Los Angeles.*

In sad contrast, the music store was empty, save for a bored-looking cashier behind a neat window display of records from the '50s, '60s, and '70s.

Unbidden, a memory of Tony popped into Jessica's head. She was sixteen the first time she'd heard Johnny Cash's iconic album *At Folsom Prison.* It was a Saturday night, and Tony had been in one of his melancholy moods when she'd returned home from a friend's house. The lights had been dimmed; a half-empty bottle of Jim Beam had sat on the coffee table next to an ashtray overflowing with cigarette butts, Cash's voice crackly and jumpy as the needle danced across the vinyl.

Tony'd had that sad, faraway look on his face he'd get sometimes when he'd been drinking, his eyes fixed on an image only he could see.

Picking up the album sleeve, Jessica had read the song listings on the back. "What's up, Tony?" she'd teased. She had always called her father Tony, never Dad. "Don't tell me you got the 'Folsom Prison Blues'?"

He'd laughed, but she'd noticed the smile didn't reach his eyes. She'd flopped on the couch and listened to a couple of songs with him for a while, then told him she thought this Johnny Cash fella must have been pretty brave, or really dumb, to play a gig in a prison full of murderers and rapists.

Tony had been silent for a few minutes, and she'd thought he hadn't heard her. Then, in a voice so low she almost couldn't hear it, he'd said, "Not everything's black and white in this world, Jess. Sometimes good people make mistakes. Sometimes innocent folk are locked up for things they didn't do. And sometimes, the really bad ones never have to pay for what they've done."

At the time, Jessica had had no idea what he was talking about, had put his ramblings down to too much liquor and jailhouse music.

Now, she wasn't sure she wanted to know.

She pushed open a heavy glass door and entered the compact reception area of the *Eagle Rock Reformer*. A large, lumpy woman with hair the color of straw and a sullen expression sat behind the front counter. She wore a shapeless black dress and a bunch of cheap metal bangles on each wrist that jangled whenever she moved. She could have been forty-five or sixty. It was impossible to tell.

The east and west walls were dominated by framed front pages depicting some of the paper's biggest stories over the years. There was the discovery of an early victim of the Hillside Strangler in an Eagle Rock neighborhood. The abduction of an eight-year-old girl by the Night Stalker. An exclusive interview with Ben Affleck, a former student of nearby Occidental College, after his Oscar win for best screenplay for *Good Will Hunting*. And there was the murder of a local woman and the disappearance of her toddler daughter.

Jessica turned away from the now-familiar image of Eleanor and Alicia Lavelle staring out from behind the glass and peered through an open doorway behind the receptionist leading to a medium-size office. Her idea of newsrooms had no doubt been influenced by old movies and television shows because she was expecting to find a bustling hub of activity, with phones ringing, keyboards clattering, and cigarette smoke hanging heavy in the air.

What she saw were four cubicles pushed up against each other in an awkward square, three of which were empty. The fourth was occupied by a young guy chewing a pencil and studying the page of a spiral-bound notepad. CNN was playing quietly in the background. The phones were silent. Jessica wondered if the other reporters were in the line outside waiting for weird ice cream.

The receptionist peered at her suspiciously over the rim of tortoise-shell-framed glasses, her eyes flitting first to the tattoos on Jessica's arm and then the piercing in her nose. She had the look of a wary woman who fully expected Jessica to leap across the counter and help herself to some free newspapers or ransack the stationery cupboard.

"Can I help you?" she asked with a frown.

The woman took off the glasses, letting them hang from a chain around her neck, the bangles jangling loudly. She reminded Jessica of a disapproving homeroom teacher in high school whom she'd hated with a passion.

Jessica offered the woman what she hoped passed for a friendly smile but what felt more like a grimace. "I sure hope so. I'm actually looking for a little favor."

The woman arched her eyebrows and pursed her lips but said nothing.

"My name's Jessica Shaw, and I'm a private investigator. I'm working on behalf of a client who is looking for some information on a couple of former Eagle Rock residents, and I was hoping I could take a look through some back copies of the newspaper to find out a little more about them?"

The receptionist was shaking her head before Jessica had even finished speaking. "This is a newspaper, not a public library," she said. "We can't just allow people to walk in off the street and access our files."

"I already tried the library," Jessica said. "They don't store old copies of the *Reformer*. Just back editions of the *Los Angeles Times* on microfilm. I was hoping for a more local angle, and they suggested I try here."

"Then I guess you're out of luck."

The receptionist put her glasses back on and turned to her computer screen, making it clear the conversation was over. Jessica turned to leave and was almost out of the front door when she heard a male voice behind her.

"A private eye, huh?"

She looked over her shoulder and saw the reporter leaning casually against the office doorframe, arms folded across his chest, an amused smile playing on his lips. He was older than she'd initially thought, closer to her own age, and kinda cute but dressed like someone's dad in a rumpled button-down shirt and tan corduroys.

"That's right," Jessica said, walking back into the reception area. "I'm doing some background research on some folks who used to live around here. I think they may have been in the newspaper once or twice, and I was hoping to have a look through some old back copies."

"Has something happened?" he asked. "I could certainly do with a good story for next week's splash. It's been a quiet news day." He laughed. "Make that a quiet news *month*."

Jessica smiled. "No, nothing new, I'm afraid. Neither of the people I'm looking into have lived in Eagle Rock for years."

He looked disappointed, and she wondered what he'd say if he knew he was possibly talking to one of the biggest scoops of his career.

Jessica went on, "But if I did happen to come across anything interesting, I'd be sure to let you know. You know, return the favor."

"Sounds fair enough to me," he said. "What did you say your name was?"

"Jessica Shaw."

He turned to the receptionist. "Darla, can you take Jessica through to the library and help her find the editions she's after, please?"

Darla's face reddened, and she glared at Jessica while addressing the reporter. "I already told Miss Shaw we don't allow access—"

"Oh, for Chrissake, Darla." He cut her off. "It's not exactly top secret information we keep back there. Every single one of those newspapers has been on sale to the general public at some point, remember? Now, please, help Jessica find what she's looking for."

He gave Jessica a cheeky wink and returned to his desk. Darla sat still for a moment or two as though debating whether to carry out his request. Or maybe she was just waiting for the red mist to settle. Finally, she stood and motioned brusquely for Jessica to follow her through the back office toward a glass door at the rear of the room. As Jessica passed by the reporter's desk, he plucked a business card from a leather tabletop holder and handed it to her.

"In case you do find anything interesting during your investigation."

She looked at the card. It read, "Garrett Thomas, Senior Reporter, the *Eagle Rock Reformer*." There were numbers for his direct office line and his cell phone. She said, "Sure, no problem, Garrett."

The library was actually a large windowless storage room with floor-to-ceiling metal shelves on three walls filled with bound volumes of every past issue of the *Reformer* filed by year. A polished wooden table with two leather-backed chairs on either side took up most of the space in the middle of the room. The place smelled musty, like old paper. It reminded Jessica of hanging out in real libraries when she was younger.

"What date do you want?" asked Darla.

"October 1992."

Jessica pulled out one of the chairs from the table, sat down, and dumped her bag on the floor. When Darla didn't move, she looked up and saw the woman was rooted to the spot, and all the color had drained from her face.

"Are you okay?" she asked.

Darla blinked a couple of times. "Yes, I'm fine. I'll go find those files."

She walked over to one of the shelving units and studied the spines for a moment before pulling out a large, heavy leather-bound volume with *July–Dec 1992* printed in gold letters on the spine and front cover. She placed it in front of Jessica on the table. The woman's hands were shaking. "I'll leave you to it," she said, heading quickly for the door.

Jessica waited until Darla pulled the glass door shut behind her before opening the book and carefully turning the pages until she came to the front page she'd seen in the picture frame in the reception area.

MANHUNT AFTER EAGLE ROCK WOMAN KILLED—CHILD STILL MISSING

By Jim Johnson, Staff Writer

Police were searching Wednesday for a knifeman they said stabbed and killed a local woman inside her Eagle Rock home.

The victim, identified as Eleanor Lavelle, 25, was pronounced dead at the scene. It is understood she suffered blows to the face and multiple stab wounds.

Her daughter, Alicia, 3, is still missing following the incident on Morrison Avenue, which took place Friday night / early Saturday.

Police were following "a definite line of inquiry," according to Detective Bill Geersen, who is heading up the investigation.

"Preliminary information would lead us to believe Ms. Lavelle knew her attacker," he told the *Reformer*.

Officers have spent several days searching the property and surrounding neighborhood.

The article ended with an appeal for anyone with information to contact a special tips line. Jessica flicked through the pages until she came to the following week's paper. The Lavelles were still front-page news.

COPS HUNT "PERSON OF INTEREST" IN EAGLE ROCK SLAYING

By Jim Johnson, Staff Writer

Police hunting the killer of local woman Eleanor Lavelle want to speak to a "person of interest" as part of their investigation.

Ms. Lavelle, 25, was laid to rest Monday at Glendale Memorial Park following a private service.

Her daughter, Alicia, 3, has been missing since the incident at the family's Eagle Rock home.

A police source told the *Reformer*, "We believe a male acquaintance of Eleanor Lavelle may hold information crucial to the investigation, and we want to speak to this man as a matter of urgency."

It is understood Detective Bill Geersen and his team have so far been unable to locate the whereabouts of the potential witness since Ms. Lavelle's tragic death.

When asked if the man was a suspect in her murder, the source added, "We are simply treating this man as a 'person of interest' for now."

Meanwhile, Eagle Rock residents spoke of their shock at the homicide/abduction.

Veronica Howe, 52, said, "It's hard to believe something like this could happen right on your doorstep. I hope the cops find who did this terrible thing so we can all sleep easier at night."

Tom Connelly, 41, said, "I live on the next street. They seemed like a nice family. It's a tragedy what's happened."

Jessica took a photo of both articles with her cell phone and then searched through every other edition of the *Reformer* for the remainder of 1992, but there were no reports of the person of interest being found or any arrests being made. She went over to the shelving unit where Darla had pulled the bound volume from and found one for early 1993. She looked through the newspapers from the first couple of months of the year, but there were still no major developments. A lack of a breakthrough in the investigation meant the story had quickly dropped off the front pages before coverage of the case had ceased altogether. Jessica packed up her things and returned both volumes to the shelf.

"Find anything?" Garrett Thomas called as she headed for the exit.

"Nothing interesting," she said.

Even as she spoke the words, Jessica's mind was whirring with the knowledge the cops had had a suspect in the murder of Eleanor Lavelle—and the disappearance of Alicia—whom they'd never been able to track down.

9

JESSICA

The meeting with Catherine Tavernier was at her home and not, as Jessica had assumed, at the woman's office.

South Oak Knoll Avenue was the kind of neighborhood where you needed a trust fund and an Ivy League education just to be allowed to deliver the mail to its residents. Multimillion-dollar homes sat back from a street lined on both sides by the eponymous oaks, many of the properties hidden away behind ornate wrought iron gates.

Jessica glanced down at her outfit and thought of Darla's earlier disapproval. Maybe she should have worn heels and a cute pencil skirt or a smart pantsuit. At least made an effort to cover the tattoos. She quickly dismissed the thought with a muttered "Fuck it" and decided she really didn't care what Catherine Tavernier thought of her sartorial choices. She was here as part of an investigation, not for a job interview.

Jessica double-checked the house number scrawled on a Post-it Note stuck to the dash and pulled up in front of twin gates flanked on either side by hedges as neat as a Brazilian wax. Before she had the chance to wind down the driver's-side window and search for an intercom, the gates swung inward, permitting entry to the grounds of a stunning Spanish colonial–style house. The place had probably been built in the 1920s, but its gleaming white stucco exterior and red clay tiled roof were immaculate.

She parked in the driveway next to a noisy water fountain feature and made her way toward the front door. It opened to reveal a thin, birdlike woman with sharp features and short gray hair, wearing a cream silk blouse and navy slacks.

"Ms. Tavernier?"

The woman looked nothing like the pictures Jessica had seen online, but she held out her hand anyway.

The woman's grip was weak and clammy. She smiled and shook her head. "I'm Iris—I'm Catherine's housekeeper. You must be Jessica?"

She nodded.

"Please, come in," Iris said, stepping aside so Jessica could enter the house. "Catherine is expecting you."

Jessica walked into an impressive entrance hall dominated by a wood and wrought iron staircase and decorated with modern art canvases and giant vases that probably cost more than she made in a year. She kept her arms straight down by her side, careful not to bump into anything, and followed Iris into a room with high beamed ceilings, leather chesterfield sofas, and bookcases stuffed full of hardcovers.

The centerpiece of the room was a large white stone fireplace with photographs in shiny silver frames spaced equally along the surface of the mantel. A sixty-inch television screen hung above the fireplace on the wall. Iris told Jessica to make herself comfortable while she went to find her employer.

Alone in the room, Jessica wandered over to the bookshelves and studied the titles but saw no books or authors she was familiar with. Not one James Patterson or Dan Brown. She went over to the fireplace and looked at the photos but found them to be only slightly more interesting than the books.

There were black-and-white shots of a young couple on their wedding day and a small blonde child on her own. A more recent photo showed a middle-aged woman wearing tennis whites and clutching a bronze trophy. The same woman was also in a photo with two friends.

They were all holding aloft champagne flutes and sitting around a cake decorated with a "50" candle and sparklers.

Jessica perched awkwardly on the edge of one of the chesterfields just as the woman in the photographs swept into the room in a cloud of Chanel No. 5.

Like the house, Catherine Tavernier was a tasteful mix of old and new. As given away by the birthday celebration photo, she was in her fifties, but there were definitely parts of her that weren't even close to seeing a half century yet.

Her nose was a perfect straight line, and her breasts, although small, were perkier than those of a twenty-year-old. Her complexion was bright and fresh, as though she enjoyed regular expensive facials or had the number for one of Beverly Hills' top cosmetic surgeons on speed dial.

She wore a sleeveless black dress that showed off broad shoulders and tanned, supertoned arms. Her silver-blonde hair looked like it had just been professionally blow-dried at the salon. Even so, she struck Jessica as a woman you would describe as handsome rather than beautiful or pretty.

Catherine strode confidently across the room, and Jessica rose to accept her offer of a handshake that was way more robust than her housekeeper's flaccid effort had been. It wasn't a bone crusher but not a weak-assed lady pump either—a handshake that had clearly been honed over many years of boardroom meetings and business deals.

"Thanks for agreeing to see me, especially at your home," Jessica said. "I had assumed our meeting would be taking place at your office."

Catherine smiled. "I'm winding down toward semiretirement, so I mostly just work mornings now. And I thought the house would be a more pleasant environment for a chat."

"It's a beautiful home," Jessica said, mainly because she felt like she had to acknowledge the lavish surroundings. But it was true—the place did have the wow factor. For a prime piece of real estate like this, she figured there wouldn't be much change left over from $4 million.

"Thank you," Catherine said. "I like it well enough. Would you like an iced tea or some coffee? Or I have a lovely 2013 zinfandel from the Napa Valley?"

"An iced tea would be great, thanks."

Catherine turned to the housekeeper, who was hovering in the doorway. "I'll have some of the wine, please, Iris. Could you bring the drinks outside? It's too nice a day to sit indoors."

Jessica followed Catherine through a set of french doors out into a backyard with a kidney-shaped pool and a hot tub enclosed by an abundance of lush trees, plants, and flowers. The whole area was thoughtfully designed, with octagonal Saltillo pavers, a vine-covered pergola near the pool, and a porch with a dining table and a corner seating space filled with plump cushions and more ornate vases and lanterns holding tiny tea lights.

The heady, sweet fragrance of honeysuckle filled the air, and it was easy to imagine how great the place would be for al fresco parties, with the pool and fairy lights all lit up and the Napa Valley wine flowing as guests mingled in the warm evening breeze.

A nice way to live if you could afford it.

They sat at the dining table, shaded from the sun but still able to enjoy what was left of a glorious afternoon, as the rays glinted off the pool's glassy turquoise surface and cicadas sang unseen in the surrounding foliage.

Catherine kicked off the conversation without waiting for any prompting from Jessica. Another business meeting tactic, no doubt. "So you're a private investigator?" she said. "That must be exciting. And a little dangerous, too, I would imagine."

Jessica smiled. "It has its moments."

"My secretary tells me Tav-Con came up as part of one of your investigations. I'm intrigued. I sold the business twenty-some years ago.

Please don't tell me you've found someone I owe money to after all this time."

Jessica laughed. "No, nothing like that. I actually wanted to ask you about one of Tav-Con's former employees. A woman named Eleanor Lavelle?"

A shadow passed briefly across Catherine's face. She nodded. "The young woman who was killed in Eagle Rock. I don't think they ever found the child, did they?" She looked at Jessica. "Or is that why you're investigating the case? Have they found the little girl or the person who killed the mother?"

"No, unfortunately not," Jessica said. "There haven't been any new developments. My client simply wants me to cast a fresh eye over the case, what with the twenty-fifth anniversary approaching."

Catherine looked wistful. "Twenty-five years. How quickly time passes."

Iris appeared with the iced tea in a tall glass and a goldfish bowl–size wineglass. She placed the drinks on a couple of napkins, like a cocktail waitress, then scuttled off back into the house. Jessica drank some of the iced tea to be polite, but it was actually pretty good.

"Did you know Eleanor Lavelle?" she asked.

Catherine took a small sip of the wine and shook her head. "I never met her. I know she worked for my father briefly, but I was at school in Boston at the time. In any case, I had no real interest in the business back then. I was far more interested in boys and parties. I rarely visited the premises, so I didn't really know any of the employees."

"But you do remember the case?"

"Of course," she said. "Everyone was shocked by what happened. A young woman attacked in her own home like that. But I don't remember a lot of the details, I'm afraid. It was a difficult time for my family.

"My father had been diagnosed with terminal lung cancer in August of that year, and his health deteriorated very quickly. My mother and I spent a lot of time at the hospital with him while he underwent various tests and treatment before eventually moving on to palliative care. All that money and they still couldn't save him."

Catherine smiled sadly, lost in the memory.

She went on. "He died in November 1992, and most of my time in the weeks after his death was spent dealing with lawyers with regard to the business and his estate. I do recall what happened to the woman and her daughter being on the news a lot around the same time, but my focus was on my father. We were very close."

"I lost my own father two years ago," Jessica said. "I don't think it's something you ever get over." Her voice caught slightly on the words, and she coughed to clear her throat. "If you don't mind me asking, why did your father leave the business to you rather than Mrs. Tavernier?"

Catherine gave a short laugh. "My mother was a lovely woman but not business minded at all. The only thing she knew about money was how to spend it. She was well looked after, of course, but both my parents were happy for Tav-Con to be passed into my hands. And I had my father's blessing to sell the company and set up my own business. He always knew the construction industry wasn't really me."

"I'm sure he would have been very proud of what you've gone on to achieve."

"Yes, I suppose he would." She smiled ruefully. "In a business sense, anyway."

According to the profiles Jessica had read online, Catherine Tavernier had been married twice but never had any children. Her first husband had been a fellow student at Boston University, and the marriage had been short lived. Her second husband, a partner in a law firm, had two sons from a previous relationship, but they didn't have any kids together.

All very interesting in a Page Six kind of way, but Jessica was keen to steer the conversation back to the Lavelles.

"Did your father ever mention Eleanor Lavelle?" she asked. "What she was like as an employee? What sort of work she did for the company?"

"She was one of three administrative staff who worked in the office," Catherine said. "I suppose her duties would have included filing, answering the telephone, dealing with customer inquiries, things like that. I believe she did the job well enough, and she was very popular with Tav-Con's clients. Quite a vivacious young woman, according to my father."

"A good employee, then? No problems that you know of?"

Catherine looked uncomfortable and took a long drink of wine before answering.

"My father thought she was personally involved with another member of the staff," she said finally. "Whenever the construction workers came into the office, she would be a little flirtatious with them, and he suspected the flirtation had spilled over into what he felt was an inappropriate relationship with one of the men. He never said who the man was or why he thought they were seeing each other, but he did ask for my advice on the matter."

"And what did you say?"

"I told him to stop being such an old bore and let them get on with it. Unless he caught them in flagrante on work premises, I didn't see how it was any of his business. Lots of people meet their partners at work. Then the woman became pregnant and left the company to be a full-time mother, so the situation resolved itself. The next time I heard her name mentioned was on the news."

Jessica nodded. She couldn't think of anything more to say, so she finished what was left of the iced tea and stood up. "Thanks for your time, Catherine. You've been very helpful."

"No problem at all. If you think of anything else you want to ask, just give me a call." She produced a business card from a pocket in the dress and handed it to Jessica. "I'll see you out."

Back in the truck, Jessica pulled her cell phone from the glove compartment and switched it on. Once the screen came to life, a text from her IT contact in New York appeared. It wasn't good news. He could tell Jessica who John Doe's internet service provider was and that the email had been sent from somewhere in the Los Angeles area, but that was about it. A dead end.

Jessica sighed and hit the redial button and tried the Hollywood Station again, but Jason Pryce was still unavailable. She left another message for the detective, again stressing how important it was that she speak to him as soon as possible. Then she eased the Silverado through the gates back onto South Oak Knoll Avenue and followed the GPS instructions to return to Eagle Rock.

Jessica had been on the Arroyo Seco Parkway for about five minutes when she first noticed the black SUV in her rearview mirror.

10

AMY

The bar on Las Palmas was all corrugated iron on the outside and exposed brick walls inside. With a dozen flat-screen TVs, spray can graffiti art, and five-dollar shots, it had a trailer park aesthetic and old-school vibe that was supposed to be ironic rather than literal.

Amy spotted him immediately because he was the only person in the place over the age of twenty-five. Frank (no last names) leaned casually on the bar, a bottle of beer in his hand. He wore a dress shirt tucked into jeans belted below a heaving belly and looked completely out of place among the surfer dudes and college kids.

The bar had been Frank's suggestion, and she felt embarrassed for him, choosing such an inappropriate venue for a man of his age. Or maybe his selection had been for her benefit, to make her feel more relaxed.

Yeah, fat chance.

Amy wove her way through the crowd until she reached the bar. She tapped him on the shoulder. "Sorry I'm late."

He was wearing too much cologne, and it caught in her throat as she spoke, making her cough, but Frank didn't seem to notice. "Cindy! You made it."

He gave her a wet kiss on the cheek, and she had to resist the urge to wipe the damp spot left behind on her skin.

"Do you want your usual?" Frank asked the question just loudly enough for other patrons nearby to overhear, as though he was trying to give off the impression Amy was his wife or girlfriend. She noticed the bartender, a hot guy with lots of tattoos and a pierced septum, give her a quizzical look as if to say, *What the hell are you doing with the old fat guy?*

"Just a Diet Coke, please."

Frank frowned. "You sure? You don't want a chardonnay instead?"

"A soda is fine."

Frank ordered the drinks while Amy gazed around the room. The place was full of kids her own age laughing, drinking, flirting, having fun. She felt a pang and wasn't sure if it was jealousy or resentment.

The soda arrived, and she took a sip, wishing she'd had some booze after all. She was torn between wanting the night to be over with as soon as possible and putting off what lay ahead.

Frank watched her as she drank, barely concealed desire in his eyes. They were small beady eyes, and they took in every inch of her body. He drained his bottle of Bud and licked his lips. "I, uh, have a place in mind for tonight. It's nearby. You ready to go?"

Amy wasn't ready to go. She didn't want to leave the bar, with its people and music and carefree fun. "I was thinking we could have another drink here? It seems like a cool place."

"Why don't we pick up some liquor on the way? Get us in the mood. A private party is way more fun."

He winked and pressed his crotch discreetly against her hip, making it clear he was already in the mood.

"Sure thing."

She moved away from Frank's excitement and placed the glass on the bar. The cute bartender caught her eye.

"Leaving so soon?" he asked.

"I guess so."

"Shame," he said with a shy smile.

"Yes, it is."

She followed Frank to the exit, feeling like a woman walking to her own execution.

Frank's Corvette convertible was parked half a block away. Amy lowered herself into the passenger seat and glanced in the side-view mirror. The soft top was up, and she twisted around to look through its tiny rear window.

She'd noticed a black SUV on two occasions recently, while out with other clients, and she was worried about being tailed by a disgruntled wife. Not Frank's, though. The poor woman apparently had no idea what her husband was getting up to while he pretended to work late and attend business conferences.

"Something wrong?" Frank looked antsy. Maybe his wife wasn't so oblivious after all.

There was no sign of a black SUV with tinted windows.

Amy said, "No, just thought I recognized someone from college."

She fastened her seat belt as Frank started the car and eased into the evening traffic. She zoned out as he bragged about a big insurance deal he'd landed at work.

Neither of them noticed the red Ford Focus that had been parked three spaces behind the Corvette follow as they turned onto Hollywood Boulevard.

11

JESSICA

The vehicle was big and wide with a silver grille on the front and tinted windows. Probably a Ford or a Subaru. It remained five cars back as Jessica continued along the freeway, her eyes flitting between the road ahead and the rearview mirror.

She took the next off-ramp, as advised by the GPS, and as she turned onto York Boulevard, Jessica saw the black SUV follow. It was now three cars back. Instead of staying on York, she hooked a quick right onto North Figueroa Street, and the SUV stayed with her. Jessica's heartbeat punched against her ribs, and her breath quickened. She signaled a left turn onto Yosemite Drive and glanced in the rearview mirror again.

The SUV was gone.

Jessica heaved a sigh of relief but remained alert for the reappearance of a tail as she continued her journey back to the motel. By the time she pulled into the Blue Moon Inn's lot several minutes later, she was sure she was no longer being followed.

If she was even being followed at all.

Maybe the SUV's driver had simply been taking a similar route to her own. Even so, Jessica decided she would keep her weapon within easy reach at all times from now on.

For a pacifist who had never even been involved in a fistfight as far as Jessica knew, Tony had always been big on personal protection.

Always insisted on having guns in the house. Once she was old enough, they'd often spend Sunday afternoons together at the shooting range on West Twentieth Street. Jessica, a beginner learning how to handle a firearm properly. Tony, brushing up on existing skills.

Some weekends, they would head out to a cabin in the woods in Upstate New York, plinking tin cans and hunting squirrels and rabbits.

"One day, you might have to shoot something bigger than a small animal," Tony told her. "You might be the hunted instead of the hunter, and you'll need to be prepared."

The night before her first day working as a private investigator, Tony had presented Jessica with a box wrapped in pink tissue paper. Inside, nestled among more folds of tissue paper, like a new pair of shoes, was a Glock 17. It had served her well during her first couple of years on the job. These days, she preferred the more compact and discreet Glock 26. For Jessica, it was about protection, not confrontation. Even though she had drawn her weapon countless times, she'd still never shot anything bigger than a rabbit.

A couple of hours later, Jessica was back in Ace's Bar armed with both the baby Glock and a Bud Light. She was in the same booth, which she was now starting to think of as her booth. She ordered a cheeseburger and fries and decided to stick with the beer and lay off the hard stuff after this morning's hangover.

The bar was quiet. No Jack Holliday. No hat guy or any of his work friends. The old man was here again, occupying what she assumed was his usual booth and playing a game of solitaire. Ace Freeman was behind the bar. Jessica hadn't spoken to him yet, other than to place the food order, but she was pretty sure he was Ace Freeman because he had the name Ace tattooed onto his right bicep above an inking of the playing card.

You didn't need to be a private investigator to figure it out.

Jessica sat and watched him for a while as he worked, chopping lemons and limes for drink garnishes, wiping down the counter, refilling the refrigerator with beer and wine.

He had long hair tied back loosely in a ponytail that was too black and too shiny to be natural, especially considering his advanced years. Like the younger bartender, he was dressed casually in jeans and a band T-shirt, this one with *Slayer* across the chest and tour dates on the back. He was slim from behind, but a beer belly from the front betrayed his fondness for sampling his own products.

He took a tumbler of whiskey and a schooner of beer over to the old man, who was now the only customer in the place other than Jessica. Then Freeman wandered over to her booth.

"Getcha anything else?" he asked.

"Another Bud Light and a couple of minutes of your time."

The man nodded. "Let me get rid of these." He picked up the plate, silverware, and empty beer bottle and disappeared in the kitchen out back before reappearing a couple of minutes later with two more beers. He slid into the booth facing Jessica.

"Razor told me a pretty little blonde was in here last night asking for me. That would be you?" His voice was husky, like he'd smoked too many cigarettes.

"Razor?"

"My part-timer; he was working the late shift."

Jessica thought of the skinny bartender and tried not to laugh. "Why is he called Razor?"

Freeman shrugged. "I never thought to ask."

"I'm going to take a wild guess here and say it has nothing to do with his sharp wit or tough-guy image."

Freeman shrugged again. "So what's an attractive young lady like yourself wanting with an old man like me? You a cop?" He grinned and wiggled his eyebrows. "Am I under arrest? You gonna cuff me?"

Jessica ignored the flirty comments. "No. Do I look like a cop?"

"You don't, but you're in here asking me questions and being all serious."

"The only question I've asked is about Razor's nickname. At least I hope it's a nickname and not his real name."

"His real name's Bruce. But you ain't here to talk about Razor, right?"

"Right."

"So who are you here to talk about?"

"Eleanor Lavelle."

"I thought you said you weren't a cop."

"I'm not. I'm a private investigator."

He eyed her up and down and nodded slowly. "I guess that's pretty cool. What do you wanna know?"

"Why don't you start by telling me how you first met Eleanor?"

"The first time I laid eyes on Eleanor Lavelle was the night she walked in here and asked me for a job. She was a stunner, all right. Cute little floral minidress and Doc Martens and all that red hair. Truth be told, I didn't really need the staff, but I gave her a job anyways. Boy, was she something else."

"When was this?"

Freeman whistled through nicotine-stained teeth and scrunched up his face like he was thinking really hard. "Now you're asking. Late '80s, maybe?"

"You remember what she was wearing the first time you met her, but you don't remember what year it was?"

"What can I say? I'm an old man. My memory ain't so good these days. I guess my brain filters out the stuff it don't need no more and holds on to what's worth remembering." He grinned, winked at her. "And that cute little outfit was definitely worth remembering."

Jessica stared at him. Here was a man who seemed to think it was completely normal to be fantasizing over a dead woman, a murder victim, as though she was this month's *Playboy* centerfold. She found it pretty fucking weird—and more than a little creepy—that Ace Freeman was still getting a hard-on over Eleanor Lavelle after all these years, but she didn't say so.

"Could this have been late 1987?" Jessica asked. "Or early 1988?"

"Yeah, maybe." He snapped his fingers suddenly. "Thanksgiving! She showed up just before Thanksgiving. I remember asking her if she wanted to join me and the wife for dinner. Figured she wouldn't know anyone else in Eagle Rock, would be spending the day on her own otherwise." He tapped the side of his head and laughed. "See, the old gray cells are still working after all."

"And did she?"

"Did she what?"

Jessica suppressed a sigh. "Join you for Thanksgiving dinner?"

"Nah, she said she was eating with Hopper. The dirty old dog."

Jessica's eyebrows arched in surprise. "Jeff Hopper? The motel owner?"

"The very same."

"Why would Eleanor be spending Thanksgiving with Hopper?"

"She was staying at the motel."

"Hopper didn't tell me she was one of his guests when I asked him about her."

"You staying at the Blue Moon Inn?"

Jessica nodded. "Yeah."

"Well, just you watch yourself with old Hopper. He's got an eye for pretty young things. And he's never been married. Says it all." Freeman twisted his own wedding ring and shook his head in apparent disgust at Hopper's bachelor status.

"He would've known Eleanor pretty well?" Jessica asked.

Freeman smirked. "I'd say so. Let's just say I don't think turkey and trimmings was all he was giving her."

"What do you mean?"

"When I said she was staying at the motel, I didn't mean she was there for a week or two. She was living there the whole time she worked in the bar. We're talking two, maybe three, months. Now, I like to think I pay my staff competitive wages and all, and she did well in tips for obvious reasons, but I don't see how she could have afforded a motel room for all that time. Not on top of food and clothes and all those fancy cosmetics and fragrances you women like to buy."

"What are you saying?"

"I'm saying maybe she was paying him some other way."

"You think they were in a sexual relationship? Do you have anything to back that up?"

"Nah, it was just a theory I had at the time."

"Did Eleanor ever talk about where she lived or worked before you gave her a job here?"

"She said she worked in a few bars in Hollywood."

"She say which ones?"

"If she did, I don't remember. It's not like I asked for references or anything. She knew how to mix a drink, she looked great, and the customers loved her. That's better than any résumé as far as I'm concerned."

"She never spoke about her life before moving to Eagle Rock?"

"I don't think so. You spoken to Darla Kennedy yet? If anyone knows about that stuff, it'd be her."

"Darla? The receptionist at the newspaper?"

"That's the one. Thick as thieves, those two were." He scratched the stubble on his chin. "Although she would've been Darla Stevenson back then, not Kennedy. Married Hank Stevenson when they were both just kids. Split up a few years back."

Darla and Eleanor had been best friends. No wonder the woman had reacted so strangely when Jessica had asked her to pull the newspapers from the time of Eleanor's murder. She made a mental note to pay another visit to Darla Kennedy.

Jessica thought of the person of interest mentioned in the article she'd read at the *Reformer* offices. "What do you think happened the night Eleanor died?" she asked. "You got a theory about that too?"

Freeman shook his head sadly. "No idea, sweetheart. Had to be some kinda lunatic, don't ya think? I mean, who else would force their way into a young girl's home and cut her up like that?"

"The newspapers at the time said the cops had a suspect, a male friend of Eleanor's. Any idea who this so-called person of interest was?"

"Sure, I do."

"Really?" Jessica tried to sound casual, like her pulse hadn't just skyrocketed through the ceiling. "Who?"

Freeman leaned across the table, all conspiratorial, and she tried not to breathe in the stench of stale cigarettes and sweat. He glanced around the room as though worried they might be overheard, even though the place was almost empty. The old man was still playing cards and was paying them no attention.

"Guy called Rob Young," Freeman said in a low voice. "He worked here in the bar. In fact, it was Eleanor who asked me to give him the job. Said she'd known him for years." He chuckled. "Hey, I guess I did know something about her life before she moved to the neighborhood."

"When was this?"

"Four or five months before she died."

"You think he did it?"

"Not a chance. Rob was a good kid. And he loved the bones of that girl."

"Why do you think the cops liked him for it?"

"In the movies, the cops always suspect those closest to the victim, don't they? Well, Rob and Eleanor had an on-off thing going on. And him splitting town like that didn't help him none either."

Jessica nodded. "The newspaper said this guy vanished around the same time Eleanor was murdered."

Freeman looked her right in the eye. "Not around the same time," he said. "The very same night."

She sat up straighter. "The same night?"

"Uh-huh. He did a late shift at the bar as usual. Left around midnight, said he was going to Eleanor's place on Morrison. That was the last time I ever saw him. The next day they found Eleanor's body, and the little girl was gone."

12

PRYCE

Tommy Getz, the manager of the Dreamz Motel, had been right about the man Amy Ong spent her last night with.

He *was* old and fat.

At fifty-six, Frank Sherman was almost three times the age of the college student. He tipped the scales at more than two hundred pounds, none of which was muscle. He had thinning gray hair, a red doughy face, and tiny beady eyes that peered warily back and forth between Pryce and Medina in Interview Room II.

They had picked him up at his place of work, a large auto insurance agency on Wilshire, where he had been employed for almost thirty years. Sherman held a senior enough position within the company to have his own small glass-fronted office overlooking an open-plan space filled with two dozen customer service advisors. His initial refusal to accompany the detectives to Hollywood to answer some questions about his relationship with Amy Ong was quickly replaced by reluctant acquiescence when offered the alternative of walking past rows of coworkers wearing handcuffs.

Once at the station, he was put in an interview room with no windows or AC and had been left there on his own for almost an hour.

"Make the bastard sweat," Medina had said.

It worked.

Sherman's face was slick with perspiration, and the collar of his smart white shirt was damp by the time Pryce and Medina sat down across from him. Medina told Sherman he was not under arrest but advised him their conversation was being recorded by the small camera fixed to the ceiling in the corner of the room.

"Do I need to call my lawyer?" Sherman asked.

"I don't know, Mr. Sherman," Pryce said. "Do you?"

"I've done nothing wrong."

"Good. In that case, we'll all be out of here in no time. We just want to go over a few things that might assist us with our investigation. Let's get started, shall we?"

Sherman hesitated, then nodded. "Okay."

"Detective Medina?" Pryce said.

Medina picked up the file he had brought into the room with him, opened it, and pulled out a photograph of Amy Ong. It was the same image as the one used to illustrate the missing person posters. He spun the photo around on the table so that it faced Sherman. "What can you tell us about your relationship with Amy Ong?" he asked.

Sherman didn't look at the picture. He stared at a spot on the gray concrete wall over the detective's shoulder. "Never heard of her."

"You've never heard of Amy Ong?" Medina asked. "Her name and picture have been all over the newspapers and television for days."

"Uh, yeah, maybe I saw something on the news about a missing girl. What I meant was I don't know her. I never met her."

"Please, take a look at the picture, Mr. Sherman."

Medina pushed the photo another inch closer to Sherman and tapped it with his fingernail.

Sherman reluctantly dragged his eyes away from the wall and glanced down quickly at the eight-by-ten image of the college student. He swallowed hard, his Adam's apple bobbing up and down above the tight collar. He shook his head.

"I told you I don't know her."

Medina sighed. "Mr. Sherman, we have an eyewitness who says a man matching your description checked into the Dreamz Motel on La Brea last Saturday night with Amy Ong."

"Yeah? Well, this eyewitness must be mistaken. Must be plenty of guys out there who look like me. I was at home last Saturday night. All night."

"Anyone who can verify that was the case?"

Sherman hesitated. "Yeah, my wife."

Medina raised his eyebrows. "Your wife? Is Mrs. Sherman in the habit of covering for you when you're out meeting with prostitutes?"

Sherman glared at him. "What the hell are you talking about?" He lifted the plastic cup in front of him, which had been filled with water. Realizing it was now empty, he scrunched the cup in his fist. Neither Pryce nor Medina offered to get him a refill.

"Do you use prostitutes regularly, Mr. Sherman?" Pryce asked.

Sherman's little eyes blinked furiously, and his double chin wobbled like a plate of Jell-O. "You've got the wrong guy. I'd like to leave now." He started to rise with some difficulty from the plastic seat he was wedged into.

"Sit back down, Mr. Sherman," Pryce said firmly. "We're not done yet."

Sherman sat back down.

Pryce continued. "You were arrested for driving under the influence of alcohol after being pulled over during a routine traffic stop in Hollywood three years ago. Is that correct?"

Sherman nodded.

The insurance salesman had pleaded guilty to the offense, paid almost $2,000 in court fines, and had his license suspended for 120 days. The DUI arrest now looked like it could cost him a hell of a lot more than a couple grand and several months of inconvenience while off the road.

"The prints you provided at the time of the DUI arrest were matched to prints lifted from the motel room where Amy Ong's body was found."

Pryce looked at Sherman. Waited. The man took his time answering.

Finally, he said, "Uh, yeah, now that I think about it, maybe I have rented a room at that motel in the past. But definitely not Saturday night."

"I'm talking specifically about prints lifted from a whiskey bottle that also had prints matching those of the victim. Likewise, plastic cups used to consume the liquor. We also matched a thumbprint from a twenty-dollar bill found in the victim's wallet to the prints we have on file from your arrest. Why don't you cut the bullshit, Mr. Sherman? What were you doing in a motel room with Amy Ong the night she was murdered?"

Sherman ran his hands through his hair and looked around the room frantically, as though searching for an escape route. "Fuck!" He banged his fists on the table, then buried his face in his hands.

Pryce and Medina waited silently.

After a couple of minutes, Sherman looked up at them, his eyes wet with tears. Beads of sweat ran down his temples; his hair was soaked. "Okay, I was with the girl last Saturday night. It was our usual agreement. We met in a bar, had a couple of drinks. Then we stopped at a liquor store for the booze and went to the motel. I paid her the cash up front, we had sex, and then I left. That's it—I swear."

"Your usual agreement?" Pryce asked. "This wasn't the first time you paid Amy Ong for sex?"

Sherman shook his head. "We've hooked up maybe a half dozen times over the last few months."

"How did you first meet her?"

"Online." He gave them the name of a website specializing in call girls of Asian appearance. "She called herself Cindy. I never knew her as Amy."

"Have you met other women through these call girl websites?" Pryce asked.

Sherman dropped his eyes. He nodded.

"All Asian?"

He shook his head. "Sometimes Latinas." He gave them the name of another website he frequently used.

"Were you the father?"

"Come again?"

"Were you the father of Amy Ong's baby? She was pregnant."

Sherman shrugged. "Nothing to do with me."

"You sure about that?" Pryce pressed.

"She always insisted on using a condom. Usually brought her own. If she got herself knocked up, it was some other guy's problem. You don't believe me, do some tests or whatever."

"We will. Does your wife know you use prostitutes?"

He shook his head. "Christ, no."

Sherman pulled at the knot on his tie until it was loose and then opened the top two buttons of the shirt. Pryce wondered if his wife ironed those shirts for him each night before work, if she helped him pick out which tie to wear to the office each morning. If Mrs. Sherman had any idea how her husband was spending his time and money.

"Let me guess?" Medina said. "Your wife doesn't understand you, but the young girls you pay for sex do, right?"

Sherman glared at him. "Look, I like screwing hot young women, okay? It's not a crime, is it?"

"Actually, engaging in a sexual act or lewd conduct with another person in exchange for money *is* a crime, Mr. Sherman." Medina pointed to the camera. "A crime you have admitted to committing during this interview, which, as you have already been advised, is being recorded."

Sherman's eyes widened. "Christ, my wife doesn't need to know about this, does she? You don't understand—she'll leave me for good this time. What with the drinking and the DUI—"

Pryce interrupted. "No, Mr. Sherman, you're the one who doesn't understand. Right now, any charges in relation to your use of prostitutes is the least of your problems."

Pryce glanced at the other detective. "Detective Medina?"

Medina opened the file again and withdrew another photograph of Amy Ong. This one was a close-up shot taken by the police photographer after her death and showed her badly beaten face. The broken nose, bruised cheekbone, and dried blood spatter on her pale skin were all clearly visible. Sherman stared at the photograph for a long time. Then choked back a sob. He reached out a hand toward the picture, his trembling fingers hovering just above Amy Ong's face but not quite touching the glossy paper.

"Cindy," he whispered.

"Did you kill Amy Ong?" Pryce asked calmly.

Sherman pushed the photo away. "No! I never touched her. Not like that. I would never hurt Cindy. Never in a million years. Fuck! You've got to believe me."

"So who did kill her?"

"How the hell should I know?" he yelled. "She was fine when I walked out of that room. She must've had another john lined up after I left. I'm telling you someone else did this to her. I'm being set up. I'm innocent."

"Why didn't you leave the motel room together?" Pryce asked. "Offer her a ride back to campus?"

"She said she wanted to take a shower, freshen up. She had her own car. Said she was parked near the bar on Las Palmas."

Amy Ong's car hadn't yet been accounted for. Pryce would put out a BOLO for the 2004 Mini in the vicinity of Las Palmas as soon as the interview was over.

"Did you kill Amy Ong?" Pryce repeated.

"No, I did not kill her. Get me my fucking lawyer right now. I'm not saying another word until he gets here."

The prints on the whiskey bottle, plastic cups, and twenty-dollar bill were compelling evidence supporting the theory Sherman had been in contact with Amy Ong shortly before her death—but they didn't necessarily put him in the motel room with her. Forensics had been unable to lift usable prints from the room itself due to multiple prints belonging to previous guests and members of staff. But Sherman had put himself in the room the night Amy Ong died, and that was good enough for Pryce.

He turned to Medina. "You want to do the honors, partner?"

"With pleasure, partner."

Medina looked at Sherman. "Francis Sherman, I am placing you under arrest for the murder of Amy Ong."

The man's expression changed instantly from rage to one of pure panic. His beady eyes widened. "You can't do this. I haven't done anything wrong."

Medina shifted in the chair and produced a small white plastic card, the size of an ATM card, from the back pocket of his jeans and began to read the Miranda warning printed on it. "You have the right to remain silent. Anything you say can and will be used against you in a court of law . . ."

Pryce placed the two photos of Amy Ong back in the file and tucked it under his arm. He stood and walked to the door, leaving Medina to continue reading Sherman his rights.

He strolled slowly down the corridor toward the squad room, thinking about what Frank Sherman had told them during the interview. He knew he should be thrilled. They had just made an arrest in a high-profile murder case a little over twenty-four hours after the body had been found. It would ease the intense media pressure weighing heavily on them to find the killer and give the Ongs some hope of seeing justice served for their daughter.

But something just felt off to Pryce.

Back at his workstation, he removed the photographs from the file and returned them to a plastic wallet inside the murder book. He picked up a stack of telephone messages that had been left on his desk and rifled through them. Most were crank callers claiming to know who had killed Amy Ong or "Confessing Sams" insisting they had committed the crime themselves. A frustrating part of the job with cases with a lot of media interest, like the Amy Ong murder, and a huge drain on police resources checking them out.

Pryce looked up as Medina appeared in the squad room with a big grin on his face.

"Now, that is what you call a slam dunk." Medina jumped in the air and mimicked dropping a shot into a basketball hoop. Then he walked over to the workstation area and raised his hand for a high five. Pryce ignored it.

"Is Sherman being booked?" he asked.

"As we speak," Medina said, lowering his hand.

"Slam dunk, huh?" Pryce rubbed at his temples with his thumb and forefinger and sighed heavily. "I don't know, Vic. It all just feels a bit too . . . easy. You know what I mean? The whiskey bottle, the cash, the prints all being left behind at the scene. Why didn't this guy get rid of anything that would tie him to the vic? Especially when he has a record and knew he would be in the system."

Medina frowned. "What, you wanting the perps to make it hard for you now, Jase? He panicked is all. Sure, he's got plenty of priors when it comes to screwing whores, but I'm betting a kill like this was his first time. Got out of there without stopping to think it through first. Trust me, man—Sherman's our guy."

"What about his theory about another john showing up at the motel after he left? It's possible, right?"

Medina shook his head. "No way. You could smell the guilt on that fat fucker like cheap cologne."

"Yeah, maybe." Pryce picked up the pile of telephone messages again and continued sifting through them.

"Hey, why don't we go grab a couple of beers?" Medina said. "Celebrate making an arrest."

Pryce didn't answer him. He was staring at a slip of paper he held in his hand. A name was scribbled next to a cell phone number, and the word *urgent* was underlined twice.

The message hadn't been left by a crank caller.

The name belonged to someone who had drifted in and out of his thoughts many times over the years. Someone he had hoped never to lay eyes on again. Someone he could not allow back into his life under any circumstances. He looked at the next slip of paper. Another message from the same woman. He thought of the heavy, gut-wrenching feeling of dread that had kept him awake for most of the previous night and knew he had been right to be worried.

"Problem?" Medina's voice broke into his thoughts.

Pryce balled the two messages in his fist and tossed them into the trash can under his desk. He shook his head.

"No problem," he said. "It's nothing important."

13

JESSICA

Jessica was about to ask Freeman for more information on Rob Young when the door opened, and Jack Holliday walked into the bar.

Once again, he looked like a guy who could give a GQ model an inferiority complex. His long legs were wrapped in black denim, and a gray athletic T-shirt showed off tanned arms and hinted at rock-hard abs underneath. His hair was still wet from the shower. He wasn't wearing the messenger bag.

"Customer," Freeman said, smiling apologetically. He slid across the leather seat and out of the booth, standing up with an exaggerated groan, hand pressed to the small of his back. He picked up his empty beer bottle, pointed to her own Bud Light. "You want another?"

Jessica had barely touched the drink during their conversation. "No thanks. This one's still pretty full."

"No problem. It's on the house."

"Cool, thanks."

Holliday caught her eye and smiled as he walked over to the bar. Jessica's cheeks burned, and she looked down and studied the label on the beer bottle like it was the most interesting thing she'd ever read. She took a long drink. Sneaked another look at Holliday while he placed his order.

Black jeans, gray tee, damp hair. No messenger bag.

Jessica took one last slug from the bottle, grabbed her own bag, and made her way quickly to the exit. As she passed him, Holliday grabbed her arm softly. "Hey, you're not leaving already, are you? I just bought you a drink."

Two beers sat on the counter, looking almost as tempting as Jack Holliday did himself.

Jessica shook her arm free. "Sorry, I gotta go."

He looked disappointed, and her stomach did a weird little flip, but she knew any interest Holliday had in her was purely about the case. She pushed open the door. The night air felt good on her flushed face as she walked briskly along York toward the motel.

Most of the shops and cafés were closed, but there were still folks around. A couple strolled arm in arm across the street. Some teenage kids careered past on skateboards. Twilight had claimed the day, but it wasn't full dark just yet, and Jessica glanced back every few yards just to be sure she wasn't being tailed by anyone on foot or by car. But she didn't have the same feeling of being watched as she'd had the night before, and she saw no one hiding in the shadows or any sign of a black SUV with tinted windows.

When Jessica reached the Blue Moon Inn, the lights in the lobby were blazing brightly, and she could see Hopper behind the desk flicking through a magazine. He looked up as she passed the window and smiled and gave her a friendly wave. She returned the gesture and made a mental note to speak to him tomorrow about Eleanor Lavelle's stay at the motel and the rumors about their relationship.

Right now, she had more pressing business to take care of.

She loped past rooms 1 through 4, and when she reached her own, she kept walking. She stopped outside room 6 and glanced around in what she hoped was a casual sort of way. Like she was a guest about to turn in for the night, instead of someone about to commit a felony.

The neon light from the roof cast a ghostly blue glow over her hands and arms, giving her skin the deathly pallor of a days-dead corpse. It was the only real light source this far back from the office, which was good news for her attempts to remain unnoticed but not so good for the job at hand.

Jessica rummaged in her bag until she found a mini Maglite flashlight and flicked the switch a couple times to make sure the batteries still worked. They did. She switched it off again and pulled a small black leather case from the bag that looked similar to the manicure sets that well-groomed, image-conscious women might carry. Inside were a dozen tiny tools held in place by strips of black elastic, but none of them were emery boards or cuticle shapers.

She considered the options for a second or two, then selected the size and style of pick best suited to the old-fashioned lock on the door in front of her. She looked around again. Satisfied there was no one watching, Jessica switched on the flashlight, inserted the pick in the lock, and within seconds heard a satisfying click.

She was both impressed and disturbed by how quick and easy access to the room had been. Her own accommodation, right next door, would be no more secure and just as easily breached by anyone with half a clue about what they were doing. Jessica decided she would sleep a lot easier with the security chain fastened in place from now on while staying in town.

Still satisfied there were no onlookers, Jessica crossed the threshold into Holliday's room and quickly and quietly closed the door behind her. Aided by the light of the flashlight and a streak of cool silver moonlight through the small window, she assessed her surroundings.

The setup was identical to her own room on the other side of the wall. A queen bed, a nightstand, a desk with an old-fashioned TV on top, and an uncomfortable chair pushed under the desktop. A coffee maker, still unused, on the top shelf of an open closet with four wire hangers on the rail. Holliday had put the hangers to good use, each one doubled up with jeans and shirts and all evenly spaced. Unlike Jessica's own room, where one of her suitcases lay open on the floor, spewing pants, T-shirts, and underwear.

The unintentional retro styling of the motel room met modern-day technology thanks to a small sleek laptop, a digital camera, and tiny white earbuds next to a pile of paperwork on the desk. Work stuff. The items on the nightstand were more personal and told Jessica a little more about the journalist.

Holliday was a man who wore expensive French aftershave, who read action thrillers by American authors, and who drank bourbon from Kentucky. He slipped his sneakers off without untying the laces first and needed glasses for reading the paperbacks by the bed. He drove a Ford, which would be the dark-green pickup truck parked in the lot outside. He took multivitamins and snacked on Snyder's mini pretzels.

And Jack Holliday had case files Jessica fully intended getting her hands on.

She swept the flashlight in a wide arc around the cramped space and spotted the messenger bag under the desk. The buckles were undone, and she threw back the flap and pulled out the folder. There was nothing else inside the bag. Pushing the rest of the paperwork on the desk to one side, she opened the folder and quickly rifled through the contents. What Holliday had in his possession clearly wasn't the original case file. Instead, the folder contained color copies of the contents of the murder book and missing person report.

Jessica froze midway through turning a page, convinced she had heard a noise right outside the door. It sounded like an empty soda can skittering across asphalt. She held her breath. Her pulse spiked. She counted five seconds, ten seconds, thirty seconds. She heard nothing else and breathed out slowly.

She held the flashlight between her teeth, pulled out her cell phone, and started photographing each page in the file, the same as she'd done with the newspaper articles at the *Reformer* offices.

The overhead light snapped on.

Jessica dropped the flashlight from her mouth and the cell phone from her hand, both hitting the hardwood flooring with a loud thud. The copies of the Lavelle case file fluttered to the floor.

"Jesus H. Christ!" she yelled.

She fumbled frantically in her bag for her gun and spun around to see Holliday standing in the doorway with a neutral expression on his face. She clutched her left hand to her chest, feeling like her heart might burst right through the rib cage.

"You seem to be in the wrong room, Miss Shaw." Holliday pointed in the direction of her own room. "I believe you are residing in room five. This is not room five."

"Jeez, Holliday. You almost gave me a heart attack. And believe me, that's not something I'd say lightly." Jessica dropped the gun back into the bag. "You're lucky I didn't shoot you."

Holliday let out an incredulous laugh and shook his head. "You really are something else—do you know that?"

"Yeah, so I've been told."

"You break into my room, and somehow I'm the bad guy? You know, I should call the cops right now."

"And tell them what? That I was looking for police files you shouldn't have anyway? Go for it. But I don't think you or your cop pal in Evidence Archives will come out of it looking too good."

Jessica bent down and picked up the flashlight and cell phone from the floor, both of which still seemed to be in working order. Crime scene photos were scattered around her feet like grotesque confetti. She picked one up. It showed Eleanor Lavelle lying on a thick plush carpet, head turned to the side, one arm down by her hip, the other outstretched toward an empty wineglass. Were it not for the five-inch gash across her throat and the blood and bruising marring her beautiful face, she could have been sleeping or passed out after a heavy night partying. She was surrounded by dark stains. It was impossible to tell from the photo if they were red wine or blood.

Holliday crouched down next to her and began collecting the sheets of paper together. He got up and tucked them back in the file, then swept the rest of the paperwork on the desk into a drawer. The edge of a photo caught Jessica's eye—something black and shiny—but he slammed the drawer shut before she could get a proper look.

They stood facing each other. Jessica handed Holliday the crime scene photo of Eleanor Lavelle she still held in her hand. "What happens now?"

"That's up to you," Holliday said. "Despite the fact you just broke into my room, and you generally speak to me like I'm shit, my offer still stands. Tell me who your client is, and I let you see the files. We agree to help each other, and we might actually get somewhere."

Jessica thought about it for a moment. "Okay. On one condition."

"Name it."

"I give you the name of my client, and that's it. No follow-up questions. No where, how, or why."

"Deal."

Holliday disappeared into the bathroom and returned a few seconds later with two small, chunky tumblers in his hands, the type used to hold toothbrushes and toothpaste in motel rooms like this one. He walked over to the nightstand and held up the bottle of Wild Turkey. "Drink?"

"Sure, why not?"

The next couple of hours were spent drinking bourbon and looking through the murder book. There were crime scene photos, autopsy reports, forensic reports, witness statements, detective notes scribbled in margins. By the time Jessica got to the end, the room was blurry and soft at the edges, thanks to the booze, but she had a clearer idea of what had happened the night Eleanor Lavelle was murdered.

The last known sighting of Alicia, as documented on the Lost Angelenos website, had taken place on a Friday, around lunchtime, at a small post office on York Boulevard, where Eleanor had stopped in with her daughter to pay a utility bill. She'd had a brief conversation with one of the mailmen, a man named Chuck Lawrence, then paid the bill and left.

As she read on, Jessica discovered Lawrence was also the one who'd found the body while attempting to deliver a parcel to the house on Morrison the next day.

Darla Stevenson, as she was known back then, confirmed in her witness statement she had spent around ninety minutes in the company of Eleanor Lavelle on the night she died. They had shared a bottle of wine at Eleanor's place and had chatted about trivial stuff, the details of which Darla couldn't remember. She hadn't seen Alicia and had assumed the child was in bed asleep. She'd left the house on Morrison sometime after eight p.m. and met her husband, Hank Stevenson, at Ace's Bar for a prearranged date night. The statement ended with a comment from Darla confirming Eleanor Lavelle was alive and well the last time she'd seen her.

Ace Freeman's statement to the police was mostly about his employee, Rob Young, whom the cops clearly suspected of the murder by the time they spoke to the bar owner. He told them what he'd told Jessica. Young was in a relationship with Eleanor, albeit probably not exclusive. He'd left the bar around midnight and told Freeman he was planning on spending the night at Eleanor's place. Freeman had never seen Young again. Interestingly, Freeman mentioned in his statement how Darla Stevenson had been visibly upset when she'd arrived at the bar, and he'd overheard her telling Young that she and Eleanor had argued. Freeman also claimed Hank Stevenson had been surprised when his wife showed up at the bar, as he had been looking forward to what he referred to as "a night off from the old lady."

In a follow-up interview, Darla Stevenson denied arguing with Eleanor and claimed they had parted on good terms.

Hank Stevenson's statement was short and to the point. He had been in Ace's Bar from around six p.m. His wife had joined him, as planned, around eight thirty, and they'd remained in the bar until eleven, when they'd both gone home and turned in for the night. He said his wife hadn't mentioned an argument with Eleanor Lavelle.

The most intriguing statements of all were provided by a married couple, Mack and Maura McCool, who were renting out their garage to Young as a small apartment space. They claimed Young had told them a few days before the murder that he was planning to leave town and head north. Portland, maybe. Or Seattle. Mack McCool had been in Ace's for most of the evening, while Maura had washed, ironed, and packed Young's clothes for him ahead of the trip while the young man worked his last shift.

He'd shown up at their house on El Paso shortly after midnight. Maura McCool had gone to bed around a half hour later, while Mack McCool and Young had stayed up and drank a few beers and watched a rerun of a football game. They'd both fallen asleep on the couch, also confirmed by the wife, who'd gotten up during the night for a glass of water. Early the next morning, Mack McCool had dropped Young off near the 5 in Glendale, where he'd been planning to hitch a ride.

The McCools had effectively provided an alibi for the prime suspect in Geersen's case. The only window of opportunity was the ten minutes or so between leaving the bar and when the McCools said Young had arrived at their home. Nowhere near enough time for him to go to the house on Morrison, kill Eleanor, and make his way back to El Paso.

And then there was the disappearance of Alicia to consider.

A search of the McCools' house, car, and the garage apartment had turned up nothing. The murder weapon had never been found. Detective Geersen had noted that the McCools' Buick LeSabre sedan had been detailed on the Saturday morning, just hours before Eleanor's body was discovered by Chuck Lawrence.

Jessica looked up from the final page. Holliday was sitting on the chair next to the desk, glasses on, also reading through the pages from the murder book, in case he had missed anything first time around.

"Who are Mack and Maura McCool?" she asked.

"You know the old guy who's always in Ace's Bar playing cards? That's Mack McCool."

"You spoken to him?"

Holliday laughed. "Yeah, if you can call 'I don't speak to asshole journalists' a conversation. Believe me—Mack McCool is not the friendliest of guys."

"What about the wife?"

"I tried her a couple of times. Wouldn't answer the door."

"I'll give Mack McCool a go. See if he's feeling any more talkative."

"Don't say I didn't warn you."

Jessica got up from the bed and stretched. It was time to call it a night. "Thanks for the drink," she said. The bottle was almost empty. "Let's get together at some point tomorrow and decide on our next move."

She headed for the door.

"Jessica?"

"Yeah?"

"You still haven't told me the name of your client."

Jessica turned to face him. "No, I haven't, have I? My client is Alicia Lavelle."

She watched Holliday's mouth drop open as she closed the door behind her.

Back in room 5, Jessica locked the door and slid the security chain in place.

Just in case.

14

JESSICA

Friday morning.

The motel room was warm and bright. Not yet nine a.m. but already the day was shaping up to be hot and heavy. It was officially early fall, but summer wasn't letting go just yet.

Jessica sat up and sipped some water from a glass on the nightstand. Her mouth felt like it was filled with cotton balls, but she'd mostly escaped a repeat of the previous day's hangover, despite last night's liquor.

Instead of throbbing pain, her head was filled with questions.

For the last forty-eight hours, they'd mostly been about the woman who could be her mother. She knew she was avoiding the ones about the man who was supposed to be her father.

The shower was still on the cold setting when she stepped into the stall. Jessica left it as it was and emerged feeling refreshed and invigorated. She dressed in denim cutoffs, a white T-shirt, and tennis shoes. After applying some makeup and finger combing her still-damp hair, she checked her reflection in the mirror. She looked okay, if a little tired.

The coffee maker was still on the closet shelf. Jessica pulled it down, set it on the desk, and got a pot going. The most recent number in the call list on her cell phone was for the switchboard at the LAPD's Hollywood Station. She hit redial and asked to speak to Pryce. She drank black coffee and waited for the inevitable invitation to leave yet another message. After a few moments of being on hold, she heard some beeps and clicks as the call was transferred, and then a man's voice came on the line.

"This is Pryce."

Jessica was so surprised to finally reach the detective that she realized she hadn't properly prepared what she wanted to say to him. So she just said, "Good morning, Detective Pryce. My name is Jessica Shaw."

A pause. Then, "How can I help you, Ms. Shaw?"

"I left a couple of messages for you yesterday."

"My apologies. I have a stack of messages on my desk I'm still trying to catch up on. Was your call regarding a case?"

"No, it's a personal matter, actually. I believe you knew my father, Tony Shaw."

Another pause. "I'm sorry—I don't recognize the name."

Pryce's voice sounded strained, or maybe it was her imagination. After all, she didn't even know the guy.

"You were at his funeral just over two years ago," she said. "Blissville, New York. I didn't have the chance to speak to you at the time, but I recognized you on TV a couple of days ago when you were interviewed at the motel where the college student was found."

There was an even longer silence this time, and Jessica thought the call had been disconnected until Pryce finally spoke again.

"Of course," he said. "Tony Shaw. Very sad. I happened to be in Manhattan and read about his passing in the family announcements in a newspaper. I thought I'd stop by and pay my respects. I'm very sorry for your loss, Ms. Shaw."

"Thank you. I was just curious as to how you knew him?"

"Tony and I went to school together."

"High school?"

"Yes, high school. I'm really sorry. I don't mean to be rude, but we've had some developments in a case I'm working on, and I really have to go now."

"What was the name of the school?"

The line was already dead.

Jessica booted up the laptop. No one had tried to jimmy the door or pick the lock during the night as far as she could tell.

On the floor was a sheet of lined notepaper that had been slipped under the door. It was folded in half and then folded again into a neat little square. She picked it up and unfolded it. The note read,

We need to talk. Call me. Jack.

He'd written a cell phone number under the short message. Jessica refolded the paper and shoved it into the back pocket of her shorts and sat down at the desk.

Tony had told her he'd grown up in northwest Los Angeles, and she tried to remember those conversations now, if he had ever mentioned which high school he'd attended. Jessica thought he might have, but she couldn't recall the name.

Most of the online biographies on Pryce focused on his LAPD career and didn't extend as far back as his high school days. But after twenty minutes of digging around, she had the name of his school in Van Nuys and the year he would have been a senior there. She pulled up the school's website and clicked on the alumni section.

At the top of the page was a gallery of photos from the class of '87's thirty-year reunion, which had taken place at a Best Western in Sherman Oaks a few months earlier. Just one year out from the class Jessica was interested in. There were links to Facebook pages dedicated to other class years and information on ordering copies of high school diplomas.

At the bottom of the page, she found what she was looking for— yearbook back issues. Many of the older ones had been donated, which meant not all years were available. Jessica skimmed through the list and was relieved to find a yearbook from 1986 was for sale. The purchase price for yearbooks three years or older was fifty bucks. Jessica winced. High school nostalgia trips clearly didn't come cheap.

There was an email address and direct telephone line for placing orders. She tapped the number into her cell phone. After a brief conversation with the office manager, a woman named Debbie Klug, Jessica had confirmation the school definitely still had a copy of the 1986 yearbook. Better still, it could be collected in person if she was in the neighborhood. Jessica figured the drive out to Van Nuys would be a lot faster than waiting for a delivery and would also save her the ten dollars shipping.

Thirty minutes later, Jessica was sitting in front of the school's main building in a parking lot crammed full of every kind of vehicle imaginable. Sensible sedans, cute little sports cars, gleaming 4X4 trucks. Most of them were more impressive than the car she'd owned before upgrading to the Silverado. When Jessica was at school, she hadn't even had a car. She'd had a MetroCard for the subway.

She went through the school's main entrance and wandered down a wide, empty hallway with cold gray lockers on either side and buzzing fluorescent lights overhead. She felt like she'd traveled back in time ten years to her own high school days and was running late for class.

The loud squeaking of her shoes on the shiny linoleum announced her arrival as she reached the office at the end of the hallway. Sitting behind a cluttered desk was a woman in her sixties with short spiky hair dyed an alarming shade of magenta. She wore turquoise glasses and a bright-green dress and looked up at Jessica with an inquisitive smile.

"Can I help you?" she asked.

"I called earlier about a yearbook."

"Oh, I didn't expect you to get here quite so soon. I'm Debbie. I spoke to you on the phone. I have the yearbook right here."

Debbie reached into one of the desk drawers and pulled out an A4-size hardback book with a faded burgundy cover and light-blue lettering. She slipped the book into a large brown envelope and scotch-taped it shut. Jessica took the yearbook and handed over two twenties and a ten and watched as the office manager locked the cash in a small metal box. Jessica was itching to get back to the truck and rip open the parcel and trawl through the photos. Just as she was about to thank the woman and leave, Debbie launched into a conversation.

"When we spoke on the phone, I assumed the yearbook was from your own senior year. But I'm guessing that's not the case." She laughed. "Otherwise I really need to know which face cream you're using or the name of your plastic surgeon."

Jessica smiled. "No, my senior year was a little later." She held up the parcel. "My father was class of '86."

"Oh, really? What's his name? I've worked here forever, so maybe I knew him."

"Tony Shaw."

Debbie's brow creased. "Nope, it's not ringing any bells. Then again, we do have one of the largest student bodies in the district, so that's a lot of names to remember when you've been here as long as I have."

"What about Jason Pryce? He was a friend of my father."

"Now that name is familiar," Debbie said. "Black fella? Very handsome? If I recall correctly, he was on one of the sports teams. Baseball or basketball, I think."

"Sounds about right," Jessica said.

Back in the car, she pulled the yearbook from the envelope and opened it. It had belonged to someone named Jimmy, and the inside front cover was filled with messages written by fellow students.

Good luck at college, Jimmy!

See you around big guy, all the best for the future!

Hey Jimmy, don't forget: life moves pretty fast!

The last comment was a line from *Ferris Bueller's Day Off*. It had been one of Tony's favorite movies and would have been the big summer hit the year he graduated high school.

Jessica and her father used to have what they called "Movie Fridays" once a month. Popcorn, pizza, beer. A choice of movie each. Tony loved anything from the '80s and anything by John Hughes. Especially *Ferris Bueller's Day Off*. Jessica suspected Tony had always secretly wanted to be just like Ferris—wisecracking, with a hot girlfriend, and always breaking the rules and never giving a damn. The reality was he was way more like Ferris's best friend, Cameron—a little uptight and frustrated, like a coiled spring waiting for a release.

Her heart leaped when she read the scribbled dedication in the yearbook, but it was signed by someone with the initials *BF*—not by Tony.

Jessica flipped through the glossy pages until she came to the seniors with surnames beginning with *P* and quickly found Jason Pryce. Debbie Klug had been right. Pryce was still an attractive man now, from what she'd seen of him on the television, but he'd been an absolute heart-breaker as a teenager. According to his short bio, he was a star of the track team rather than basketball or baseball, but there was no doubt Debbie Klug was thinking of the same person.

Jessica turned some more pages, all of which were filled with photos of spiral-permed girls, boys with bad mullets, and both sexes sporting ugly feathered dos. There were big glasses, bigger shoulder pads, and lots of light-blue eyeshadow and frosted lipstick. She came to the surnames beginning with *S* but couldn't find Tony Shaw.

With a growing sense of dread, Jessica kept on turning the pages until she came to those students whose surnames began with a *Y*. She ran her finger slowly down the page and came to a Bobby Yang and a Rachel Young and a Tina Young and a Bill Younger.

But there was no Rob Young.

And there was no photo of her father on the page.

15
PRYCE

Pryce had been partners with Medina for more than a decade, and in all that time, he had never lied to him.

At least, not about anything serious.

Sure, there had been the little white lies. Like turning down a ticket to the Lakers game because he "had plans" when he actually just wanted to spend the evening curled up on the couch with Angie. Or pretending to like the cologne Medina had bought him one Christmas even though the smell reminded Pryce of cat piss.

Little white lies. Not giant black ones. Not until yesterday, when he'd told Medina there was no problem with the phone messages he held in his hand.

That lie had been as big as the Empire State Building.

Pryce had kept tabs on Jessica and Tony Shaw over the years, even though he knew it was risky. Occasional online searches from computers that wouldn't be traced back to him. Internet cafés. Libraries. Never at home or at the office. It was during one of those searches he had learned of the unexpected and premature death of Tony Shaw. Pryce hadn't been anywhere near New York City when he'd found out the news, despite what he'd told Jessica.

Another lie.

He had feared Tony's death had been violent, that the past had finally caught up with him. Discovering his friend had died of a massive heart attack, with no suspicious circumstances involved, had brought a sense of overwhelming relief. Quickly followed by a profound sadness. They hadn't just been best friends—they'd been as close as brothers when they were kids. Family without the blood connection, with an unbreakable bond that meant they would've done anything for each other.

It was the reason why his friend had reached out to Pryce the night it had all gone wrong in Eagle Rock.

After reading about the death of Tony Shaw, Pryce had immediately decided to make the trip east to say goodbye to his "brother" in person. It had been his first mistake—emerging from the shadows of the internet into plain view at the funeral.

He'd made his second mistake this morning when he'd taken Jessica's call and told her he'd gone to school with her father.

This time, telling the truth could cost him—and her—everything.

He knew she worked as a private investigator and was a damn good one by all accounts. She'd spent several years under the tutelage of a senior investigator named Larry Lutz, working out of a shop front in Blissville, before branching out on her own following Tony's death. He knew it wouldn't take Jessica too long to figure out Pryce had no classmates by the name of Tony Shaw.

He tried to convince himself her curiosity would have been sated by the information he had given her, that maybe she wouldn't feel the need to dig any further. But somehow, Pryce knew she wouldn't stop, and the thought made his stomach churn.

He slammed the palm of his hand hard against the steering wheel and cursed.

He was sitting in his Dodge Charger in the lot of the Dreamz Motel, two spaces along from Tommy Getz's beat-up Chevy. Theirs were the only two cars in the lot. Clearly a high-profile homicide hadn't been good for business.

Pryce turned off the engine and pocketed the keys. He climbed out of the car, swapping the refrigerator cool of the AC for a blistering heat that radiated off the sidewalks. Jessica Shaw wasn't his only problem right now. He had another one in the shape of a 220-pound piece of lard by the name of Frank Sherman. And Frank Sherman was a problem because Pryce was convinced the man was telling the truth when he said he hadn't killed Amy Ong.

Truth and lies.

Pryce strode toward the motel room where Amy Ong's body had been found. Crime scene tape crisscrossed the door. It had come unstuck at the bottom edges and fluttered gently in the warm breeze. Even though Pryce knew the crime scene cleaners would have completely sanitized the room by now, he was sure he could still smell the sharp tang of her blood, could almost taste it on his tongue. He stood with his back to the door and looked out over the lot, rotating in a slow semicircle from left to right, his gaze taking in all of the surrounding properties in his line of vision.

To his left was the Dreamz Motel office with its busted camera. To the far right, beyond the stretch of rooms, was the redbrick side of a coin laundry. Dead ahead was the rear of a shiny new seven-story apartment behind an eight-foot perimeter hedge.

Pryce headed toward the office and kept going, past the building and a bored-looking Tommy Getz at the desk, until he reached the street. He took a right and, after twenty yards, turned right again into a back alley running between the rear of the apartment block and the hedge. A couple of graffiti-smeared dumpsters were tucked flush against the wall of the building between two emergency exits. The alleyway most likely provided access for fire trucks and other first responders in the event of an emergency.

Pryce looked up and saw what he hadn't been able to see from the parking lot at the Dreamz because of the overgrown foliage obscuring his view—two security cameras on opposite sides of the apartment block at second-floor level. They were compact and discreet and looked expensive. Pryce was sure that, unlike the cameras at the motel, these ones actually worked. The purpose of the cameras was undoubtedly to protect tenants and homeowners from any untoward activity taking place in the alley, but Pryce felt excitement build inside him at the possibility that one, or both, might cover some of the motel's lot and its rooms.

He left the alleyway and found the entrance to the Urban Heights apartment complex next to a vegan bistro. The reception was all glass and granite, with sleek leather couches and ugly modern artwork. Floor-to-ceiling windows revealed an outside communal pool area. A stairwell led to a state-of-the-art basement gym. A little fancier than Pryce's own condo at Los Feliz Towers, but he figured this place couldn't compete when it came to the views he enjoyed over the city.

The woman behind the front desk looked more like the kind of receptionist you'd meet in the foyer of a global banking firm rather than an apartment block just off La Brea. Slim, midtwenties, brunette. White blouse and tight black skirt. If Medina were here with Pryce, he would definitely leave his card with the woman and try to get her number.

The brunette's face creased in a delicate frown as her eyes went to the badge on Pryce's belt as he approached the desk, before the crumpled brow was quickly swapped for a well-practiced sunshine smile. "How can I help you, Officer?"

He gestured to his badge, even though he knew she had already spotted it. "Detective Pryce from the LAPD," he said. "Would it be possible to have a look at some footage from your security cameras out back? We're investigating a serious crime that took place in the neighborhood last weekend, and the footage might help us out."

Pryce hoped the woman wouldn't insist on calling the apartment complex owners for permission to view the footage; otherwise he could be looking at days wasted filing, and then waiting for, a search warrant.

She hesitated for a second, then gave a tiny shrug. "Sure, we have a security manager who looks after our surveillance cameras. Let me take you to his office."

In Pryce's experience, security managers employed by retail outlets, hotels, and apartment complexes like this one were often former military personnel or ex-cops. Or those who weren't good enough for a career in the armed forces or the police. He hoped he wasn't about to deal with the latter, or he would probably be heading back to his desk empty handed and having to apply for that search warrant after all.

The receptionist's stiletto heels clicked loudly on the tiled floor like the staccato burst of a machine gun as Pryce followed her down a narrow corridor. She knocked on a door and then opened it without waiting for an answer. "Mr. Delaney, are you free to help out this detective?"

A man wearing black pants, a white shirt with black epaulettes, and a black tie sat flicking through the sports section of the *Los Angeles Times*. In front of him were two computer screens, each split into four sections, showing various black-and-white scenes from the apartment complex, including the front entrance and lobby Pryce had just walked through. Any fears he had about being denied access to the security camera footage evaporated when the man looked up from his newspaper.

Chip Delaney was a former LAPD detective who had worked the Rampart area before taking his pension the previous year. A good cop with a good reputation, and his rugged mustachioed looks and dark curly hair had often drawn comparisons with Tom Selleck in his *Magnum, P.I.* days. The mustache and the hair were still there, albeit both a little grayer than before, and Delaney looked like he had managed to buck the trend of most other retired cops by losing a few pounds instead of gaining them. Retirement clearly agreed with him.

"Hey, Pryce, how's it going?" Delaney got up from the chair and shook his hand enthusiastically and slapped him on the back.

"Not too bad, thanks. You're looking well, Chip. Nice little number you've got yourself here."

Delaney leaned against the desk and grinned. "It pays the bills."

Pryce knew Delaney's gig at Urban Heights was less about the money and more about filling his days with something productive to do, about still feeling useful. Hours spent on the golf course soon lost its appeal after the first couple of weeks.

"I'll leave you two gentlemen to it," the receptionist said.

She retreated from the office and closed the door behind her. Pryce could hear the sharp snap of her heels quickly fading as she hurried back to her post at the front desk.

"You still working the Hollywood beat?" Delaney asked.

"Sure am. That's why I'm here. I was hoping you might be able to help with a case I'm working on."

"If I can, I will."

Pryce explained about the busted security cameras at the neighboring Dreamz Motel and how he was checking out other surveillance cameras in the area that might have picked up something useful from the night Amy Ong had been murdered. He told Delaney he was hoping the cameras attached to the rear of the apartment building might cover the motel's lot or even some of the rooms.

"Remind me when this all went down?"

"Last Saturday night."

"You're in luck," said Delaney. "We only keep the footage for a week. Another couple of days and Saturday's recording would have been wiped."

Delaney gestured to a leather swivel seat identical to his own. "Pull up a chair, and let's have a look."

He clicked a couple of buttons on the keyboard, and one of the four images filled the screen with a view of the back alleyway. At the bottom of the screen were white digits showing the date and time and the word *REAR1*. What Pryce saw was an excellent real-time view of the alleyway and the hedge but none of the motel. Delaney hit an arrow key, and the screen changed to an alternative view of the alleyway, this time from camera *REAR2*.

Pryce felt his pulse quicken. The second camera's view of the alleyway was more restricted than the first had been, but this one picked up part of the Dreamz Motel's parking lot and office and about a third of the rooms. Pryce counted four doors along from the office. The room Amy Ong had died in.

"Jackpot," he said.

"Yeah?" Delaney hit some more keys, and the date stamp in the bottom right corner changed from today's date to the previous Saturday's. "What time you looking for?"

"Why don't we start at seven p.m.?"

"You got it."

Delaney scrolled through the recording, and they watched cars and people arrive and leave the motel at an exaggerated, almost comical, speed. He hit the play button when the footage reached early evening. The minutes between 7:00 p.m. and 8:45 p.m. showed nothing of interest. Then, at 8:46 p.m., a sports car pulled into the lot and parked next to Tommy Getz's Chevy.

A heavily built man got out of the driver's side. Frank Sherman. He walked around the rear of the vehicle and opened the passenger door. Pryce held his breath. A petite female of slim build with long dark hair and wearing jeans and a white tank top emerged from the car. She had a purse slung over her shoulder and was carrying something in her hands. The whiskey bottle. Pryce breathed out slowly.

"That her?" Delaney asked.

Pryce nodded. He felt a chill wash over him. It was like looking at a ghost. Except this was the flesh-and-blood and full-of-life version of Amy Ong, completely oblivious to the fact she would be dead within a couple of hours.

He watched the screen as the couple disappeared into the office before reemerging three minutes later and making their way to what Pryce knew would be room 4. The positioning of the camera meant the view of the office and the cars parked outside it was reasonably sharp, but the picture grew grainier where the rooms stretched out away from the camera's lens.

By the time they reached the room, Amy Ong and Frank Sherman were little more than gray smudges on the screen. Pryce leaned in closer and could just make out the two figures crossing the threshold before closing the door behind them. He checked the time: 8:51 p.m.

Delaney hit fast-forward, and the time stamp jumped ahead quickly until, finally, the door to room 4 opened again. He backed up the tape slightly. At 10:02 p.m., the larger of the two figures emerged from the room. The door closed behind him. They saw him amble toward where his car was parked. He looked unsteady on his feet.

Sherman pulled his car keys from his pants pocket, dropped them, and leaned against the car for support as he stooped to scoop them up. The rear lights flashed as he pressed the fob to unlock the car before clambering into the driver's side with some difficulty. The man was clearly in no fit state to drive. Pryce wondered if someone as intoxicated as Frank Sherman appeared to be would have been capable of carrying out an attack as brutal as the one that had ended Amy Ong's life. The car backed slowly out of the space before turning toward the parking lot exit and driving out of shot.

"That your guy?" Delaney asked.

"Maybe," Pryce said. "Let's keep watching."

The time stamp read 10:07 p.m.

Two minutes and thirty-seven seconds later, a figure walked into view wearing plain dark-colored pants, sneakers, gloves, and a loose, long-sleeved hoodie. The hood was pulled up, covering the wearer's hair and obscuring their face. The person carried a duffel bag.

He looked to be similar in height to Frank Sherman but was seventy or eighty pounds lighter. Pryce was certain he was not the same man who was locked in a cell at Hollywood Station right now. This one walked purposefully in the direction of the motel rooms, head tucked down, bag swinging by his side.

Pryce could hardly breathe as he watched the person stop in front of room 4. The door opened, and he saw a flash of white. The terry cloth bathrobe. The figure in black entered the room, and the door closed again.

"Can you back that up a few seconds and zoom in?" Pryce asked.

"Sure."

Both men watched again, but the grain was too heavy to determine if there was any interaction with Amy Ong before the figure in black disappeared into the motel room. Delaney hit fast-forward. Twenty-seven minutes later, the door opened, and the unknown person was back out in the lot. He pulled the door shut behind him and jogged toward the office. Again, the hood was up, head bowed toward his chest, face hidden. Still carrying the bag, he ran past the office in the direction of La Brea. Just before he moved out of the shot, Pryce noticed the white logo of a well-known sports brand emblazoned across the front of the hoodie.

"Can you back up all the way to when this guy first makes an appearance?"

"No problem."

They watched as the dark-clad figure first walked into shot, confirming what Pryce had suspected. The sweater was plain black or navy. No sports logo. Pryce now knew the purpose of the duffel bag. A change of clothes. The guy had switched his clothing while in the motel room. Swapped blood-soaked items for fresh ones. Pryce remembered the empty bathroom. The figure in black had probably cleaned up and taken the motel's towels with him, before later discarding all of the bloodied items.

The murder had been planned.

The killer had come prepared.

"I'm going to need a copy of this recording," Pryce said.

"Sure thing," Delaney said. "I'll do it right now."

As the security manager went to work, Pryce leaned back in the seat and thought about Medina's description of Frank Sherman's arrest as a slam dunk. Pryce had been in the job long enough to know when to trust his gut, and his gut had been telling him something was off. Now he knew they had dropped the ball into the wrong net.

Truth and lies.

Frank Sherman had been telling the truth when he'd said he hadn't killed Amy Ong.

16

JESSICA

Jessica and Holliday met for lunch at a place called Pat and Lorraine's on Eagle Rock Boulevard.

The restaurant had been Holliday's suggestion after she had texted the invitation. Jessica parked in the lot out back next to Holliday's Ford pickup and found him at a table for two, wearing his reading glasses, and already studying the menu. He looked up and grinned as she sat down on the seat facing him.

"Cool place, huh?"

Jessica took in the plain Formica tabletops and tomato-red leatherette seats. The exposed white brick walls were adorned with mismatched framed pictures, and high wooden shelves were stuffed full of kitschy ornaments. She shrugged. The place was nothing special as far as she could see.

"It's okay," she said.

"You don't recognize it?"

Jessica picked up a menu and began browsing the selection of meals. Her stomach growled, and she remembered she'd only had the black coffee for breakfast. She weighed the options. Order a full all-day breakfast and worry about being judged by Holliday in the pathetic way women did when eating in front of a hot guy. Or just have eggs and then have to stop by an In-N-Out for a burger on the way back to the motel.

"Why would I recognize it?" she asked.

"Well, it's not changed much since '92," Holliday said casually. "I thought you might remember the place."

Jessica felt a chill creep down her back. She swallowed hard and lowered the menu. Holliday was looking at her intently, head cocked slightly to one side.

"What did you just say?" she asked.

Had Alicia Lavelle been to this restaurant with her mother shortly before the woman's death? Had Holliday made the connection between Alicia and Jessica? Was bringing her here his idea of a sick joke?

"*Reservoir Dogs*," he said.

Jessica stared at him blankly.

"The tipping scene," he said. "You know, when Steve Buscemi's character, Mr. Pink, refuses to leave a tip for the waitress, and the others call him out for being a cheap bastard? It was filmed right here, in this restaurant. Man, I can't believe it was twenty-five years ago."

"I've never seen the movie."

"You've never seen *Reservoir Dogs*?" Holliday asked incredulously. "It's a classic. I'm not sure we can be friends if you've never seen *Reservoir Dogs*."

"I didn't realize we were friends."

Holliday's cheeks reddened, and he turned his attention back to the menu. "I'm going for a full all-day breakfast. How about you?"

"Ditto."

He nodded approvingly.

The waitress took their orders and brought over a couple of Diet Cokes. They sat in awkward silence for a few minutes, sipping their sodas, before Holliday spoke again. It was the conversation Jessica had been waiting for.

"Your client is Alicia Lavelle?" he said in a low voice. "What the fuck is that all about, Jessica?"

"I told you I wasn't going to discuss any of the details with you. A deal's a deal. You agreed."

He ran his hands through his hair in frustration. "That was before you told me you're working for someone who's been missing for the last twenty-five years. If you'd pulled the pin on a grenade and thrown it into my motel room, I'd have been less surprised."

Jessica shrugged and said nothing.

Holliday glanced around the restaurant and leaned in closer. "People have been searching for Alicia Lavelle for more than two decades, and you know exactly where she is. You don't think you should be sharing that information with the authorities?"

"No. At least not yet. And if you don't change the subject fast, then I'm walking out of here right now."

Just then the waitress appeared with two plates heaped with eggs, sausages, bacon, and toast. They ate in silence.

"Just answer one question," Holliday said eventually. "If you already know where Alicia Lavelle is, why are you even here in Eagle Rock?"

Jessica put down her fork and sighed. "Because she doesn't know who killed her mother or who took her from the house. That's why."

"She doesn't know who abducted her?" Holliday shook his head in disbelief. "Who the hell has she been living with for the last twenty-five years?"

Jessica picked up the fork and shoveled some bacon into her mouth and chewed slowly. Instead of answering his question, she asked one of her own. "Why are you so interested in the case?"

"You already asked me that."

"You didn't give me a proper answer."

"It's an interesting case."

"This is LA. There are hundreds—*thousands*—of interesting cases you could be writing about. Why this one?"

Holliday fiddled with the sugar dispenser. "I lived in Eagle Rock when it happened. I was just a kid at the time, fifteen or sixteen, but I remember the fear that gripped the town. Suddenly people were locking their front doors during the day. Kids weren't allowed out on their own. Everybody was suspicious of everybody else."

"You said you've been looking into the Lavelle case for a while. Who have you spoken to in Eagle Rock already?"

"Other than the cops? Just Hopper and Ace Freeman. I already told you I didn't have any luck with the McCools."

"That's it? I thought you'd written all those anniversary articles?"

"The information was mostly from newspaper cuttings and phone interviews with sources in the LAPD. I'd only been here once before this visit."

"Other than the time you lived here as a kid."

"Right."

"Your folks still here?"

"No, we moved to West Hollywood years ago."

"Where do you live now?"

"Venice Beach. You're based in New York, right?"

Jessica shook her head. "I was. Not now."

"Where do you live now?"

"Around. I travel from place to place."

"Sounds lonely. Any family?"

Jessica shook her head again. "Not anymore."

"Shit, I'm sorry. What happened?"

"My dad had a heart attack two years ago. I found him. I don't remember my mom. She died in an automobile accident when I was a baby."

"Hey, that's rough." Holliday reached across the table for her hand, and as his skin touched hers, she felt an electric current charge through her veins, like she'd just stuck her fingers in a live socket. Jessica pulled her hand away.

"You okay, kiddo?" Holliday asked.

"Yeah." She smiled weakly.

"Okay, time to change the subject. What's the story with the tattoos?"

Jessica's left hand instinctively went to her right arm, which was entirely decorated with brightly colored artwork. Just over two years ago, the skin had been untouched by a needle. Now it was filled with hearts, skulls, and roses. She touched an anchor on the center of her forearm. It was her first tattoo and had been inked just hours after they'd put Tony in the ground.

She had lasted less than an hour at the wake at a neighbor's house before telling sympathetic almost-friends and complete strangers that she needed to go home and lie down.

Jessica had headed for the nearest bar instead.

Three double Scotch on the rocks later and she'd known booze alone wasn't going to cut it. She'd needed to feel something real, something that would prick the anesthetized bubble she'd been bouncing around in for the best part of a week. Jessica had wanted to feel pain that she was in control of.

After leaving the bar, she'd stumbled outside into the rain, the booze and torrential downpour combining to make it difficult to focus on the blinking sign across the street. After she'd squinted at the letters for a few moments, they'd eventually formed into words, and she'd known she had found what she was looking for.

Before the tattoo artist had been able to comment on her whiskey breath, Jessica had flopped onto the seat and presented her arm to him. He'd eyed the naked, milky flesh hungrily. It was clear he wasn't going to pass up all that unspoiled virgin terrain, whether she was drunk or not.

"Have a look through these," he'd said, thrusting a folder at her. "See if anything catches your eye."

The book was full of designs clearly aimed at first-time female customers—tiny pink roses, pretty butterflies, Japanese symbols. Shaking her head, she'd pointed to a big rockabilly anchor in shades of black, silver, and blue on a poster on the wall.

"I'll have that one." She'd tapped the exact spot on her arm. "Right here."

Then she had sat back, closed her eyes, and savored the exquisite pain of the needle.

The choice of design had been ironic, Jessica realized now, because she felt like she had been drifting ever since.

"The tattoos are a story for another day," she told Holliday. "Why don't we get the check?"

"Sure thing. It's my treat."

"I don't need you to buy my lunch."

"I know you don't." He grinned. "You're picking up the check next time."

"Deal," Jessica said. "Just make sure you tip the goddamn waitress."

Jessica and Holliday emerged into the afternoon sun, hands raised to their faces to shade their eyes from the glare. As they turned around the side of the building toward the lot where their trucks were parked, a car sitting at the curb farther down the street caught Jessica's eye.

It was a black SUV with a silver grille and tinted windows.

"Son of a bitch," she said.

"What's wrong?"

Jessica hesitated. "I think I left my cell phone in the restaurant."

Holliday frowned. "I didn't notice it on the table when we left."

"I'd better go check. I'll catch you later."

She walked back to the entrance to Pat and Lorraine's and waved as Holliday drove past a few seconds later. The SUV was still parked farther along the street, behind a silver Honda, outside a hair salon. Towering palm trees lined the street and threw long shadows into her path as Jessica strode toward the car.

As she closed the distance between herself and the SUV, the calmness of the afternoon was shattered by the roar of an engine firing up and the growl of the gas pedal being pumped. She had almost reached the hair salon and the SUV. A high-pitched squeal filled the air as the SUV suddenly pulled away from the curb. Its tires burned, black streaks left in its wake, as the big vehicle careered into the road.

The SUV blew past at batshit crazy speed as Jessica stood rooted to the spot. Then she was running, legs pumping, feet pounding on asphalt, lactic acid exploding in her thighs, as she tried to make out the license plate. She realized the driver could be John Doe and the plate could be the lead she needed. But the car was already almost out of sight.

She returned to the parking lot and climbed behind the wheel of her truck. The quickest and most direct route back to the Blue Moon Inn would be to travel south along Eagle Rock Boulevard and then hook a left onto York at the ARCO station.

Instead, she took North Avenue Forty-Six and looped around the campus of Occidental College before turning down random streets until she hit York and approached the motel from the opposite direction. The whole time, Jessica checked the rearview mirror at regular intervals for a black SUV, or any other suspicious vehicles, but saw nothing that gave her cause for concern.

As she pulled off the street and into the lot, she spotted Hopper through the office window, behind the desk, working on some paperwork. Jessica parked next to the motel's neon sign and smoked a cigarette and watched him for a few minutes.

Then she made her way across the lot to the office. Hopper looked up when he heard the door open and offered what looked to Jessica to be a sheepish smile.

"Good afternoon, Miss Shaw," he said hesitantly.

"Please, call me Jessica."

"I, uh, changed your bedsheets earlier and left some fresh towels in the bathroom."

"Great, thanks, Hopper."

He looked uncomfortable. "And I guess I owe you an apology."

"Why—what did you do?" she asked sharply. Had he been snooping through her stuff while attending to the room? Saw something he shouldn't have?

"Jack told me you were pissed that I told him you were in Eagle Rock working the Lavelle case." Hopper cast his eyes downward. "You were right to be upset. It was damn unprofessional of me to give out information on my guests like that. I completely understand if you want to seek alternative accommodation for the remainder of your stay in town, and I'll be happy to refund the days you already paid for."

"Forget about it." Jessica dismissed his apology with the wave of a hand. "Actually, I was hoping to have another chat? If you're not too busy, that is?"

"Sure. You want some coffee?"

"I'd love some. Black. No sugar."

"Grab a seat. I'll bring it over."

Jessica sat awkwardly on one of the wicker couches, trying to make herself as comfortable as possible while it creaked loudly in protest under her weight. Hopper placed two steaming paper cups of coffee on the table in front of them and took the seat facing the one she sat on.

"What do you want to chat about?" he asked.

"Did Eleanor Lavelle stay here at the motel for a while when she first arrived in Eagle Rock?"

"Yes, she did. That's right."

"You didn't mention she was a guest here when I first asked you about her."

"I didn't think it was relevant."

"According to Ace Freeman, Eleanor was more like a resident than a regular guest. Long-term stay."

"Yeah. A couple of months. Maybe three."

"He also said some other stuff."

Jessica noticed Hopper's jaw clench.

"I'll bet he did," he said.

"He said there were some rumors about you and Eleanor. Rumors you were in a relationship and she was staying here for free."

Jessica expected an angry response from Hopper, but he just drank some coffee and then set down the cup with a weary sigh.

"Those rumors were started by Ace Freeman himself."

"Why would he do that?"

"Because he's a spiteful, jealous man who hates my guts. Has for more than forty years."

"Why?"

"A cute little blonde by the name of Crissy Smith, that's why. She and Ace dated a few times in high school, but it was nothing serious at the time. At least not to her it wasn't. Ace was a different story altogether. When I asked her to senior prom and she said yes, he was furious. He's never forgiven me."

Jessica remembered Freeman's comment about Hopper having never married.

"What happened to this Crissy Smith?" she asked.

Hopper smiled sadly and looked at her with eyes filled with pain.

"She married him," he said. "Goes by the name of Crissy Freeman these days. Damn near broke my heart, but he's the one who's still holding a grudge after all these years."

"So you were never romantically involved with Eleanor Lavelle?"

"Absolutely not. We never had that kind of relationship. What I said about Eleanor before—maybe I gave you the wrong impression when I said she was something special. She *was* special, but the way I felt about her wasn't sexual or romantic."

"How did you feel about her?"

"Protective, I guess. The first night she turned up here, she tried to come across all sassy and sure of herself. But I could see it in her eyes."

"See what?"

"She was lost. Eleanor never told me much about her past, but I know this much: that girl didn't have it easy. She was a hell of a lot more vulnerable than she liked to let on."

"Is that why you allowed her to stay at the motel for free?"

Hopper shook his head vigorously. "Uh-uh. Another of Freeman's lies. Eleanor paid her way, same as everyone else. I don't know where she got the cash from, and I never asked. None of my damn business. But she paid me a week's lodgings in full every Monday without fail."

"Okay, I get that you and Ace don't get along. But why would he make this stuff up about Eleanor? She worked for the guy. He gave me the impression they got on well."

Hopper laughed bitterly. "I already told you—Ace Freeman is spiteful and jealous. I think he truly believed something was going on between Eleanor and I. You know, history repeating itself."

"How so?"

"According to Eleanor, Ace was all roaming hands. A pat on the backside here, a squeeze of the arm there. Then he went too far and tried to get it on with her one night and earned himself a good hard slap for his troubles. She told him she already had a fella and she'd quit the bar if he laid a finger on her again. I guess he thought I was her fella."

"Could this boyfriend she was referring to have been Rob Young?"

"Nah, this was way before the Young kid arrived in town. I never asked her who the guy was. Again, I figured it was none of my business. I wouldn't have been surprised if she'd made the boyfriend up just to get Ace off her case."

"That bad, huh?"

"Worse," he said. "The guy is a grade-A creep. If you're going to be spending any more time at that bar, just keep an eye out for him."

"Seriously?"

Hopper nodded grimly. "Young, pretty, and sassy—you're just his type."

17

JESSICA

Jessica was relieved to find Razor, rather than Freeman, behind the bar when she slid onto a stool at Ace's later that evening.

As she waited to order her drink, it occurred to her she'd spent every night in the place since her arrival in Eagle Rock. If she didn't clear the case soon, she'd be in danger of ending up with a drinking problem. A bit like Mack McCool, who seemed to be as much of a permanent fixture in Ace's as the pool table and the ripped leatherette seats. He occupied his usual booth, a schooner of beer and a whiskey chaser on the table and his deck of cards laid out in front of him.

"What're you havin'?" Razor asked, slinging a bar towel over his shoulder. He was wearing another obscure band tee with musty armpits and skinny jeans.

"Beer, please."

He smirked. "Let me guess. Cold, right?"

"Yes. In fact, no."

Jessica figured she might need something stronger if she was going to attempt a conversation with Mack McCool. "Scratch that," she said. "I'll have a Scotch instead."

"Decent?" Razor sighed.

"That's right." Jessica pointed to where Mack McCool was sitting, studying the playing cards. "And whatever he's having too."

Razor didn't even bother trying to hide his surprise, but he said nothing and set about pouring the drinks.

While she waited, Jessica fired off a text to Holliday.

In Ace's. You around tonight?

A few seconds later, her cell phone vibrated with a response.

Sorry, working to deadline. Catch you tomorrow?

Jessica felt as though she'd just been turned down for a date.

No problem. Speak tomorrow.

She slipped the cell phone into her bag and balanced the beer glass and two tumblers of whiskey in her hands. She slowly crossed the room toward Mack McCool's booth, careful not to slosh any of the contents over the sides. He didn't look up when Jessica approached or when she slid into the seat across from him.

He continued to play his card game for what felt like a long time. Finally, Mack McCool looked at her. "Can I help you?"

The hot room suddenly got a whole lot chillier. The way he'd said those four words seemed to Jessica to be more of a challenge than a question.

She stared back at him, tried to show she wasn't intimidated.

McCool had the complexion of a man with too much fondness for the whiskey bottle. Broken capillaries gave his cheeks a permanently flushed, weather-beaten appearance, and a porous nose the color of a fresh bruise completed the booze lover's look. His pale, watery eyes were bloodshot. He looked away, unable to hold her eye.

"My name is Jessica Shaw. I'm a private—"

"I know who you are."

"I'm investigating the Lavelle case, and I've been speaking to some local residents about what happened that night. I hoped we might have a chat about Eleanor and Alicia."

Jessica thought she saw his face twitch involuntarily at the mention of Alicia's name, but he said nothing.

She went on. "I specifically wanted to ask you about a man called Rob Young. I believe he was a lodger of yours at the time of the incident?"

McCool ignored her and turned his attention back to the cards. A minute passed in silence. Then two minutes.

Then he said, "You need to leave now."

"If you don't want to talk to me, that's fine. I'll leave you alone. But I have as much right to drink in this bar as you or anyone else."

"I'm not talking about the bar. I'm not even talking about Eagle Rock. I'm talking about LA. Get out of town tonight if you know what's good for you."

"Is that a threat?"

McCool shrugged and took a slug of beer from his own glass. The two drinks Jessica had bought for him remained untouched. "If you say so."

"And if I don't leave town?"

McCool stunned her by swiping his hand across the table, sending the cards fluttering onto the floor. He squeezed out of the booth and leaned over her, palms pressed against the table. He was so close Jessica could smell the whiskey on his breath.

"Game over," he said. "That's what."

Jessica watched him leave, then picked up her own whiskey and drank it in one go. Then she sank the one she'd bought for Mack McCool.

"That went well," Razor said, eyeing the cards scattered around the booth as she returned to the stool.

She placed the empty tumbler on the counter. "Stick another one in there, will you?"

Razor poured generously from the bottle of Royal Emblem and placed the drink on a napkin. "Don't take it personally," he said. "Old McCool isn't exactly known for his social skills around here. First time I've seen him lose his shit like that myself, to be fair, but I hear he has a real mean temper."

As Jessica rummaged in her bag for her wallet to pay the bartender, she became aware of movement out of the corner of her eye. The construction worker from her first night in Ace's Bar had parked himself on the popped-pimple stool right next to her own.

"Oh, great," she muttered under her breath.

The guy leaned into her, completely invading Jessica's personal space. He pointed to her drink. "That one's on me, sweetheart."

His breath smelled minty, like he'd just popped a couple of Altoids. He signaled to Razor to pour the same again for himself. Jessica was about to tell the construction guy where to get off when he introduced himself.

"Hank Stevenson," he said. "I saw you in here a coupla nights ago. You got a name?"

Hank Stevenson. Ex-husband of Darla Kennedy, who was the one-time best friend of Eleanor Lavelle. Suddenly, Jessica wasn't quite so desperate to get rid of him.

"Jessica Shaw. You probably know by now why I'm in town."

"Yeah, I heard."

Stevenson was still wearing the ball cap but had swapped his work gear for jeans and a short-sleeved plaid shirt. The jeans were sharply creased down the middle of each leg, and she noticed the left one had a double fold where it hadn't been ironed properly. Jessica pegged him as someone who still lived alone after the breakdown of his marriage.

Her eyes instinctively moved to his left hand. No wedding ring. She couldn't decide whether Hank Stevenson was trying to hit on her or was just a nosy old bastard trying to find out information about her investigation. She guessed a bit of both.

"Found out anything interesting yet?" he asked.

"Bits and pieces."

"Yeah? Can't see how digging up the past is going to help anyone now. Me? I prefer to focus on the here and now."

He scratched three-day-old gray stubble on his chin with dirty fingernails and gave her a smile that made Jessica's flesh crawl.

"Your wife was best friends with Eleanor?" she asked.

"Ex-wife. And yes, she was."

"What about you? Did you know Eleanor well?"

"Well enough. Not as much as Darla seemed to think, though."

"What do you mean?"

Stevenson picked up his whiskey, studied it for a moment, and then took a long, slow drink. He emptied the glass, and Jessica followed suit. She caught Razor's eye and indicated she wanted two more drinks. Stevenson watched the bartender pour, then continued with his story.

"Darla worshipped the ground Eleanor walked on," he said. "What you need to understand about Darla is she never had many girlfriends before Eleanor showed up in town. She was quiet and lacked confidence, and the other girls at school never showed much of an interest in her. If they did, it was to make fun of her. Me and Darla, we were childhood sweethearts and got married a week after graduation, so she didn't really need anyone else."

Jessica watched as Razor walked over to Mack McCool's booth and began collecting the playing cards from the floor before leaving them in a neat little pile on the table. She hoped he wasn't expecting the old man back in the bar tonight. She wasn't in the mood for round two.

Jessica turned her attention back to Hank Stevenson.

"We used to come along here to Ace's every Friday night, and that's how Darla got to know Eleanor," he said. "They'd talk about women's stuff—you know, like clothes and movie stars and all that kind of shit.

Then they started hanging out together away from the bar. Next thing, Darla's wearing makeup and changing the way she dresses to look more like Eleanor, even though she didn't really have the figure, truth be told. These days, you women would probably call it a girl crush. Don't get me wrong— it wasn't sexual or nothing. I guess Darla just wanted to be like Eleanor."

"What did you mean when you said you didn't know Eleanor as well as Darla thought you did?"

"That's the other thing you need to know about Darla: she's jealous as hell." Stevenson laughed. "When that green-eyed monster rears its ugly head, boy, you'd better take cover. It's the reason why we split up in the end. What self-respecting man puts up with his wife checking his cell phone and rummaging through his pockets when he's been out at work all day earning a living? I only stayed as long as I did because of Hank Junior. When he left for college a few years back, I was outta there."

"Do you think Darla was jealous of Eleanor?"

"Hell yeah. What broad wouldn't be? Eleanor had every guy in Eagle Rock after her. And Darla thought that included me too. At one point, she even convinced herself we were having an affair behind her back."

"And were you?"

Stevenson snorted. "Not a chance. Girl like Eleanor wouldn't have looked twice at a guy like me." He picked up the refilled tumbler, took a sip, then looked at Jessica. "In any case, I loved my wife. I had no interest in screwing her best friend."

They both drank in silence for a few minutes. Then Jessica remembered what Catherine Tavernier had told her about her father's suspicions that Eleanor was having an affair with a coworker.

"You're a construction worker, right?" she asked. "Did you ever work for Tav-Con?"

"Yeah, back in the '90s, before Premium Construction took over the contracts. Still work for Premium now."

"You ever remember hearing any rumors about Eleanor being involved with any of the staff when she worked in the office there?"

Stevenson shook his head. "Can't say that I do. And believe me, if any of the boys were getting jiggy with Eleanor Lavelle, they wouldn't have kept something as juicy as that to themselves. Whole place woulda known about it."

"Maybe she wanted to keep the relationship on the down-low?" Jessica said. "From what I hear, the owner wasn't too happy about the idea of coworkers getting it on together."

"Lincoln Tavernier? Yeah, doesn't surprise me. Old bastard walked around with a poker stuck up his ass most of the time. He wasn't just the boss—he was the fun police. I don't want to speak ill of the dead or nothing, but things improved a lot when his number came up and Premium took over the company. Still don't think Eleanor was involved with any of the guys, though." He rubbed his thumb and forefinger together. "Not enough dinero for Eleanor."

"What does that mean?"

"Eleanor liked money. And she liked men with money. Ones with big bank balances and fat wallets and dumb enough to spend all their cash on her."

"Sounds pretty shallow."

"Yeah, well, she had a really shit life growing up in those kids' homes, didn't she? I guess she just wanted some financial security, a better future for herself. Who could blame her? What I could never understand was how she wound up slumming it in this dump and then working in an office for peanuts. The way she spoke, it sounded like she was earning a fortune when she lived in Hollywood."

"What did she do in Hollywood?"

Jessica tried to keep her tone neutral despite the excitement suddenly bubbling up inside of her. Hollywood. Eleanor's missing years. The years off the radar.

"Worked in a few of the topless bars. You know, a bit of 'exotic dancing,' as she called it. Skimpy panties and high heels and not much else. Reckoned she could make a hundred bucks on a good night and even more on weekends and holidays."

"You know which bars?"

"Never asked. Not my scene." Stevenson laughed raucously, as though the topless bars in Hollywood were exactly his scene.

"Did she have an apartment in Hollywood?"

"Nah, from what she told Darla, she crashed on couches mostly. When she wasn't spending the night in motels and hotels with the customers, that is."

Her excitement at finding out more about Eleanor's past evaporated as Jessica listened to the details. She started to feel sick to her stomach. Hopper had been right about Eleanor—she had been lost. It seemed to Jessica that Eleanor Lavelle had been a young woman who thought she was playing all these men when she was the one who was really being exploited.

Jessica drank some Scotch, hoping the burn of the whiskey might wash away the bile rising in her throat.

"The police report mentions Darla had a fight with Eleanor the night she died. Did she?"

Stevenson whistled through his teeth in a way that set her own teeth on edge. "You've seen the police file? I'm impressed."

"Yes, I have. Did they fight?"

"Physically? I don't know about that. But they did have one helluva argument."

"According to your own witness statement, you told the police you didn't know anything about a fight."

He shrugged. "Darla was my wife. I was just trying to look out for her."

"Lying to the police doesn't bother you?"

Stevenson chuckled. "It didn't then, and it wouldn't bother me none now either. Not one little bit."

"Even though Darla was the last person to see Eleanor alive?"

"Now, that's where you're wrong, sweetheart. The guy who slit Eleanor's throat was the last person to see her alive. I was with Darla the whole night after she left the house on Morrison. Hours before the cops said Eleanor died. I know Darla didn't do it, and I didn't see any point in telling the police about the fight and having them point the finger at her. Poor gal was in a bad enough state as it was when she found out Eleanor was dead. The last words they'd spoken to each other were said in anger. Can you imagine how that made Darla feel?"

"What did they argue about?"

"Eleanor was planning on splitting town. Darla got upset. They argued. She left. That's all I know."

Jessica was silent for a moment, then said, "I need to go powder my nose."

She moved off the stool and stumbled slightly as she grabbed her bag. The room had taken on a warm, fuzzy glow. She squinted at the far wall and saw two doors and a pink neon sign for restrooms behind the pool table.

"Same again?" asked Stevenson.

"Yeah, whatever."

Jessica headed for the rear of the room and paused at the pool table to allow a cute college guy to hit his shot before squeezing past and heading for the ladies' room. Sandwiched between the two restroom doors was an old bulletin board made up of a cork surface behind a locked glass panel, designed to prevent drunken patrons from tampering with the displayed contents. The glass was covered in a layer of grime, and the gig flyers and drinks promos behind it were decades old. The bulletin board, like the rest of Ace's Bar, hadn't been updated in years. There were photos, too, the fashion and hairstyles suggesting they'd been taken a long time ago. Back in the days when people actually went to those one-hour photo places to have their film developed, before the rise of social media meant sharing pictures online instead.

Jessica immediately spotted a couple of photos of Eleanor Lavelle, her long red hair making her easy to pick out among the dozens of smiling faces. In one, Ace Freeman stood grinning behind the bar with his arm slung across Eleanor's shoulders. In another, Eleanor and a much younger Darla Kennedy held up shot glasses in each hand to the camera. They were both laughing, their cheeks flushed with booze and youth and happiness.

A third picture of Eleanor, partially obscured by a flyer, caught Jessica's eye. She reached into her bag and pulled out the picklock set. Looked around, saw the college guys were busy with their game of pool, not taking any notice of her. The amount of booze she'd consumed made springing the lock a trickier task than it should have been, but eventually it yielded.

Jessica cracked open the frame just wide enough to carefully slide her fingernail under the thumbtack, pulling it out along with the photo. She held the glossy print under the restroom sign's neon light for a closer look.

Eleanor Lavelle's arms were wrapped protectively around the neck of a slightly awkward-looking guy in his early twenties. He had piercing blue eyes and long dark curly hair that fell around his face. He wore an Alice in Chains T-shirt and baggy, ripped jeans. Even in the '90s, the bar staff's uniform at Ace's appeared to have been a band tee and jeans, with only the fit of the pants changing in the ensuing years. Jessica flipped the photo over and saw some words written in neat capital letters on the back: *Eleanor and Rob, Aug '92.*

She shoved the photo into the back pocket of her cutoffs and pushed open the door to the ladies' restroom. Jessica stumbled against the washbasin and retched a couple of times, but nothing came up. She turned the cold tap on full and splashed water onto her face and wiped her hands on her shorts. Then she pulled the photo from her pocket and looked at it again under the glare of the fluorescent lights.

The writing on the back told Jessica the couple captured by the camera's lens were Eleanor Lavelle and Rob Young.

The photo itself told her they were Eleanor Lavelle and Tony Shaw.

18

ELEANOR

Eleanor filled Darla's glass to just below the rim. The deep-burgundy liquid was almost black in the dimness of the candlelit room.

"Why are we drinking fancy red wine anyway?" Darla giggled and took another sip of the expensive merlot. "It's definitely an improvement on our usual Friday-night beers."

Eleanor smiled mysteriously. "Because we're celebrating."

Her friend raised an eyebrow over her glass. "Really? What are we celebrating?"

They had drunk a full bottle between them already, and Darla's cheeks were flushed the same color as the wine.

Eleanor took a last hit of weed, licked her thumb and forefinger, and doused what was left of the joint. She dropped it in an ashtray and wafted her hand in front of her to clear the air.

"Let me just get rid of the evidence first, and then we'll talk." She winked at Darla, picked up the ashtray, and headed for the hallway. "Stick some music on. But not too loud."

Upstairs in the bathroom, Eleanor emptied the joint end and ash down the toilet, flushed, and rinsed out the ashtray. The bedroom next to the bathroom was illuminated by the faint glow of a nightlight. Eleanor pushed open the door and stepped inside. Alicia was sleeping, her Barbie doll tucked under her arm. Eleanor crossed the room and sat on the edge of the bed. She watched her daughter sleep for a few minutes. Listened to her soft snores.

"My precious baby girl," she whispered.

She brushed aside a chocolate-colored curl and leaned down and kissed Alicia on the cheek.

Back downstairs, Alice in Chains was playing on the stereo system. Eleanor returned the ashtray to the coffee table and rolled her eyes theatrically at Darla. "Job done. He'll never know."

"Oh, c'mon, Ellie. Robbie's a good guy. You could do a lot worse."

"I could do a lot better. He's a total square. You know what happened the last time he found weed in the house. He didn't speak to me for two days, and it's not even his house."

"He just wants what's best for you and Alicia."

"Yeah? Well, so do I, and we deserve better than the life we have here in this dump."

Darla frowned. "Eagle Rock ain't so bad."

"It ain't so great either. That's why we're getting the hell out of here. Just as soon as I get the cash together."

Darla's hand stilled, the wineglass paused halfway to her mouth. She stared at Eleanor. "Going where? For how long? Like a vacation?"

"I haven't decided where we're going yet," Eleanor lied. "Or for how long." She looked Darla in the eye and shrugged. "Maybe forever."

Darla slammed the glass on the table, spilling wine over the side. "You mean you're leaving town? For good? When did you make this decision?"

"Don't be upset, sweetie," Eleanor soothed. "We can always write each other. Speak on the phone. You can come visit anytime you like once we're settled." Darla's eyes brimmed with tears, and Eleanor sighed. "You know we can't stay here. The situation has changed. You know that."

"You could try giving your relationship with Robbie a chance," Darla said. "Let him move in here instead of renting that garage apartment. You know he'd jump at the chance to marry you and adopt Alicia. To make it all official."

Eleanor could feel the anger well up inside her. Tonight was supposed to be a celebration. About looking to the future, a *better* future, for her and her daughter. Trust Darla to kill her buzz. She was as bad as Rob.

"Look, sweetie," she said, "if you want to stay in Eagle Rock forever, answering phones at the local newspaper and popping out babies for the first guy who showed an interest, that's your call. It's not for me. There's nothing keeping me here anymore."

"What about the people who care about you?" Darla shot back. She was shouting now, black mascara tears streaking her flushed cheeks. "Do we count for nothing?"

"Darla, keep your goddamn voice down," Eleanor hissed, glancing at the ceiling. "Alicia is asleep upstairs."

"What about Robbie?" Darla demanded. "What's he saying about all of this? I take it he's being left behind too? Dumped like a piece of trash?"

"He doesn't know, and he ain't gonna know. Not until we're gone." She gave Darla a hard look. "And he still ain't gonna know. Do you understand what I'm saying?"

Darla shook her head and snatched up her purse from the couch. "I can't do this. I'm going to meet Hank."

"Good luck with that." Eleanor snorted. "He's probably already picked up someone else for the night."

The slap caught her by surprise. Hard and sharp. Eleanor held her hand to the spot on her cheek where it smarted. She stared at Darla, her mouth open. The other woman stood over her, spit foaming in the corners of her mouth, her lips stained pink by the wine.

"You're a nasty, selfish piece of work, Eleanor Lavelle. You think you're too good for Robbie? For me? The truth is you're not good enough for either of us. We both deserve better."

Darla strode toward the front door and threw it open.

"Don't bother coming back," Eleanor yelled after her.

Darla glanced over her shoulder. "The way you fuck around with people, Eleanor? One day someone is gonna make you pay for it. Then you'll be sorry."

19

JESSICA

Tony Shaw had been shy and awkward and gentle, a man of few words who preferred to express himself through his photography rather than conversation. He appreciated art and books, and he enjoyed watching old movies with his daughter on a Friday night.

He was also a murder suspect.

For twenty-five years, he had been a wanted man. Evading the detectives who hunted him, haunting their sleepless nights, taunting them with his absence, leaving them feeling impotent due to their inability to track him down.

For twenty-five years, Jessica's father had been a key player in one of LA's most notorious unsolved crimes, and she'd never had any idea.

Some private investigator.

It hit her now just how little she had really known about the man she'd thought she was closer to than anyone else in the world. She hadn't known his real name. Or where he grew up. Where he went to high school. Who his friends were. And she had known nothing about the woman he had supposedly loved. The woman who had given birth to her.

Above all else, Jessica had no idea if Tony Shaw was capable of cold-blooded murder.

She left the restroom, and then the bar, in a daze. She heard Hank Stevenson yell something about a drink, and Razor ask if she was okay, but Jessica felt like she was deep underwater and their muffled voices were drifting down from the surface.

Then she was running along York. Sweat dampened her hairline and the back of her neck. Her chest ached, and her breath came in ragged bursts. The photo in her pocket felt heavy and accusatory, like a lipstick stolen from a drugstore. When she reached the Blue Moon Inn, Jessica doubled over, hands on her thighs, trying to catch her breath.

Her truck was still parked next to the neon sign. Jessica couldn't face her tiny, claustrophobic motel room, so she dropped the Silverado's tailgate and used it as a makeshift step to clamber onto the truck bed's hard tonneau cover.

She lay down flat on her back, her chest heaving. Above her, the sky had deepened to shades of lilac and heather that she might have found beautiful on any other night. But not this night. She pulled the pack of Marlboro Lights and lighter from her bag and lit a cigarette. The gray-white wisps of smoke briefly obscured the perfect sunset before evaporating.

The first time Jessica had heard Rob Young's name and had been made aware of his possible involvement in the murder of Eleanor Lavelle and the abduction of her daughter, a thought had ignited somewhere in the dark recesses of her brain. Like a flare being fired into the night from a boat stranded in the middle of the ocean. The trails had lingered in the depths of her subconscious until finally being snuffed out by the absence of Rob Young's name, or her father's photo, in Jason Pryce's high school yearbook.

She flicked the butt over the side of the truck and watched the orange glow of the tip arc through the air before disappearing from view. She lit another cigarette. Jessica used to be the kind of girl who would have the occasional smoke when she'd had a few drinks at a party. After Tony died, it had become twenty a day. Same with the drinking and the tattoos. Everything to excess.

She had found him dead on the kitchen floor after arriving home from work one evening. He had been about to make dinner. There were chopped vegetables on a wooden block next to a knife, a saucepan filled with water waiting to be placed on the stove, an open packet of dried pasta.

She'd pumped his chest with shaking hands, thirty compressions, before delivering two rescue breaths. His lips were already blue and felt ice cold when pressed against her own, but still she repeated the procedure over and over again with no response.

Then she was hitting him and holding him and begging him not to leave her.

Tony Shaw had suffered sudden cardiac death caused by hypertrophic cardiomyopathy—a genetic heart condition that had, to the best of Jessica's knowledge, been undiagnosed. A ticking time bomb inside his chest waiting to explode. She had been advised to undergo screening for signs of a similar heart condition, as well as genetic tests to determine whether she had inherited the same faulty gene. They'd hooked her up to machines and computers and eventually told her she had nothing to worry about. Her heart was strong and healthy and absolutely fine.

They were wrong. Jessica's heart wasn't fine. It had been smashed into a million pieces. She would never be fine again.

She had cried hard the day Tony died as she'd cradled him in her arms on the cold tiled floor. She hadn't shed a single tear since. Not at the funeral. Not when she'd handed in her notice and told her boss she was leaving the job she loved. Not even when she'd handed over the keys to the Realtor and walked out of the home she'd shared with Tony for the last time without so much as a backward glance.

There were ghosts lurking in every corner of every room of that house in Blissville. They were on every street Jessica walked down, every corner she turned. Whether she was picking up lunch at the deli on the corner of Greenpoint and Starr, having a beer at the Jar Bar, or taking in an old movie at the Film Noir Cinema, she couldn't escape the memory of Tony. He was everywhere. She had known she would have to get as far away from New York as she possibly could.

Now, it seemed to Jessica she had been running from a life she knew nothing about. A past that belonged to someone else. She wasn't Jessica Shaw, New York PI, daughter of shy and talented local photographer Tony Shaw. She was Alicia Lavelle, notorious missing daughter of a murdered woman, a child whose face had been as synonymous with the early '90s in Eagle Rock as Calvin Klein perfume and Nirvana CDs.

Jessica already had a mother, of course, but the sanitized version proffered up to her by Tony had been a million miles away from the real one: a redhead who'd ended up with her throat ripped open after a life spent in care homes and seducing men in topless bars.

Tony hadn't liked to talk about the past. So for a long time, all she'd known about Pamela Arnold—the woman she'd grown up believing was her mom—was that she'd died in a car accident before Jessica and Tony had moved to New York.

She'd found out more about Pamela when she was fifteen. It had been a Wednesday, and Tony had taken her to her favorite Mexican restaurant. They would go there often on weekends but never on a school night, so she'd known something was up.

They'd ordered chicken fajitas and burritos, and when Tony's margarita had arrived, he'd gulped down half the cocktail in one go. When Jessica had pointed out he had salty frosting stuck to his lips, he'd dabbed at his mouth awkwardly with a napkin, as though he was on a first date. Then he'd told her about her mother and the night she'd died.

The first time he'd laid eyes on Pamela Arnold was at a night class on portraiture techniques. She wasn't a photographer, like Tony. She'd been booked as the model. Pamela had been pretty, but to Tony, the instant attraction had been about a lot more than just looks. She'd had an energy about her, something he couldn't quite put his finger on that placed her in a league of her own. They had quickly become inseparable, and Jessica had come along soon after.

She was less than a year old, Tony had said, when the accident had happened. Then he'd told Jessica about the trip to the grocery store, the discovery of the destroyed car, the speculation about what could have caused such a tragic end to a young mother's life.

Sitting in the restaurant, her burrito half-eaten and completely forgotten about, Jessica had asked Tony if he had any other photos of her mother. Pictures he had taken of her during their photography class or during their own time together. He'd shaken his head, told her he had burned the lot the night Pamela had died. All except one. The photo that was now cracked and creased and curling at the edges and still tucked safely behind the dollar bills in Jessica's wallet.

But the woman in the photo was not Eleanor Lavelle, and the kid cradled in her arms was not Jessica. Her best guess was "Pamela Arnold" had been one of Tony's photography clients, and he'd kept a spare print from the family portrait shoot to make his lies more convincing. The extent of his deception took her breath away.

Looking back now, maybe she should have been able to smell the bullshit among the jalapeños and pico de gallo in that Mexican restaurant. But Tony had been her rock, the one person she could always count on. He was her dad, and he'd never once given her any reason to believe she couldn't trust him. Until now.

Finally, the tears came.

Like a field that hadn't seen rain for years, Jessica hadn't realized just how much she needed the release until her cheeks were sodden and her body spent from the wracking sobs.

She cried for the man she thought Tony was and the man he might really have been.

And she cried for herself because she felt like she had lost him all over again.

Jessica must have fallen asleep lying there on the truck bed because it was full dark when she opened her eyes. The lilac sky replaced by inky black. The moon was a tiny cold jewel far in the distance, and there were no stars. The red and blue of the neon sign washed over her in calming, rhythmic waves.

Jessica sat up and rubbed eyes that were puffy and sticky with tears and sleep and globs of mascara. She lowered herself onto the tailgate and dropped to the ground. After securing the tailgate back into place, she fished in her bag for the key fob and made her way across the parking lot to her room in the Blue Moon Inn.

Once inside, Jessica flipped the light switch and fastened the security chain in place. The room smelled strongly of floral detergent from the fresh bedsheets. She dropped her bag on the neatly made-up bed. Her bones felt like they were a hundred years old, and she dragged herself wearily to the bathroom.

The image staring back at her from the vanity mirror above the sink was not a pretty one. Her eyes were bloodshot, and the lids were red and swollen as though she'd been punched. Sooty mascara streaks tracked the tears that had fallen down her cheeks. Her nostrils were clogged with snot. She cleaned up and swapped her clothes for an oversized T-shirt that would be cool enough to sleep in.

As she left the bathroom, Jessica saw a shadow pass across the main room's window.

It was a fleeting movement, no more than a split second, but she knew what she had seen. A darker shade of black standing out against the starless night.

Jessica dropped to her knees and crawled over to the bed and grabbed the Glock from the bag. She checked there was a full magazine in the gun. There was. She scrambled toward the door, keeping herself out of sight of the window; reached up; and killed the light. Slowly and silently, she rose and pressed her face against the door. She screwed one eye shut and peered through the peephole with the other.

A pair of eyes stared back at her.

Jessica pulled back from the door with a gasp. She tightened her grip on the weapon and quickly weighed her options. She could call 911 and report a snooper and wait forever for a patrol car to respond to the call. She could exit the motel room through the bathroom window and make her way to the safety of the office. Or she could take a more direct approach and challenge the guy face on.

She opted for the direct approach.

Jessica unfastened the security chain and unlocked the door silently. She planted her feet shoulder width apart, one foot slightly forward of the other, and raised the baby Glock with her right hand. With her left, she threw open the door and screamed, "Don't fucking move!"

Standing in front of her was Mack McCool.

His watery eyes widened, and his mouth dropped open, and he raised his hands slowly in a gesture of surrender. Jessica brought her left hand to the gun to steady her grip on the weapon.

"What the hell are you doing sneaking around outside my motel room in the middle of the night?"

The sharp, foul stench of urine reached her nostrils, and her eyes flicked downward for a split second, long enough to see a dark stain spreading across the inside thigh of McCool's tan chinos.

"Christ," she muttered.

"Please, lower the gun," McCool said. "I didn't mean to frighten you. I'm not going to hurt you."

"Damn straight you're not." Jessica kept the weapon trained on his forehead, her hands steady, wrapped tightly around the stocky grip. "What do you want?"

"I just . . ." McCool shook his head, didn't finish the sentence.

"You just *what*?"

"You're not safe here."

"Look, buddy: I'm the one holding the gun. I don't think you're in any position to be making any more threats."

McCool sighed. Looked at Jessica. She couldn't read those pale, watery eyes. "I'm not threatening you."

"But you've been following me?"

He nodded. "I just wanted to make sure you were okay is all. I was looking out for you. I know I handled things badly earlier. But you need to believe me. I'm telling you the truth."

"You call following someone with a big fucking SUV looking out for someone?"

McCool appeared confused. "What SUV? I haven't had a car for years. I followed you on foot from Ace's the first night you showed up in Eagle Rock. Then I came back again tonight. That's it."

"So who's the guy in the car?"

"I don't know anything about a guy in a car. But if someone else is following you, you need to take my advice and leave town tonight. If he knows who you really are, you're in danger."

Jessica felt light headed. "Who I really am?"

"Took me about two minutes to figure it out after you walked into the bar the other night. If I worked it out, others will too."

"What about the email?" Jessica asked. "Are you John Doe?"

McCool shook his head. "I have no idea what you're talking about." He slowly lowered his hands and let them hang loosely by his sides. "I've spent the last twenty-five years worrying this would happen. That you would show up one day looking for answers."

"Did Tony—*Rob*—kill Eleanor Lavelle?"

McCool shook his head. "No."

"Was he my real father?"

The old man stared at his feet. He couldn't bring himself to look her in the eye.

This was a very different Mack McCool from the aggressive one who had yelled at her in the bar just hours earlier.

"Tell me," she said.

"I don't know for sure, but I don't think so."

"Who is my real father?"

"I don't know."

"Who the hell was Rob Young?"

"Believe me—the less you know, the safer you'll be. He loved you, and he loved Eleanor. That's all you need to know."

"Bullshit." Jessica took a step toward McCool, the gun still raised. "Tell me who he was and why he took me from that house."

"No."

"I'll find out anyway. It's what I do."

McCool shook his head. "You won't find out about him. Rob Young wasn't his real name. You'll get nowhere. Go back to New York, Jessica. Forget about Eagle Rock. Just remember the man who loved you like you were his daughter."

She took another step closer to McCool and pressed the barrel of the baby Glock to his forehead. "I want to know the truth."

"You're not going to shoot me, Jessica." He put his hand to the barrel and gently lowered the gun. He backed away from her. "I hope this is the last time I see you. Stay safe. And trust no one. Including your journalist friend."

"What does that mean?"

McCool didn't answer her. He just turned and walked away in the direction of York Boulevard without looking back. Jessica watched him shuffle off into the darkness until she couldn't see him anymore.

She had no intention of taking his advice.

Jessica's eyes fell upon her truck, still parked next to the motel sign. She pulled on sneakers and a pair of jeans. Stuck the Glock in the waistband and made her way to the Silverado. The yearbook was on the passenger seat where she'd thrown it after leaving the high school in Van Nuys.

Jessica climbed onto the seat and left the door ajar so the dome light would illuminate the truck's interior. Then she opened the yearbook to the first page of seniors and scanned each and every photo.

She didn't have to search for too long. There, with the other students whose surnames began with *F*, was the man she'd shared the best part of her life with.

Eighteen years old. Dark curly hair and a shy smile. Piercing blue eyes. An awkwardness that suggested he preferred to be behind the camera rather than in front of it.

Tony Shaw.

Rob Young.

Murder suspect.

Liar.

Jessica remembered the scribbled dedication in the yearbook's inside front cover—*Life moves pretty fast!*

His real name was Brad Ferezy.

20

JESSICA

The murder house was easy to spot.

All the other properties on Morrison were well-tended Craftsman cottages painted in complementary shades of cream and light gray and moss green with gleaming white trim around doors and windows. Ornate porticos hung over front doors, and empty rocking chairs sat on uncluttered porches overlooking tidy, pretty lawns.

Wrecking any hopes the street's residents might have of ever achieving curb appeal was the ugly, dilapidated mud-brown house at the end of the block.

Paint blistered and cracked and peeled from the siding, and old leaves filled the corners of the porch like snowdrifts. The front lawn had been scorched bare by a long-ago fire, and wooden boards were nailed haphazardly over the big front window to cover the broken pane.

Jessica and Holliday stood on the sidewalk in front of Eleanor Lavelle's former home. She had decided not to tell him about discovering Rob Young's real identity. Or that the number one murder suspect in the Lavelle case and the man she'd thought was her father were the same person.

She also kept the previous night's altercation with Mack McCool to herself, especially his warning not to trust Holliday. As far as Jessica could tell, the journalist was on her team. The team who wanted to know who killed Eleanor Lavelle. Not like a drunk old man who seemed determined to hide the truth.

Holliday frowned. "Remind me why we're here?"

"You don't want to get a feel for the place where Eleanor died?"

"Not really. It's not like we can just walk in and take a look around anyway."

"Why not?"

"The house is still owned by the company Eleanor rented from. Some small-time property firm with a handful of rental properties in east LA."

"They never sold it?"

Holliday shook his head and pointed to a couple of signs lying prostrate on the front yard's dead lawn, their wooden stakes corroded by the elements. One was a **FOR SALE** sign; the other warned trespassers the premises were protected by Smith & Wesson. Jessica shuddered. She didn't know if the gun warning had simply been for show or if Eleanor really had had a weapon in the house. If she had, it hadn't been enough to save her life.

"No sale," Holliday said. "But it certainly wasn't for lack of trying. No one wanted to live in a house where a young woman was slaughtered. Even for a reduced price."

"I'm surprised there weren't any property developers willing to swoop in and take advantage of the low selling price. Surely they're hard nosed enough not to give a damn about what happened in the house?"

"You'd be surprised. Folks are superstitious. In any case, no real development potential. Not enough land and too close to other residential properties for any substantial projects."

"So the place has just been left to rot?" Jessica asked.

"Exactly," Holliday said. "The owners gave up on a sale a long time ago. Haven't even carried out showings for years. Not that I ever tried. I've never had any desire to look around inside. Still don't. The thought of it gives me the creeps."

"I do want to look around. Come on."

Holliday hesitated for a moment, then reluctantly followed Jessica up the driveway. She tested the ball of her foot on the first step of the porch. It held firm. She walked up the other two steps and tried the door handle. It was locked.

"At least we tried," Holliday said. "Let's go."

"Not so fast." Jessica produced the picklock kit from her bag and waved it in front of Holliday.

"Oh, jeez," he said. "Why am I not surprised?"

"Keep watch," she ordered.

The lock was old and hadn't been used for a long time, so it took longer than expected to breach with the pick. But her perseverance paid off after thirty seconds when she heard the click. Jessica pushed the door open and grinned triumphantly at Holliday.

"After you," she said.

Holliday didn't move.

"What are you so scared of?"

"Right now? You."

He pushed past her and entered the murder house.

The living room was just off a small entrance vestibule. The big front-facing window was bare, but the wooden slats prevented the morning's bright sunshine from filling the room. Slim shards leaked through the cracks in the wood and provided some meager light, but the farthest corners of the room remained hidden in shadow. A filthy, stained couch, sagging in the middle, was pushed up against the wall. Next to it was an upturned crate with empty beer bottles and an ashtray spilling cigarette butts and old joints.

"Junkies?" Jessica asked.

Holliday shook his head. "Kids partying. Geersen told me there had been dozens of complaints about loud music and general frivolity over the years. Not his department, obviously, but he was always kept up to speed with anything to do with the house. Neighbors even petitioned for the place to be razed to the ground."

"Why wasn't it?"

"Money. What else? A demolition would not have been cheap, and the owner didn't want to pay the cash. Why would they? They don't have to live here."

"I guess."

Jessica looked around. Empty beer and liquor bottles were discarded across the rotten wood flooring. Dozens of burnt-out votive candles in glass containers were dotted around the room. On a wall, someone had written *RIP Eleanor* in big black letters with a Sharpie. A chill crawled down Jessica's spine. She closed her eyes and tried to get a feel for the woman who had died here. Tune into the evil that had once filled the space.

As though reading her thoughts, Holliday said, "Place gives me the fucking creeps."

Jessica sighed and opened her eyes. "The couch is different from the one in the crime scene photos."

"The leather couch was ripped apart and submitted for evidence," Holliday explained. "Bloodstains belonging to Eleanor and black fabric that was never identified were both found on the seat covers. Of course, the case never went to trial anyway."

Jessica nodded. She remembered reading about the evidence samples being collected from the house when she'd gone through the murder book. "How'd this couch get in here, then?"

"Kids probably salvaged it from a dump site," Holliday said. "Smuggled it in here for their parties."

"How did they even get in? Front door was locked."

Holliday shrugged. "Beats me. Can we leave now?"

Jessica crossed the living room and disappeared inside the adjoining kitchen. She reappeared a few seconds later. "Back door lock's busted."

Holliday folded his arms across his chest and smirked. "If only you'd known, huh? Would've saved you committing a felony for the second time this week."

"I'm going upstairs," she said.

"Is that an invitation?" he asked.

She ignored him.

The stairs creaked and groaned as they both carefully made their way up to the first floor. At the top of the stairway, they found a small hallway with three doors, two of which were ajar. The middle one was a family bathroom. The compact space was entirely taken up by an avocado-colored bathtub and matching sink and a toilet with no lid. The walls had been decorated with pink tiles that were now cracked and faded.

The door to the left led to the master bedroom. It was empty of furnishings other than a stained double mattress with exposed springs dumped on the floor. Surrounding the mattress were more votives and used condoms and empty liquor bottles.

Holliday made a tutting sound behind her from the doorway. "Kids these days, huh? No respect for themselves or anyone else. God, how I miss those days."

Jessica turned and pushed past him back into the hallway and stood in front of the final door. Alicia's room. The door was closed. She could feel the heat from Holliday's body close behind her, his breath on her neck. She reached out a hand and turned the doorknob and crossed the threshold into the smaller of the two bedrooms.

It was dark and empty, but she could imagine a small bed with a pink cover and the window framed by matching curtains. Stuffed toys on the bed, maybe a dollhouse in the corner of the room.

Without knowing why, Jessica made her way to the closet and threw open the slatted doors. She pulled the Maglite from her bag, flicked the switch, and trained the flashlight's beam inside. It wasn't quite a walk-in closet, but it was still fairly deep. There were no hangers on the rod, and the floor was covered with a rectangle of thin beige carpet crusted with rat droppings. On the walls were messy crayon scribbles in rainbow colors at toddler height.

Jessica crawled into the cramped space and pulled at a corner of the carpet, ripping it all the way back until the hardwood flooring underneath was fully exposed. She ran her hands across the wooden boards, pressing and testing each one. The one closest to the wall in the back corner was slightly looser than the rest. Pressing down on one end of the board, she saw the other end pop up a half inch. It was enough to dig her fingers underneath into the tiny gap. She was able to get just enough purchase to wiggle the floorboard completely free. Jessica threw it behind her and shone the Maglite into a space that was about ten inches long, five inches wide, and three inches deep.

Inside, under a layer of thick dust, was a tightly folded plastic bag.

"Well, I'll be damned," Holliday said at her back. "How did you know where to look?"

Jessica couldn't explain the pull toward the closet to herself, never mind Holliday.

"The house doesn't have a basement or an attic," she said. "The next logical hiding place is in the closet. I've seen this kind of thing a lot in my job."

Holliday crouched down next to her and watched as she pulled the bag free from its hiding place. Jessica shook it clean of dust to reveal a red-and-white logo.

"Thrifty Drug Store," Holliday said.

"Never heard of it," she said.

"I think they were more of a West Coast chain. Sold the usual drugstore items, like deodorant and toothpaste. Candy too. But what I remember most about Thrifty's was the ice cream. It tasted amazing, and it was really cheap. As a kid, I couldn't get enough of it. Haven't seen a Thrifty's for years, though. Probably not since the '90s."

"Do you think this bag has been here since Eleanor was the tenant?"

"Only one way to find out."

Holliday held the Maglite while Jessica carefully unwrapped the plastic bag. She peeked inside and then looked at Holliday with wide eyes.

"Holy shit."

"What?"

She reached into the bag and pulled out a thick bundle of crumpled dollar bills bound tightly together with an elastic band.

"Holy shit," Holliday said.

Jessica thumbed through the cash. Tens and twenties and fifties and hundreds. "There must be thousands of dollars here." She handed the money to Holliday. "There's something else in here."

She retrieved a brown envelope from the Thrifty's bag, opened the flap, and looked inside.

"Looks like photographs," she said.

Jessica carefully slid the contents from the envelope. About a dozen photos. She immediately recognized Eleanor Lavelle in the one at the top of the stack. It had been taken at night, on the street, and showed the young woman arm in arm with a much older man.

The prints were stuck together, and she had to prize them apart carefully. The hiding place in the closet where they had been stored had been cool and dry, so there hadn't been much natural deterioration of the photos over the years, just some slight discoloration.

The next photo showed Eleanor with the same man. This time, her arms were around his neck, pulling him in close for a kiss. The backdrop was a brick wall, with a dumpster just in the shot. Jessica guessed the image had been captured in an alleyway.

The rest of the photos told a similar story: Eleanor Lavelle with a bunch of different men in intimate situations. They looked a little like paparazzi shots of celebrities, where the subjects were unaware of the camera's lens. The back of each photo was blank. No names written to identify the men. No photo developer stamp either. Jessica held up one of the images to Holliday.

"Recognize this guy?"

He studied it for a few seconds, then shook his head. "No, should I?"

"I don't know. He seems kind of familiar, but I can't place him."

Holliday gestured for her to hand over the pile of photos. He rifled through them. "This, I do recognize," he said, holding up one of the prints.

He showed Jessica the photo. Frozen in time was Eleanor Lavelle emerging from a bar or a club, laughing and leaning into a white-haired man. He had his arm around her shoulder, and she had her own arm snaked across the front of his fat belly. Holliday tapped what looked to be part of a neon sign shaped like a palm tree in the top-left corner of the shot.

"What is it?" Jessica asked.

"The logo for a topless bar in Hollywood," Holliday said. "I've been there before. I know exactly where this place is."

21

PRYCE

Medina looked like a guy who'd just walked into a bar only to be told last orders had already been called.

"I still think Fat Frank is involved," he said, sulking.

Both detectives were studying the surveillance footage from Urban Heights on Pryce's computer screen. Pryce froze the image of the figure in black and tapped it with his pen.

"We both agree this guy is not Frank Sherman, yeah? I know they say TV cameras add ten pounds, but I've never heard of a situation where someone looks almost a hundred pounds lighter."

"Okay, not Sherman," Medina agreed.

Pryce let the footage run on and hit the pause button again when the motel door opened. He zoomed in on the flash of white in the doorway.

"Lots of grain, but I think we can also be as sure as we possibly can be that Amy Ong answered the door while wearing the white bathrobe, so she was still alive when Sherman left the motel."

Medina was silent for a few seconds. "Maybe Sherman was working with this guy? Like a tag team. Or he paid someone to kill her? Could be Amy Ong was trying to blackmail Sherman, threatened to tell his wife what he was up to, and he had to shut her up."

Pryce shook his head. "If this was a paid hit, he wouldn't have been anywhere near that motel room himself. And he definitely wouldn't have left his prints all over the scene."

Medina's shoulders hunched in dejection. "I thought we had this one nailed."

Pryce turned back to the computer screen. He swapped the surveillance footage for his email inbox and hit refresh. No new emails. He pulled up the surveillance footage again and sat back in his chair, hands clasped behind his head.

"Let's run through some alternative scenarios that don't involve Frank Sherman."

Medina said, "Okay, shoot."

"An opportunist killer who picked a motel room at random and struck gold when a defenseless young woman answered the door."

Medina dismissed the theory immediately. "The change of clothing and knife suggest a degree of planning that doesn't fit with a random attack."

"I agree," Pryce said. "How about another one of her regular johns, someone like Sherman? Something happened, and things went bad quickly."

Medina shook his head. "Again, the clothes and the weapon mean an unplanned attack by someone she knew doesn't stack up either."

Pryce nodded. "Any ideas?"

Medina said, "How about a regular john, like you said, but someone with a serious grudge against Amy Ong? Maybe the baby daddy? Someone who planned the attack in advance. We know the roommate only told us about Amy Ong meeting with someone named 'Frank.' No mention of a second john. But she also made it clear she didn't want to know the sordid details about what her friend was getting up to, so it's possible Kasey Taylor didn't know anything about the double shift."

"I like it," Pryce said.

They both fell silent, lost in thought.

Pryce said, "What if it was nothing to do with her work as a prostitute?"

"I'm listening."

"Our guy could be a stalker who'd been watching Amy Ong for a while. He saw her meet with Sherman, followed them to the motel, waited for Sherman to leave, and then made his move."

"It's possible," Medina said. "But why would she open the door to a strange guy? The motel rooms were equipped with peepholes. The poor gal might have been desperate enough to turn tricks for cash, but she wasn't dumb, as far as we could tell. The roommate said she was real smart."

Pryce said, "Seems to me a regular john with a grudge against Amy Ong is the most plausible scenario. Some guy she knew, who she felt safe with and assumed posed her no threat, who took advantage of her trust."

"Sounds good to me."

"But not Frank Sherman."

Medina shrugged. "I guess."

"Kick him loose, Vic. Caution him for using prostitutes, and give him a rocket up his ass for drunk driving again. He's lucky he didn't wind up with another DUI or in the hospital, the mess he was in. But we've got nothing else on him."

Pryce watched Medina trudge down the corridor toward the holding cells, then got up and wandered over to the break room. He poured some coffee into a foam cup and drank it while thinking about their next move.

The call girl website Frank Sherman used was a waste of time. Even if they were able to track down premises or an owner for Hot Asian Angels and then subpoenaed a list of their clients, most of the profiles would be attached to burner phones and untraceable email accounts.

Pryce thought of Frank Sherman's glass-fronted office and the lack of privacy afforded to him each day. Throw into the mix nosy coworkers and computer glitches and IT departments, and there weren't many guys dumb enough to risk using a computer at work to arrange hookups with hookers. Home computers and email accounts were just as off-limits for guys with wives and kids. The kind of guys with a lot to lose who might need to silence a prostitute with a big mouth.

He would speak to Kasey Taylor again. Find out if Amy Ong had mentioned any details about any of her other regulars. First names, occupations, if they were married, bars or motels where they regularly met. Anything at all. And he would push her on anyone Amy Ong might have had a problem with. Maybe someone she'd tried to blackmail for extra cash or a john she had refused to see again. Kasey Taylor had held out on them once already, and Pryce wouldn't be surprised if she was still holding something back. He trashed the coffee cup and returned to his workstation.

He checked his emails again. There was a new message. More surveillance footage to trawl through, this time from the LAPD's own cameras. Many of them were mounted on top of traffic signals and light poles around the city, the feeds monitored by reserve officers and volunteers in tiny, windowless control rooms. The email was from one of those reserve officers, responding to Pryce's request for feeds from cameras situated in the vicinity of the Dreamz Motel. There were links to footage from two cameras. One south of Hollywood Boulevard on La Brea, the other on the corner of La Brea and Hawthorn.

He let the footage from the first camera run from 10:30 p.m. onward. He saw families making their way home after dinner, young folks heading out to bars and clubs, and a handful of tourists wandering around, identifiable by the expensive cameras hanging around their necks and street maps purchased from gas stations clutched in their hands.

Then, after about ten minutes, a figure dressed in black strode into the shot. Hood up, carrying a duffel bag, back to the camera, head down. About five ten, with broad shoulders. Walking with purpose on La Brea. There was something slightly off about the way he walked, but Pryce couldn't put his finger on what it was. The figure in black quickly disappeared from the shot.

Pryce turned to the feed from the second camera and sped through the tape until 10:40 p.m. showed on the date stamp. He held his breath until the perp appeared in shot. Breathed out slowly as the figure in black immediately turned down Hawthorn.

The camera's lens covered only the entrance to the street. He watched as the perp climbed into a red car parked by the curb outside a small strip mall and drove off. Pryce zoomed in, but the shot only picked up the first three digits of the license plate. He couldn't be sure of the make or model of the car either.

"Dammit." He slammed his fist against the desk.

"Hey, what's up, partner?"

Pryce hadn't noticed Medina return to his own workstation.

"All done with Sherman?" he asked.

"Yup," said Medina. "Our pal Fat Frank looked like he'd just been offered a free weekend in Vegas with a high-class hooker when I broke the news. Then he threatened to sue the department. What's up with you? Your application for Hot Asian Angels get rejected?"

"Very funny." Pryce motioned for Medina to join him at his desk. "Have a look at this." He played the feeds from both cameras on La Brea for the benefit of the other detective before freezing the shot on the red car. "Any idea what the make and model is?"

Medina leaned closer to the computer screen. He stabbed a finger at a small dark oblong smudge. "Looks like a Ford badge to me." He screwed up his eyes. "Can't tell which model. Probably a Focus." He moved his finger to another tiny smudge on the rear window. "And that looks like a barcode."

"A barcode?"

"Rental car," Medina explained. "Allows the rental car company to scan the vehicle when it goes in and out of the lot so they can keep track of it." He looked at Pryce. "This is good news, partner."

"How so?"

"We have three digits from the license plate," Medina said. "We also have the color and make and possible model of the car. My bet is on a short-term rental, picked up the day of the killing and returned the day after. I've got a buddy at QuikCar. I'll call him now with what we've got, and hopefully we get a hit." Medina saw the doubtful look on Pryce's face. "It's a long shot, I know, but it's gotta be worth a try."

"You're right," Pryce said. "I'll try Avis and Hertz, and then we can work our way through the other major rental companies."

Medina called QuikCar, and Pryce spoke to three different staff members at Avis before reaching someone senior enough to handle his request.

Ten minutes later, they reconvened.

Medina said, "My buddy at QuikCar tells me if the car was rented from his store, then he should come up with a match fairly quickly. I told him this guy could have rented from any QuikCar in LA or even out of town. Hell, out of state even. In which case it's gonna take hours for colleagues at other QuikCar locations to check through their fleets and report back with possible matches."

"Same story at Avis."

Medina looked at his watch. It was a little after noon. "Want to break for lunch and draw up a list of other rental companies to call this afternoon?"

"Sounds good to me. Los Balcones?"

"If you're paying."

Medina grabbed his leather jacket from where it was slung over the back of his chair. Pryce didn't bother with a jacket of his own. The temperature had dropped a couple of degrees since yesterday, but it was still warm enough for shirtsleeves. They strolled out onto Wilcox into sunshine bright enough for both men to put on their sunglasses, Medina opting for his usual Ray-Bans and Pryce trying out the new classic Armani aviators Angie had bought him as a surprise gift.

Medina turned left in the direction of De Longpre. Pryce froze on the spot in front of the station entrance.

He looked directly across the street. There, standing in front of Potter Bail Bonds, under the shade of an old oak tree, was a woman in her twenties. Slim, blonde, five foot five. She wore a white cotton dress, black Converse sneakers, and dark shades. Her right arm was covered with colorful tattoos. She leaned casually against the hood of a black truck and smoked a cigarette.

Pryce stared at her.

She stared right back at him.

Even with the sunglasses obscuring part of her face, he knew he was looking at Jessica Shaw.

22

JESSICA

Jessica saw Pryce emerge from the station and felt her heart punch against her rib cage.

She took another drag on the cigarette and tried to give off the impression of being relaxed. Like she didn't feel as though she was about to prove those heart docs wrong when they'd told her the organ was strong and healthy. She needed to show the cop she was in control of the situation and wasn't going to be brushed off so easily this time.

Pryce was with another man who looked Latino but was dressed like the guy from *Happy Days*. Jessica assumed he was Pryce's partner. She dropped the cigarette to the sidewalk and removed the sunglasses. Pushing herself slowly off the hood of the truck, she checked both ways for traffic, then crossed the street toward the two detectives. Pryce looked shaken, while his partner wore a confused expression.

Good, Jessica thought. At least she had the upper hand for now.

When she reached them, she didn't bother with an introduction. The look on Pryce's face told her he knew exactly who she was.

"We need to talk, Detective Pryce," she said. "I know my father's real name was Brad Ferezy, not Tony Shaw."

Pryce nodded gravely. "Yes, we do need to talk." He turned to his partner. "Vic, this is Jessica. She's the daughter of an old school friend of mine. We have some stuff to sort out. I'm going to have to take a raincheck on lunch."

"Okay, no problem." The other detective set off down Wilcox, but not before throwing Pryce a look over his shoulder that made it clear he would be expecting an explanation later.

Pryce watched him go, then turned back to Jessica. "Can you give me five minutes? There's something I need to find."

"Sure," she said. "I'll wait in the truck."

Pryce was back in front of the station seven minutes later.

Jessica knew exactly how many minutes she had waited because she had watched every one of them click by on the dash's clock, wondering if he was going to show or not. Pryce jogged across the street, nipped around the rear of the truck, then slid into the passenger seat beside her. He was holding a sealed white envelope in his hand. Sweat dampened his brow and upper lip, and Jessica nudged the AC up a few notches.

"Thank you," he said. He shifted in his seat to face her. "You look well. I know you might find this hard to believe, but despite everything, it's good to see you. To meet you properly after all this time." He was drumming his fingers nervously on the envelope.

"What do you mean, 'despite everything'?" she asked.

Pryce sighed. "First off, I apologize for not offering to take you someplace for lunch or coffee, but I don't think this is a conversation that should be happening around other people. Secondly, I apologize for being so evasive when you called these last couple of days. I guess I panicked. I was thinking about what was best for myself, not what was best for you."

"And what's best for me?"

"The truth, I guess. I'd always agreed with Brad when he said the less you knew about your past, the better. Now? I think you'll be safer if you do know."

With that comment, he glanced in the rearview mirror, then checked the side-view mirror. Jessica did likewise. There were no folks hiding in the shadows. No black SUV with tinted windows.

"I'm listening," Jessica said.

Pryce shifted awkwardly in the leather seat and nodded.

He said, "Brad and I grew up on the same street in a neighborhood in Van Nuys. Our moms were friends, so it was always likely we would become best friends, too, even though we were totally different. Brad was into reading and cameras, whereas I've barely picked up a book my whole life. I was always a jock who played sports and was a member of the track team all the way through school. Brad hated sports. But we were tight. Closer than brothers, you could say. Then things changed."

"What happened?"

"A couple of things. Brad's mom died a few weeks before graduation. Massive heart attack. It was completely unexpected, and it totally floored him. He never knew who his dad was, and I was about to head off to college in San Diego on a track scholarship. I guess he felt like he was on his own. He told me he was planning to move to Hollywood to try to make some cash from his photography. With all the big stars in Tinseltown, he thought he'd be able to sell his pictures to newspapers and photo agencies, like those paparazzi guys who drive around in Beemers and Ferraris. But I don't think he had much success. Spent most of his time mixing drinks and serving up shots in a bunch of different bars, as far as I could tell."

"You kept in touch?"

"We wrote each other from time to time. Met up occasionally for a beer when I was back in LA for the holidays. One time, he told me he'd met a girl. She worked the bars in Hollywood, too, and he seemed real sweet on her."

"Eleanor Lavelle?"

Pryce nodded. "Then we lost touch for a while. By then, I was back in LA for good. I'd suffered a cruciate ligament injury while training for a big race. The medics patched up the knee pretty good, but I couldn't hit anywhere close to my previous PRs. My track career was over. I joined the academy, decided to become a cop instead. The day I graduated, me and a few of the other guys went out for a drink to celebrate. We walked into a place in West Hollywood, and guess who was behind the bar?"

"Brad Ferezy."

"Right. We shot the shit for a few minutes while he prepared the drinks. He couldn't believe I was a cop now. We swapped numbers and promised to keep in touch. I didn't hear from him again until the night it all went down in Eagle Rock."

Jessica noticed her hands were gripping the steering wheel, her fingers wrapped so tightly around the knotted leather the knuckles had turned white. Pryce noticed too.

"You sure you want to hear the rest?" he asked.

She nodded. "Yeah." Jessica stared straight ahead through the windshield. She was looking out onto Wilcox but was seeing the murder house as it would have been twenty-five years ago.

"I was woken in the middle of the night by the telephone ringing," Pryce said. "I'd assumed the phone call was work related, even though I wasn't on call that night. The riots had happened just a few months earlier, so we were all on high alert, ready to be called into action at a moment's notice again, if need be. But it wasn't my boss calling—it was Brad. He was upset and not making a lot of sense. He told me Eleanor was dead and he was going to be framed for her murder. He said he had to go on the run with her kid—and he needed my help to do it. If it wasn't for the panic in his voice, I'd have thought it was a drunken joke."

"What did you do?"

"I told him to meet me at a motel on La Brea, a place I knew by reputation. The kind of dump where a black guy could show up in the middle of the night and book a room with no questions asked. On the way to the motel, I called a contact of mine, a gangbanger turned snitch, and set the ball rolling on the things I knew Brad would need."

"Which were?"

"A car no one would be able to trace to him and some new IDs for Brad and the kid."

"The kid being me."

"Yeah, you. Sorry."

"Please, go on."

"You were both dropped off at the motel by a middle-aged couple. Brad said he was renting a room from them. The woman had bought some new clothes for you at a twenty-four-hour Walmart on the way to the motel, and they'd packed a bag with some of Brad's stuff so they could tell the cops he'd left town on a planned trip. Then they gave him some cash and left to have their car detailed. They were going out to a deserted highway someplace to burn the clothes Brad was wearing when he found Eleanor."

"Brad found Eleanor?"

Jessica could see Pryce nodding from the corner of her eye.

"He said he went to Eleanor's place after his shift at a local bar had finished. He had his own key and let himself in. Right away, he saw Eleanor lying on the living room floor, covered in blood. She wasn't moving, didn't look like she was breathing. And then things got really weird."

Jessica turned in the seat to face him. "You mean more weird than his girlfriend lying dead in a pool of blood on the living room floor?"

Pryce looked her in the eye, his expression serious.

"The killer was still there," he said. "Sitting calmly on the couch, holding a gun in one hand and a knife in the other. The gun was pointed at Brad. The knife was soaked in blood. He recognized it as the knife he used in the bar—you know, for cutting fruit garnishes for the drinks? The killer told Brad he had two choices. Take the kid and get as far away from Eagle Rock as possible, and never speak of what happened. Or get a bullet in the brain, before the kid died the same way the mother had, with Brad's knife and his prints all over it left at the scene."

"Christ," Jessica whispered. "All those years, he knew who killed Eleanor? Who was it?"

Pryce shook his head. "I don't know. He wouldn't tell me, and he wouldn't tell the couple who'd helped him either. He said it would be safer for us all if we never knew. I begged him—told him I'd go and arrest this guy's ass and back Brad one hundred percent with the knife thing. But he wouldn't listen. He was terrified this lunatic would come after you."

Jessica was stunned. They sat in silence for a few minutes.

"You think he was telling you the truth?" she asked. "You're sure he didn't kill Eleanor himself?"

"As sure as I can be without actually being there. I told you we were like brothers. Brad was a good guy. He didn't have it in him to kill someone."

"But you'd drifted apart. You said as much yourself. Maybe he'd changed."

"No chance," Pryce said firmly. "You seriously think I'd risk everything to help Brad if I thought for even one second he was capable of murder? Think about it. I'm not just talking about my badge; I'm talking about my own ass being thrown in jail if anyone ever found out what I did. That gangbanger I told you about? The guy was killed in a drive-by shooting six months later, and you know how I felt when I heard the news? Relieved, that's what. I no longer had to live with the constant worry he would call in a favor one day. So, yeah, that's how sure I was of Brad's innocence."

"The counterfeit IDs. Paper tripping?"

Pryce nodded.

Jessica knew paper tripping—or ghosting—was a form of identity theft where someone stole the identity of a dead person who would've been around the same age as the "ghoster" had they still been alive. The practice was far less common these days because of the increased computerization of government records and the sharing of information by different agencies. But back in the early '90s, it would just about have still been possible to assume the identity of a dead person and go on to apply for passports or Social Security benefits in their name.

"Jessica Shaw and Tony Shaw—who were they?" she asked.

"I don't know the exact details," Pryce said. "I'm pretty sure the girl was born the same year as you were and died around a year later. I think Tony Shaw was actually born the year before Brad, and he died when he was about fifteen. Their births were registered in LA, but they were both out of state when they died. I do know the real Jessica Shaw and Tony Shaw shared a surname, but they weren't related in any way. The gangbanger had an excellent counterfeit contact who had a whole bunch of potential "ghosts" lined up—with fake birth certificates to match—just waiting to be sold for the right price to anyone who had to disappear for a while."

"And who paid for all of this deception?"

"Me. I used my own savings to pay for the IDs and the car. I know Brad would've done the same for me if I was ever in trouble."

"Do you also know why he was going by the name of Rob Young while living in Eagle Rock?"

Pryce shook his head. "I don't. The first I knew anything about anyone called Rob Young was when I heard some talk between other cops about the prime suspect in the Lavelle case. It threw me at first before I realized they were talking about Brad."

Jessica's head was starting to hurt, and her throat felt tight, but she had to ask the next question. "Do you think there's any chance at all Tony—*Brad*—was my biological father?"

"I really don't know, Jessica," Pryce said gently. "Maybe this will provide some of the answers you're still looking for."

He handed Jessica the envelope.

"What is it?" She turned it over in her hands. It was blank on both sides.

"A letter from Brad to you," Pryce said. "I don't know what it contains. I never opened it. It was mailed to me at the station around ten years ago, along with a note asking me to make sure you received it only if something happened to him and you showed up in LA one day asking questions. I guess today is that day."

Jessica stuffed the envelope into the glove compartment next to the Thrifty's bag.

"I'll read it later. I can't face it right now."

"Of course. You've had a lot to take in already."

"Earlier, you said I'd probably be safer knowing the truth about my past. What did you mean?"

"I don't want to frighten you, Jessica, but the killer could still be out there. Or they might be dead or in prison for another crime. We just don't know. But you're going to have to be more careful, more vigilant, from now on, just in case. Do you have a weapon?"

Jessica nodded. The baby Glock was in her shoulder bag. "I have a gun."

"Good. Where are you staying while in town?"

"The Blue Moon Inn in Eagle Rock. I've been looking into the case."

"Shit, Jessica." Pryce stared at her in disbelief. "What you're doing is dangerous. You need to get as far away from LA as possible. And you need to do it right now."

23

JESSICA

Jessica assured Pryce she would return to the Blue Moon Inn and start packing up her stuff right away.

She lied.

She had no intention of leaving LA just yet.

As she pulled into the motel's parking lot, Hopper gestured through the window for Jessica to join him. She nodded and held up two fingers, indicating she would meet him in a couple of minutes. She parked outside room 5 and strolled back the way she had just driven. Entering the lobby, she saw an old man sitting on one of the wicker seats.

His face was a weather-beaten tan and creased by a million wrinkles. He reminded Jessica of a shar-pei. Just like a dog's, his head bobbed up, and he sat up straighter at the sound of the door, his eyes tracking her all the way to the counter.

"Visitor here to see you," Hopper said in a hushed tone. "Chuck Lawrence. He heard you were in town asking about the Lavelles."

"The guy who found Eleanor's body?" Jessica whispered back.

"That's the one. Must be real keen to speak to you. He's been here for more than an hour already. We've gone through two pots of coffee and spoken about everything from the weather to how the Lakers will fare next season to the price of groceries at Ralph's." Hopper lowered his voice even further. "I think the old boy's just a bit lonely and wants someone to talk to."

"Lucky me."

Jessica walked over to Chuck Lawrence. He was at least ten years older than Hopper, just about justifying the motel owner's reference to the man as an "old boy." Chuck had thinning silver hair, neatly parted and combed, and kind brown eyes. A walking cane was propped against the couch next to him.

"Mr. Lawrence? I'm Jessica Shaw. I believe you wanted to have a chat about the Lavelles?"

Lawrence struggled to his feet with the help of the cane.

"Please, call me Chuck," he said, over the sound of the seat creaking. His voice was surprisingly strong, in contrast to his frail appearance. "You mind if we talk outside? It's a beautiful day, and I'm gasping for a smoke."

"Sure, no problem."

Jessica followed slowly at his back as Chuck shuffled toward the door, leaning heavily on the cane. Once outside, he lowered himself carefully onto a bench next to a soda machine with a satisfied sigh and stretched out his legs.

Jessica fished some change from her wallet and keyed in the code for a Diet Coke.

"You want a soda?" she asked.

Chuck shook his head. "Thanks, but no. I've had about five cups of Hopper's coffee. Between my bladder and the caffeine, I'll be up all night buzzing and pissing as it is."

He found some cigarettes and a lighter in the breast pocket of his shirt. As he lit up, Jessica realized she was all out.

"Mind if I bum a smoke?" she asked.

Chuck grinned. "My kinda girl. Bet you like a drink too."

Jessica laughed. "Only if it's a decent Scotch." She popped the tab on the soda can. "I guess this'll have to do for now." She took a sip before leaning in close to Lawrence so he could light her cigarette. "So you're here to tell me about the day you found Eleanor?"

Chuck nodded. "Ace Freeman told me a young lady PI was in town asking about the murder. Or maybe it was the kid with the crazy ears who told me. No, wait a minute—it was Hank Stevenson. He said you were real pretty but feisty."

He saw the concerned look on her face and tapped his temple with the hand holding the cigarette.

"Don't you worry about old Chuck," he said. "I've still got all my faculties. Sharp as a thumbtack. Okay, maybe I don't remember what I had for supper last night, and I sometimes forget to buy milk when I'm at Ralph's, but I remember everything from way back. Believe me— what I saw that day ain't gonna leave me until the day they dump me in the ground."

"I can imagine."

"You know I was the mailman, right? More than forty years I spent pounding these streets. Up and down porch steps, climbing apartment stairwells." He waved the cane in front of her. "It's the reason why my knees are busted now, but it was worth it. I loved the job. I'm a sociable guy, always been up for a chat and cup of coffee. As the local mailman, I knew everyone, and everyone knew me. After Eleanor, it was never the same."

Jessica waited for Chuck to continue.

"It was an early fall day on the weekend," he said. "Bit cooler than today but pleasant enough. I'd been whistling a cheerful tune as I made my way up the porch steps. The reason I remember I was whistling is because suddenly the tune seemed too loud in the still surroundings. The song died on my lips but seemed to linger in the air for a few seconds before being swept away by the breeze. You know what I mean? When a song or a burst of laughter is followed by silence so still the sound seems to just hang there for a moment or two?"

Jessica nodded. She knew exactly what the old man meant.

"Anyways, I walked up the rest of the steps onto the porch. My ears alert, listening for any sounds. You see, I'd been at that house on

Morrison countless times since Eleanor moved in, and the place was always a riot of noise. Especially on a weekend. Usually a radio would be playing, or those kids' cartoons were blaring on the TV. You'd hear Eleanor and little Alicia laughing and shouting. Usual family stuff. Not that day, though. I remember thinking that brown house looked like a giant bear in the midst of a winter hibernation."

Jessica shuddered, knowing all too well how the story was going to end.

"What did you do next?" she asked.

"I wasn't too concerned at first," he said. "I assumed they'd overslept. It was Saturday, after all. Then I checked the time on my watch. It was 10:37 a.m. exactly. I told you, I can remember every little detail. I was much later making my rounds than usual. Old Mrs. Knight, who lived at the end of the street, had insisted on making me coffee before providing a detailed update of her arthritis problems. Mrs. Knight's ailments were of absolutely no interest to me, but her coffee was the proper stuff, not that crap from a jar, and a half hour had passed before I'd even realized how late it was."

Chuck stubbed out his cigarette on the arm of the bench and lit another. He offered Jessica the pack again. She shook her head.

"All of a sudden, it didn't seem so likely they'd just overslept," he said. "My own two kids were teenagers by then, but I remembered all too well how sleeping in was a rare thing when you had little kids. Always up early and jumping around, and from my own experience of visiting the house in the past, little Alicia was no different. It was too soon to make the trip Eleanor had spoken about, so I racked my brain, tried to remember if she had mentioned going away for the weekend. But the station wagon was parked in the driveway, and she was expecting the parcel I was delivering, so I didn't think so. That's when I started to worry."

Jessica noticed his eyes were wet. He took a long drag on the cigarette.

"The curtains were still drawn," he said. "There was a gap in the middle where they didn't quite meet properly, so I stuck my face against the window and tried to look inside. Couldn't see much. Some burnt-out candles, a half-empty bottle of wine on the table. It struck me then that Eleanor might have been entertaining the night before. You know, a young man. Maybe that's why she was still in bed. I jumped back from the window, feeling like a Peeping Tom, and gave the front door a couple of good, hard knocks.

"I expected to hear the sound of her footsteps in the hallway, for Eleanor to answer the door in her dressing gown, maybe a little embarrassed. But I heard nothing. The parcel was a new Barbie doll for the little girl, so I shouted, 'Hey, Barbie's out here, and she wants to meet her new family!' But still there was no response. It was eerie, like the house was empty, but somehow, I knew that wasn't the case. I was debating with myself whether to try again after lunch or leave a note asking Eleanor to pick up the parcel herself from the post office in town when I heard it."

"What did you hear?"

"A weird click, click, click sound. I knocked again. Still nothing. The noise bothered me. I started thinking Eleanor might have had an accident. A bad fall, knocked herself out, couldn't reach the phone to call for help. All sorts of dreadful scenarios went through my mind. My wife was always telling me I watched too many of those dumb TV movies they show in the afternoon. But I tried the door anyway, and it was unlocked."

"And that's when you found her."

Chuck nodded. "She was on the carpet, in front of the couch. That's why I couldn't see her from the window. I knew just from looking at her she was dead. I didn't even touch her. I thought of the little girl, and I screamed Alicia's name a few times and got no answer. I was terrified what I might find in her bedroom, so I just went straight for the telephone in the kitchen and dialed 911. I hid in there until the cops arrived, like a coward. I couldn't face seeing Eleanor again. All that blood. And her beautiful face all beaten up."

His chin dropped to his chest, and he shook his head as though trying to rid himself of the memory.

"They had to take my statement out in the yard. They said Alicia was missing, and they told me the clicking sound I'd heard was a cassette in the stereo system that had come to the end of the tape. That bastard had slaughtered Eleanor like a pig while her goddamn music played in the background."

Jessica wanted to reach out a hand and comfort Chuck Lawrence, but she couldn't move. "You mentioned Eleanor was planning a trip?"

"I spoke to her in the post office on York the day before," he said. "You know I was also the last known person to see little Alicia before she vanished?"

Jessica nodded, shifted uncomfortably on the bench, and averted her gaze.

He said, "Eleanor and I spoke for a few minutes about the usual kinda stuff, like the weather. She told me she was expecting a parcel so would probably see me again over the weekend and would make sure to have a nice pot of coffee ready for me when I made the delivery. Then she made a comment about how she'd miss our chats when she was gone."

"Gone where?"

Lawrence shrugged. "She didn't say. All I know is she was planning on leaving town for good. Said she wanted a better life for her and her daughter. Told me she was just waiting on some news, and then they would be off. The way she spoke, we're talking a matter of days or weeks rather than months."

"Did you tell the police about her plans to leave Eagle Rock?"

Chuck frowned. "No, they never asked. Didn't seem too interested in what we spoke about in the post office. All their questions were about finding Eleanor the next day and whether I'd seen Alicia at all on the

Saturday morning. Which I hadn't. Why? Do you think her planning on leaving town was important?"

"I'm not sure, Chuck," she said. "How did Eleanor seem when she spoke about the trip?"

"Excited, I guess. Maybe . . . something else too."

"Like what?"

"Not fear exactly." Chuck looked at Jessica and frowned. "But I'd say, thinking back now, she was definitely on edge about something that day."

24

PRYCE

Pryce slowly turned the pages of Eleanor Lavelle's murder book.

He had requested the file—and then made a copy—years ago, and it had been well thumbed since then. He didn't read novels, like Dionne and Angie did, but he read murder books. From cover to cover, over and over again. He knew the contents of every page of this one by heart—the autopsy report, the newspaper cuttings, the witness statements from the bar owner and the best friend and the McCools. He had searched every single line for any indication, anything at all, suggesting Brad Ferezy could have been a killer.

Less than an hour ago, he had looked Jessica Shaw straight in the eye and told her he had never once doubted his best friend's innocence.

It had been yet another lie to add to the growing collection.

It was a question he had asked himself dozens of times over the last twenty-five years. On those nights when sleep wouldn't come, or during moments he spent gazing out of the window, the thought would manifest itself deep inside his brain, like a worm burrowing under soil.

The whole Rob Young name thing had always bothered him. Why adopt a new identity unless you'd done something pretty bad or had some particularly nasty folks after you? Either way, the need for an alias didn't fit with the Brad Ferezy Pryce had known. He simply could not reconcile the shy kid who had gladly helped him with his schoolwork with being a cold-blooded murderer.

Pryce sat back in his chair and looked around the squad room as it buzzed with activity.

Phones rang, cops discussed cases with each other or spent a few minutes just shooting the shit, news channels reported the same stories over and over again on an hourly loop on wall-mounted television screens. The smell of microwaved Chinese food wafted from the break room, carried around the squad room by desktop fans.

Rodriguez caught Pryce's eye and offered him a sympathetic smile. News of Frank Sherman being kicked loose was common knowledge by now. The congratulatory backslaps had been replaced by awkward nods and strained smiles. Worse still, Grayling was back from her vacation and was applying even more pressure for a quick result.

Amy Ong's car had been found where Frank Sherman had said it would be, close to the bar on Las Palmas, and was currently being pulled apart by Forensics, but Pryce wasn't hopeful it'd be the lead they were looking for.

He turned another page in the file and found himself staring at the face of three-year-old Alicia Lavelle. She was the one part of the Lavelle investigation that wasn't a mystery, at least not to him. For once, he hadn't been lying when he'd told Jessica he was pleased to meet her properly and see she was doing okay. The kid had been a part of his life longer than his own daughter had, albeit from a distance. He decided he would swing by the Blue Moon Inn after he'd clocked out for the night, just to make sure she'd taken his advice and left town.

Pryce looked up from the photo as Medina entered the squad room. He closed the murder book and dropped it into the bottom drawer of the desk and locked it.

Medina screwed up his face. "This place stinks something bad. Has someone been eating Chinese takeout at their desk again?"

"How was lunch?" Pryce asked.

"Oh, just swell, thanks," Medina snarked, slumping into his chair. "Nothing I like more than a table for one during the lunch rush. I must've looked like a guy whose blind date had taken one look at him through the window and decided not to bother. Although I definitely can recommend the *clásico* ceviche if you do decide to join me next time."

"Sounds a lot better than the carne asada I picked up at the burrito stand."

Medina looked at Pryce, crossed his arms. "How was it?"

"Not too great, to be honest. It's definitely given me a touch of heartburn."

"Not the freakin' burrito, you moron. The chat with the girl. You know, the cute blonde with the tattoos who had you all spooked earlier. You gonna tell me what that was all about?"

Pryce sighed. Truth and lies. He decided to split the difference.

"Her father was an old school friend of mine. Seems he got himself into a bit of bother years back and changed his name. The kid's just found out and managed to track me down, wanted to find out if I knew what trouble he had been in, but it was after I knew him. Turns out the guy's dead now, so nothing to worry about. No big deal."

Medina looked doubtful but didn't push it. He logged onto his computer and groaned.

"Aww man, have you seen this shit all over the internet?" He turned the screen around so Pryce could see the website of a well-known newspaper.

Pryce nodded. "Yeah, I saw it."

The media had gotten wind of the arrest, and subsequent release, of a suspect. They'd also found out details of Amy Ong's injuries and knew she was working as a prostitute and had been pregnant at the time of her death. There was no mention of Frank Sherman's name anywhere in the coverage. Pryce suspected he had traded the information in return for his name being kept out of the papers. As well as a nice big tip fee, of course.

Pryce knew the insurance salesman wouldn't follow through on his threat to sue the department—too much unwanted publicity for a guy already trying to save his marriage—but it looked like he had managed to hit pay dirt all the same. Pryce was willing to bet Sherman would be cruising the streets later, looking for a good time, with a fifth of whiskey in his pocket and a wad of bills stuffed in his wallet.

Medina turned his computer screen back around. "I'm going to give ViCAP another shot, even though we've had nothing so far."

The FBI's Violent Criminal Apprehension Program—or ViCAP, as it was more commonly known—was used by state and local law enforcement to identify possible links between seemingly unconnected violent crimes such as homicides and sexual assaults.

Medina went on. "A search for homicides involving known prostitutes, where the murder weapon was a knife or similar, resulted in hundreds of hits. Way too many to follow up on. Add *dark hoodie* and *duffel bag* to the search terms, and it goes the other way. We get nada. I suppose we could take a look at the first lot of hits and start with the most recent in the Hollywood area and work—"

Medina was interrupted by a low vibrating sound as his cell bounced across the desk. He grabbed the phone and checked the caller ID. "My buddy at QuikCar," he told Pryce. "Let's hope he has some good news for us."

Pryce had already come up with a blank with Avis. He watched as his partner's expression changed from hopeful to disappointed, then switched briefly back to hopeful again, before finally settling on frustration as he killed the call.

"No joy so far," Medina said. "Ken reckons the red Ford is definitely not one of his. He's gone through the entire fleet, and there's no match with the plate number."

"Ditto Avis," Pryce said. "They called back while you were having a romantic lunch for one."

"Ken's based at QuikCar's La Cienega location, but we still might get lucky with one of their other places," Medina said. "He's got a friend at LAX checking their own fleet as we speak, but the airport's their biggest and busiest operation, so it could take a while longer for a definitive answer. Another buddy works out of West Hollywood, but he's on a day off and says he'll check their cars when he's back on shift tomorrow. He knows they have a couple of red Fords but won't have access to the plate numbers until he's behind the computer."

"Tomorrow?" Pryce asked. "Isn't there someone else who can do it?"

Medina shook his head. "Ken's doing me a favor. This is all unofficial. We start getting other staff involved, and the big bosses find out what's happening, the next thing we know, they're demanding a search warrant to access their customer databases."

"I guess. While we wait, maybe we should both go through ViCAP again? See if anything stands out."

The two detectives worked in silence at their respective workstations. As he scrolled through the results from the database search, Pryce thought about their guy and how he was sure he had killed before, how other victims could be languishing somewhere in the system.

And if he was right, Pryce knew the killer might already have his next target firmly in his sights.

25

JESSICA

The girl was about twenty, but the thick makeup made her look five years older.

Silver platform stilettos added an extra few inches to her five-six, size-two frame. Her hair hung to her waist in thick chestnut waves, a mix of her own and clip-on extensions. She swung her head as she danced, the long hair providing the only cover for bare breasts that seemed to defy gravity even when she was upside down, with her legs wrapped around the pole, thigh muscles straining to hold the position.

She was naked except for the shoes and a red lace thong. A single spotlight followed her as she moved, dry ice rising around her. Her back arched and her legs kicked, and her hands caressed the pole like it was her lover as she worked through a series of languid movements in time to the beat of the music.

The song was "Naughty Girl," by Beyoncé. As the last notes played out, the girl dropped to her knees and flipped her hair again. She parted her lips slightly as her heavy-lidded eyes gazed out at the audience. A final seductive act for those closest to the stage but also the perfect position to scoop up the dollar bills scattered in front of her as the song ended. They were tens and twenties. She was good enough to avoid the single-digit dollars but not good enough for any fifties.

The performance over, Jessica and Holliday turned back to the bar, and both ordered a bottle of beer.

Outside, the Tahiti Club had looked dated and more than a little rough around the edges. Inside, the clientele was much the same. Most of the men were older than Holliday, while the women working the bar, the stage, and the room in general were all younger than Jessica.

"You said you'd been to this place before," she said. "Bachelor party?"

Holliday shook his head. "No special reason. I guess I just like it here."

It was Jessica's first time at the Tahiti Club, but she'd been in plenty of strip bars in the past. Sometimes it was for a case; other times she'd tagged along with guys she worked with, showed them she was one of the boys. Then there were the times she just wanted a quiet drink without the hassle of being hit on by men who took the sight of a woman drinking on her own in a bar as some sort of invitation. Topless bars were different. Why bother with her when they could ogle all the prime flesh on show instead? An added bonus was never having to wait in line to use the bathroom.

The sound of a saxophone solo filled the room now from hidden speakers. George Michael sang about loneliness and deception, his voice as smooth as silk sheets on naked skin. "Careless Whisper."

The place was small and dimly lit. Holliday glanced at her. He had a look on his face that she couldn't read. His gaze traveled slowly up and down, taking in her appearance. She was wearing tight black leather pants, a white satin shirt, and sandals that showed off bloodred toenails.

Holliday wore dark jeans and a navy shirt, with the sleeves rolled up to the elbows. Jessica caught a trace of the now-familiar spicy scent of his cologne. He tossed back a swallow of beer and nodded to the bartender.

She was black, around twenty-five, and beautiful. Bouncy curls and glossy lips. Tight tube top and tighter hot pants. The woman sauntered slowly from the other end of the bar toward Holliday, hips swaying, never taking her eyes off him.

"What can I do for you?" She asked the question in a way that sounded like she wasn't talking about getting him another beer.

Holliday dropped a ten onto the counter along with one of the photos of Eleanor Lavelle emerging from the Tahiti Club.

"Anyone around here who can tell me about this woman? She used to work here."

The bartender tucked the cash into the tube top, then leaned her elbows on the counter and looked down at the photo.

"She sure is pretty. Don't look familiar, though. When did she work here?"

"Around thirty years ago."

The woman straightened up and pushed the photo back toward Holliday with a throaty laugh.

"Honey, I wasn't even a twinkle in my daddy's eye thirty years ago."

"Anyone else who might know her?"

"Uh-uh. None of the staff anyways. Bobby, the doorman, he's been here longer than anyone, but you're talking ten, maybe fifteen years."

Holliday scooped up the photo. "Thanks anyway."

"There is someone who might be able to help."

"Yeah? Who?"

The bartender stared at Holliday, raised a perfectly sculpted eyebrow. He pulled another ten from his wallet, and the bill quickly disappeared into the tube top. She pointed a scarlet talon in the direction of a man sitting on his own in a booth close to the stage.

"Johnny Blue. Been coming here forever. Buy him a drink, and he might give you a few minutes of his time." She glanced at the wall clock behind her. "Better make it quick, though. Clio is on at midnight. She's his favorite."

"His name is Johnny Blue?" Jessica said. "Seriously?"

The bartender shrugged, gave her a cold, hard stare. "It's what everyone calls him, and it's what he answers to."

"Well, I guess you'd better pour old Johnny Blue a drink of whatever he usually has, and we'll have the same again too." Jessica jerked a thumb at Holliday. "He's paying, seeing as he seems to be so generous with his cash this evening."

The woman pulled a couple of beers from a refrigerator and then reached for a bottle of Scotch on a glass shelf. Glenlivet. Speyside single malt, aged eighteen years. Just like half the girls employed by the Tahiti Club. The whiskey was better than decent. The bartender poured a double, added a splash of water.

Holliday winced. "You take American Express?"

The woman smiled. "Plastic or paper is fine by me, honey."

Johnny Blue was around the same age as Ace Freeman and Hopper but fitter and sharper than both. He was small and wiry and alert, like he'd been a bantamweight boxer or at least a decent street brawler in his youth. Silver hair and matching mustache. A chunky gold necklace and a big Rolex watch. The Rolex might have been the real deal, or it might have been purchased from a Venice Beach hawker. Jessica's money was on the former. The lapels on his blue satin shirt were too big, the hems on his cream slacks a little too wide. If he had wheels parked in the lot outside, her best guess would be a Mustang or a Pontiac Firebird.

Johnny Blue was clearly a man with a taste for all things retro, except when it came to women, judging by the way he was eyeballing the young blonde onstage.

Jessica and Holliday each took one of the seats facing him, blocking his view of the girl.

"Mind if we join you?" Holliday asked.

Johnny Blue kept his expression poker-face neutral. No hint of surprise or worry or even curiosity.

Holliday pushed the whiskey toward him. "Glenlivet."

Johnny Blue picked up the glass, sniffed it, and nodded like he approved.

"What do you want?" he asked.

Holliday produced the photo of Eleanor Lavelle from the back pocket of his jeans. Placed it on the table. "You recognize this girl?"

"You cops?"

"No," Holliday said.

"Private?"

"Yes," Jessica said.

Johnny Blue paused for a beat. Then said, "Yeah, I recognize her. She was a dancer here a long time ago. Eleanor something. I don't remember her surname."

Holliday and Jessica exchanged glances.

"You mind if we ask you a few questions about her?" she said.

Johnny Blue picked up the whiskey Holliday had placed in front of him. He took a small sip, closed his eyes, licked his lips, and sighed with satisfaction.

"The thing that makes this Scotch so unique is the mix of casks," he said. "American and European oak, first and second fill." He opened his eyes. "A rich fruity aroma with toffee notes and a burst of sweet oranges with a spicy finish." He smiled, exposing a gold tooth. No doubt also the real deal. "The thing is when I do a lot of talking, it makes me thirsty."

Holliday sighed, withdrew a ten from his wallet, dropped it on the table.

Johnny Blue glanced at the dollar bill and looked at Holliday. "I mean *real* thirsty."

Holliday turned to Jessica and shrugged. "I'm all out. I'm going to have to hit an ATM."

Jessica rummaged in her bag for her own wallet and pulled out another ten. Johnny Blue nodded and pocketed the cash. He drained the whiskey he'd been drinking before they joined him, then swapped the empty glass for the full one.

A redhead wearing a burgundy fishnet dress and black thong and nothing else appeared with a silver tray balanced on steepled fingers. She scooped up the empty glass and placed it on the tray next to a bottle of champagne and two flutes.

"Everything okay here, Johnny?" she said, eyeing Holliday and Jessica.

Johnny Blue made an O symbol with his thumb and forefinger. "Everything is A-okay, Lola. Will you be a sweetheart and keep an eye on my whiskey while I head out back for a smoke?"

"Sure thing, Johnny." Lola threw another curious look over her shoulder before heading for another stage-side booth with the Moët.

"Is your name really Johnny Blue?" Jessica asked.

"It's what everyone calls me, and it's what I answer to." He stood up. "Let's go outside."

They followed him down a dark corridor, past a men's restroom, and through an emergency door out into an alleyway. Johnny Blue nudged half a brick against the doorframe with the toe of his loafers, propping the fire door open.

"Damn regulations mean a guy has to come out here every time he wants a smoke these days." He produced a pack of Camels from his breast pocket and lit a cigarette, without offering one to Holliday or Jessica.

A smaller version of the neon palm tree sign at the front of the premises blinked green and yellow above the back door, giving Johnny Blue's lined face a sickly, jaundiced appearance.

"So what you wanna know?" he asked.

"Anything at all you can tell us about Eleanor Lavelle from the time she worked here," Jessica told him.

He snapped his fingers. "Lavelle. That's it. Let me see that photo again."

Holliday handed him the photograph, and he held it up to the light from the neon sign.

"Yeah, I liked her a lot," Johnny Blue said. "She was all natural, both the red hair and the titties, and she had bundles of personality.

When she joined you for a drink, you got the feeling she was enjoying herself, rather than just going through the motions like some of the others. I also liked that she used her real name, even though it wasn't a particularly sexy name. None of this 'Angel' or 'Coco' nonsense. That, in itself, was sexy as hell."

"How long did she work at the Tahiti Club?" Jessica asked.

He shrugged. "A year, maybe. Give or take." Johnny Blue sucked on the cigarette, blew out the smoke impatiently. "I was real sad when I found out she'd met a sticky end, but I can't say I was completely surprised."

"You weren't surprised she was murdered?" Holliday asked.

"Well, yeah, I was surprised someone went as far as cutting her up like that. What I meant was I wasn't surprised she ended up getting herself into trouble."

"How so?" Holliday said.

"Far as I could tell, Eleanor did okay for money here. It wasn't just me who liked her. She was a popular girl. That stage was always covered in cash after she finished every performance. But it wasn't enough for her, if you believe the rumors."

"What rumors?" Jessica asked.

"From what I heard, she was entertaining some of the regulars outside of work, and it wasn't just a lap dance she was offering, if you catch my drift? What went on behind closed doors I don't know for sure. All I can tell you is what I saw with my own eyes. More than once, there would be a cab waiting at the curb out front, engine running, one of the regulars in the backseat, waiting for Eleanor to finish her shift."

"She was turning tricks?" Holliday asked.

"If she was, that's not all she was doing. Again, if the rumors were to be believed, that is."

"What do you mean?" Jessica said.

"Blackmail." Johnny Blue took a final deep drag on the cigarette and flicked the butt away. "The story doing the rounds was that Eleanor had a boyfriend. Some kid who would snap photos of her with the customers looking all cozy going into hotels or kissing on street corners. Anything that might get a guy into bother with his wife if she were to come into possession of photographic evidence of him getting up to no good."

"You recognize any of these guys?" Jessica pulled the envelope containing the photographs they'd found at the murder house from her bag and handed them to Johnny Blue.

He looked through them all and laughed. "So the rumors were true, huh? Yeah, one or two look familiar. Don't ask me for names, though. It's the girls I remember, not the other guys."

Jessica pointed to the photo of the man who had looked familiar to her. "What about him?"

Johnny Blue shook his head. "Nah, don't recognize him. But it was a long time ago. I've seen a lot of faces come and go over the years."

"You're not in any of these photos," she said. "You were never involved with Eleanor Lavelle beyond drinks and dancing at the club?"

He grinned. "Believe me, I'm way too smart to get involved with any of these girls after hours. In any case, most of us steered clear of Eleanor once the rumors started circulating."

"Is that why she left the Tahiti Club?" Holliday asked. "Did she get fired because word got out she was trying to blackmail some of the customers?"

"She wasn't fired. It was her own choice to leave. Said she was giving up the stripping and moving away from Hollywood to shack up with some guy she'd met who she reckoned was going to look after her."

"I don't suppose you have a name for this guy?" Jessica asked.

Johnny Blue shook his head. "None of my business. As I said, I've seen a lot of faces come and go over the years. The girls included. There's always someone younger and prettier who comes along and replaces your favorites." He consulted the Rolex. "Speaking of which, it's almost midnight, and Clio is due onstage. Smoke break is over."

He opened the emergency door and kicked the half brick to one side. Just before closing the door behind him, he turned to them and said, "I meant it when I said I liked her. I hope you find the bastard who did it."

The door swung shut behind Johnny Blue. Holliday and Jessica stood there facing each other in the alleyway. Neither of them spoke. The neon sign blinked. The music continued to pound through the wall. A sultry beat with a heavy bass. They looked at each other. She opened her mouth to speak, but before any words came out, Holliday's mouth was on her own. Lips that were soft and firm all at the same time.

Jessica kissed him back. There were clashing teeth and tongues and the taste of beer. He pushed her against the wall, and she felt the rough scratch of the bricks through her satin shirt. She ran her fingers through his hair and pulled him closer and bit his lip. His hands explored the skin under her shirt. Then his fingers were down the back of the leather pants, pulling her into him. His mouth moved from her lips down to her neck, and she heard him groan under urgent kisses.

Right man, wrong place, wrong time.

Jessica's eyes snapped open. The thought had come from nowhere and lodged itself at the front of her brain. She gently pushed him away.

"We can't do this. At least, not right now."

He looked at her with eyes filled with heat for a long second. Then nodded. Backed away reluctantly.

"Okay," he said softly. "Let's go."

He took her hand and led her from the alleyway to the parking lot. Two spaces down from her Silverado was a Pontiac Firebird.

They drove back to the motel in silence.

26

JESSICA

For the first time in days, Jessica didn't think about Tony Shaw or Eleanor Lavelle or Alicia Lavelle when she opened her eyes. Only one person had dominated her thoughts, both asleep and awake, for the last eight hours.

Jack Holliday.

Her lips still felt tender and bruised where he'd kissed her. Her skin tingled where he'd touched her. The parts of her body where he hadn't yet placed his hands ached at the thought of it. She spread her hand over the coolness of the empty space in the bed next to her, knowing it could have been filled with his warmth instead if she hadn't put the brakes on outside the Tahiti Club.

It wasn't as though she had taken a vow of celibacy during the time she had been grieving for Tony. There had been men, some more memorable than others. The lonely guy listening to sad songs on a Wurlitzer in a bar on the edge of a small town in Alabama. The cocksure Texas cowboy who'd thought he was doing the seducing when she'd been the one calling all the shots. The professional poker player in Vegas, with a suite in the Bellagio overlooking the fountains, who'd lost all his chips and then the contents of his minibar while he'd slept.

Men with nothing in common, except for being spared that awkward conversation over breakfast about whether they should see each other again. Jessica was always long gone by then, slipping silently into the dawn streets, carrying her shoes and her shame, hours before they stirred in soiled sheets that stank of cheap sex and perfume. She couldn't even remember the last time she'd spent the night with a man when sober or when she had actually liked the guy.

Maybe Jack Holliday would be different.

Maybe, once this was all over, she could find out if he really was right for her.

It wasn't the kiss that made Jessica hope. Or the crackling electricity that had flowed between them outside the strip bar. It was the way he had held her hand, his fingers interlaced with her own, refusing to let go until they reached her truck.

Back at the motel, he had kissed her softly on the cheek under the glow of the blue neon lighting, and she'd wondered why the hell she wasn't dragging him into her room. Into her bed.

After showering, dressing, and a cup of black coffee, Jessica sat at the desk and thought about the other man in her life.

Tony Shaw, a.k.a. Rob Young, a.k.a. Brad Ferezy.

Despite Pryce's unwavering belief in his innocence, Jessica still needed to be convinced. She had to know if his status as person of interest was simply down to splitting town so soon after the murder or if there was more to it.

She needed to speak to Bill Geersen.

She could waste the next hour trying to track down the retired detective's cell phone number herself, or she could text Holliday and have the number in two minutes. Jessica picked up her cell phone and tapped out the message. Her finger hovered over the send button. She read the text again.

Need to speak to Geersen. Can you send me his cell no. please? JS.

She paused. Should she reference what almost happened last night? "Oh, just send the damn text, will you," she muttered.

Jessica hit send. Then spent the next seventy-three seconds staring at the tiny screen waiting for a reply. Even though she was expecting the text, she still jumped when the cell beeped and bounced across the desk. She snatched it up and read the message.

Hey there! Bill's on a cruise and can't be contacted by cell, he wants to get away from it all with the anniversary approaching xx

Two kisses. Jessica felt slightly embarrassed by the thrill of delight that coursed through her at the gesture.

She mentally crossed Bill Geersen off her list for the time being. She found Garrett Thomas's business card in her wallet and punched in the number for the reporter's direct line. Nobody answered, and she remembered it was Sunday. She tried his cell. He picked up after two rings.

"This is Garrett."

"Hey, Garrett, it's Jessica Shaw. I spoke to you the other—"

"The pretty PI. I remember. Please tell me you're calling with a story or offering to take me to lunch later. Or both. That would work."

Jessica laughed. "I'm afraid not on both counts. I'm actually trying to get hold of someone and thought you might be able to help. A reporter by the name of Jim Johnson. Does he still work for the paper?"

"Nah. Johnson left the *Reformer* way before my time. Worked for the *Los Angeles Times* for a while. A fantastic operator in his day, from what I've heard. Probably retired now, though."

"No idea how I can contact him?"

"Nope, sorry. Never had any dealings with him myself. Is this about the case you're working on? What was it about again?"

"Oh, just a woman who lived in Eagle Rock for a short spell with her kid years ago. A family member is trying to trace her. Some small inheritance involved. No big deal but I thought this Jim Johnson guy might have been able to help me track them down."

"You sure there's no story there? Because right now I'm writing about Eagle Rock's annual music festival, and unless anything better comes up, it's going to be next week's splash."

"Sounds pretty cool," Jessica said, changing the subject. "When's it happening?"

"Last night. And it was pretty cool. Lots of live bands and dancing and food trucks along Colorado Boulevard. But not exactly 'hold the front page' kind of stuff."

"I'm sorry I missed it. I was at a strip bar in Hollywood last night."

"Okay, your Saturday night sounds way more fun than mine."

"Would you believe me if I said it was work related?"

"Not for a second. Hey, I'm sorry I can't help with a number for Jim Johnson, but you have my cell phone number if you do fancy lunch or drinks while you're in town. Or another visit to that strip club. I'm easy."

Jessica laughed. "Sure thing."

She ended the call and booted up the laptop.

Jim Johnson had his own website, but Garrett Thomas was right: the man was now effectively retired. According to his bio page, he'd started out as a cub reporter at the *Reformer* in the late '70s before working his way up to the role of senior reporter. The latter part of his career had been spent covering the crime beat for the *Los Angeles Times*. He'd officially retired last year and returned to his native England, where he was still available for the occasional freelancing opportunity.

Jessica figured journalists were just the same as PIs and cops. Never quite able to give up the job completely. Her old boss, Larry Lutz, still had a ways to go before retirement, but she knew he would be one of those guys, just like Jim Johnson, who would still be available for "free-lance opportunities" when the time came to clear out his desk.

Jessica? She'd make like Bill Geersen and spend her twilight years sipping mojitos on a cruise liner somewhere exotic. But hopefully without the excess baggage of unsolved cases weighing her down.

Johnson had a contact page, but there was no cell phone number. The only way of getting in touch with him was by sending a message via a contact form. It was already Sunday evening in the UK, and Jessica had no idea how often Johnson checked his messages. She composed a brief note anyway, explaining who she was and how she wanted to speak to him about the Lavelle case. She submitted the form.

The contact page was illustrated with a photo of Johnson and two other men at what appeared to be some sort of press awards ceremony. All three men held crystal trophies, their faces flushed with booze and triumph, their bow ties slightly askew. All three looked like they were in their sixties, with plenty of miles on the clock. Jessica was about to close down the web browser when the caption below the photo caught her eye.

She felt her heart stop.

Jessica reread the one-line sentence, unable to believe what she was seeing. She opened Google, typed in a name, and searched for images. The results provided confirmation of what she suspected, and her cheeks flamed with anger.

Jessica hooked up her portable printer to the laptop and printed off the photo of the three men, with the caption identifying each of them, and snatched the page as soon as it fed through the machine. She slammed the laptop shut, stuffed the gun into her waistband, threw open the door, and marched out into the blinding morning sunshine.

Holliday's Ford pickup was parked in front of room 6. The curtains were still drawn. Jessica banged her fist hard on the door. Holliday opened the door wearing only a pair of boxer shorts. A goofy grin spread across his face when he saw who his visitor was. Jessica stood with her hands on her hips, not returning the smile.

Then she punched him as hard as she could square on the jaw.

Holliday blinked and staggered backward. "What the hell was that for?" He stared at her in astonishment. "Is it because I kissed you?"

"No, it's because you lied to me."

"You're going to have to help me out here, Jessica. I have no idea what you're talking about."

"Who the hell are you?" she demanded.

"What? You know who I am. Are you okay? What's happened?"

"Oh, I know what you told me. Jack Holliday, superstar journalist, huh?"

"I wouldn't say superstar . . ." Holliday laughed, but it sounded forced. Suddenly he didn't look so sure of himself anymore.

Jessica threw the printout at him, and it landed faceup on his bare feet. He glanced down at the photo. The craggy, ancient face of Jack Holliday smiled back at him. He closed his eyes and ran his hand through his hair.

"Look, Jessica, I can explain."

"Damn straight you can."

He leaned out of the doorway and looked up and down the row of motel rooms.

"Can we have this conversation inside, please? I'm not even dressed yet."

"I'm not setting foot inside that room until you tell me who you really are."

He sighed. "My name is Matt Connor. I'm a private investigator. Same as you."

Jessica stared at him for a long moment. Then she looked past his shoulder to the desk and the items sitting on top of it. Slim, sleek laptop. Tiny white earbuds. Digital camera. No Dictaphone or shorthand-filled notepad or any other tools of the trade you would associate with a journalist.

The camera was small and compact, nowhere near as expensive or effective as the Nikon Jessica used for her own surveillance work, but it would still do the job. She pushed past him and ripped open the top drawer of the desk. The papers he had swiftly swept inside the night she had broken into his room were still there. She rifled through them.

"Jessica . . ."

She remembered how she had caught a glimpse of something black and shiny. She found the photograph and felt another surge of anger hit her like a steam train when she saw what it contained.

Her truck.

She looked at the next photo. And the next. All of them were shots of Jessica or the Silverado.

"You've been watching me?"

Connor said nothing for a long moment. Then he nodded. "I know you're Alicia Lavelle. I've known all along."

27

AMY

The terry cloth bathrobe felt rough against her skin, like the motel used cheap detergent in the laundry room and didn't bother with any softener.

The sheets she'd lain on were the same. Frank's bulk pressing her into the rough, scratchy fabric as he'd moved clumsily on top of her. Drunk and sweating, fueled by whiskey and lust. Thankfully it had been over quickly, like it always was.

Amy found her panties on the floor, twisted into a tiny black ball. She pulled them on, wrapped the bathrobe tighter around her body, and sat on the bed. She watched Frank silently as he dressed. He swayed precariously as he bent over to tie his shoelaces.

"You sure I can't drop you off on campus?" he asked.

"My own car is parked near the bar. I want to take a shower before I leave anyway. Freshen up."

She'd had no more than a sip of the whiskey he'd poured for her, Frank happily finishing off her drink before taking care of the rest of the bottle on his own. He pitched sideways now while picking up his belt from the floor. She had no intention of getting into a car with him in his inebriated state. In any case, Amy couldn't stand the thought of spending a single second more in his company than she had to.

He leaned over her. Kissed her wetly on the lips. Slipped a meaty hand inside her bathrobe and caressed her breast.

"I'll be in touch soon, sweetheart."

"Sure thing, Frank."

Amy followed him to the door, locked it behind him, and slid the security chain in place. She bit her lip. She wouldn't cry. She knew it wouldn't be forever. Couldn't be forever after what had happened.

She looked at her clothing, folded neatly on an easy chair, and considered ditching the shower. Getting the hell out of this dump as quickly as possible. She shook her head. The smell of Frank on her was making her nauseous.

Amy was about to head for the bathroom when a knock on the door startled her.

"Shit," she muttered, looking around the room. She couldn't see anything Frank might have left behind. He had never requested sex more than once on the same night before, but maybe he wanted an encore tonight. The thought made Amy's stomach lurch.

She pressed her eye against the peephole.

It wasn't Frank.

It was a stranger.

Amy breathed a sigh of relief. Wrong room probably. There was another soft knock. She decided to ignore it. No point opening the door, getting into a conversation. She headed for the bathroom.

"I know you're in there, Amy. Or should I call you Cindy?"

Amy froze. "Shit."

She walked back to the door and looked through the peephole again. Realized the face partially obscured by the hooded top wasn't that of a stranger after all.

"We need to talk about the baby, Amy. Find a way to sort out this mess. A solution that suits everyone. That's what you want, isn't it?"

A tear slid down Amy's cheek, and she brushed it away with trembling fingers. "Yes," she whispered. It was exactly what she wanted.

She scraped aside the security chain and flipped the lock. Opened the door and stepped aside to allow her unexpected visitor into the room. Heard the door close behind her as she walked over to the pile of clothes on the chair.

"I want to get dressed first," she said. "Then we can talk."

For a split second, she mistook the fingers in her hair for a gesture of affection. Then the grip tightened, and her head was wrenched painfully to the side, her face smashing into the desk. White lights exploded in front of her eyes as her nostrils filled with blood.

She fell to the carpet and felt a gloved fist come down hard on her cheekbone. Then she was being dragged by strong hands from the floor onto the bed.

The first blow from the knife landed between her breasts, and she gasped for breath. Held her hands in front of her in what she knew was a futile gesture. Felt the blade slice through flesh and bone. The knife sank deep again and again, and blood exploded in her mouth.

Amy's eyes closed. Her breathing slowed, wet and wheezy.

She thought of her mom and dad. She thought of her younger sisters.

And she thought of the life that had been growing inside of her.

Her baby.

His baby.

The child she'd thought she didn't want.

In those final moments, she knew she would have kept her baby. Knew in her heart she would have loved it if she had only been given the chance.

28

JESSICA

Matt Connor closed the motel room door, and Jessica immediately withdrew the gun from the waistband of her pants. She kept her hand down by her side, not pointing the weapon at him.

Not yet, anyway.

"Relax, Jessica. I'm not going to hurt you."

Connor reached for a pair of jeans and a T-shirt, both of which had been hanging neatly on evenly spaced hangers in the closet. He perched on the edge of the bed and slipped one long leg into the jeans and then the other. He winced as the neck of the T-shirt brushed against his swollen jaw as he pulled it over his head. The tiny bubble of sympathy Jessica felt was quickly crushed like a bug under her shoe.

"Start talking," she said coldly.

Connor looked up at her. "It's really not as bad as it seems. You were going to find out about me sooner or later. Things just became more complicated than they should have."

He tried the lopsided grin thing. It didn't work this time.

"Who are you working for?" she asked.

"Bill Geersen."

"You said he was retired."

"He is—that's the point. The guy should be playing golf, spending time with the grandkids. But he can't draw a line under the job and enjoy his retirement without knowing what happened the night your mother was murdered. You know what it's like with some cops. The cases they were never able to solve, they eat away at them. They don't ever give up hope of cracking them one day."

"So Geersen isn't on a cruise? I want to see him. You need to set up a meet."

"He is on a cruise. Hawaii. Probably lounging by the pool with a tequila sunrise waiting for me to check in with an update for him. Sorry—I lied about him not having his cell phone."

The lopsided grin again.

"How long has he been your client?" Jessica asked.

"Around eighteen months. He's spent a fair amount of his retirement fund on my fees. He was determined to find you."

"How did he know I was even still alive? I could have been buried up in the Eagle Rock hills for decades for all he knew, while he was throwing his money at a case he wasn't good enough to solve first time around."

"Bill always figured there were three possible scenarios to explain what had happened to you," Connor said. "The first was you'd died the night Eleanor Lavelle was murdered, as you said, and the body would likely never be found. But he was convinced you were still alive. Cop instinct, he called it. Said he could feel it in his gut."

"Yeah? Probably a bad case of gas. His gut wasn't much help twenty-five years ago. What was the second option?"

"You were being held against your will in a cellar or basement somewhere. You know, like Ariel Castro, who kidnapped three young women and kept them captive for years in his own home. If so, it was a nightmare scenario for the cops. The only real hope of finding you after so many years would be down to dumb luck. A successful escape bid or discovery after the captor died or took seriously ill."

"And the third theory?"

"You already know the answer to that question, Jessica," he said softly. "Alicia Lavelle grew up leading a normal life. She either knew her real identity or was completely oblivious to her past. It was the theory Geersen and I always liked best. I began my search on the basis Alicia Lavelle was living somewhere under a different name and probably unaware folks had been searching for her for more than two decades. I guess we were right. What we still don't know is whether you always knew you were Alicia Lavelle?"

"I'm the one asking the questions. I'm also the one holding the gun. How did you track me down? Paper tripping?"

Connor nodded. "Back then, it was a good way to disappear. I can't tell you how many weeks I spent trawling through birth and death certificates at the Department of Public Health's Vital Records office." He laughed. "The girls who worked there even knew me by name and used to bring me coffee each day."

"I bet they did."

He went on. "I started off searching for girls born a year or so either side of Alicia Lavelle's birthdate who had died by the time they were three or four years old. Then I went through the same process for males born around the same time as Rob Young. Of course, we had no date of birth or anything official on the guy, so I had to guess his age and search a couple years either side of that estimate. This time, I was looking for young men who had died before they'd been assigned a Social Security number."

"Yeah, I know how it works."

"Of course. Once I had two lists drawn up, I cross-referenced them for surnames in common and ended up with six possible matches, so I started checking each of them out, including a Jessica and Tony Shaw in New York. Your own website was easy to find, but I couldn't be certain the woman in the profile photo was the same person as the three-year-old kid I was trying to find. Then I got lucky and found a photo of Tony Shaw."

Jessica was confused. "Tony never liked having his photo taken. He always preferred to be behind the camera. I can't believe there would be any photos of him floating around on the internet."

"There was," Connor said. "It appeared in an online newspaper article about a photography exhibition in Williamsburg."

Jessica knew exactly which photo Connor was referring to. It was a candid shot of Tony mingling with friends and fellow art lovers at the small gallery where his work had been on show. The exhibition had featured in several local arts publications. She remembered how happy he'd looked in the photo and how proud she had been of his achievement, and she felt like her heart was breaking all over again.

Connor said, "I printed off the photo of Tony Shaw and made my way immediately to Eagle Rock. I'd already shown the local motel owner pictures of another father and daughter who I'd thought might be the ones I was looking for, with no luck.

"I tried Hopper again, and this time, he identified the guy in the photo as Rob Young. A fair bit older and grayer, with shorter hair, and carrying a little more weight around the middle, but definitely the same guy who'd dated Eleanor Lavelle and split town around the time of her murder.

"I told him I was an investigative journalist, working closely with Bill Geersen, and slipped him fifty bucks to keep quiet about what I'd shown him. I told him there would be more 'tip fees' for contacting me right away if anyone else showed up in Eagle Rock asking questions about the Lavelles."

"Why not just tell him you were a PI?"

Connor shrugged. "It was the cover story Geersen and I came up with. Journalists seem to be less intimidating than PIs. Some folks think of us the same way they do the cops. They're edgy, on the defensive. With journalists, you'd be surprised how many people are willing to open up to you if they think there's a chance their picture might appear in the paper."

Connor stood suddenly and walked over to the nightstand. It wasn't yet noon, but he cracked the seal on a bottle of Wild Turkey anyway.

"I need a drink," he said. "You want one?"

"I don't want anything from you."

"Suit yourself."

Connor returned to his spot at the end of the bed and sipped the liquor.

"I was excited," he said. "I thought I was about to crack one of the most famous unsolved cases in LA. I never actually lived in Eagle Rock, but I wasn't lying when I said I remembered it being all over the news, the effect it had on local communities. A lot of bad shit goes down in LA, but people were genuinely shocked by what happened and worried they might be next."

He took another swallow of bourbon. Jessica kept her finger on the trigger, the gun still pointing at the floor.

"I booked the first flight to New York I could get a seat on," he said. "I was buzzing. I was about to find Alicia Lavelle. Of course, it didn't turn out that way. Before I'd even sat down to my pastrami sandwich for lunch, I'd discovered Tony Shaw was dead and you were in the wind again. Sold up, left town, no forwarding address. You can imagine my disappointment."

"My heart bleeds for you."

Connor at least had the good grace to look embarrassed.

"I almost found you another couple of times," he said. "DeKalb County, Alabama. Granbury, Texas. Both times, I showed up less than twenty-four hours after you'd left town. I started to believe I'd never track you down, that you'd always be two steps ahead. From what I've heard, you're a good PI. I got to thinking maybe you knew exactly who you were, and you were making damn sure no one ever located you. I took on other jobs that occupied my time and attention. The Lavelle case went on the back burner. Then I got a Google Alert. Jessica Shaw's name had popped up in a local newspaper after helping cops find a missing teenager in Simi Valley. Suddenly, Alicia Lavelle was the priority again."

"You're John Doe," she said. "You sent the email. Lured me to Eagle Rock."

Connor nodded. "I knew it was a long shot. Then, Wednesday night, I'm sitting having a beer in a bar in Venice, and I get a call. It's Jeff Hopper. Turns out a female PI from New York is in town, and she's working the Lavelle case. Blonde, pretty, little diamond stud in her nose, and a lot of tattoos. I felt like I'd won the lottery. And here we are."

Jessica said, "What I don't understand is why all the pretense? Why not just call in the LAPD once you'd tracked me down? Why goes as far as . . . what you did last night?"

"I know this is a fucking mess, Jessica," he said. "It was supposed to be a job—that's all. It was never meant to be personal. But it is."

Connor got up from the bed and walked toward her. Jessica backed up and felt the rough edge of the desk press hard against her kidneys. She raised the gun, and Connor stopped, his hands held up, more in disbelief than surrender.

"Don't come near me," she said. "You don't get to lay a finger on me again."

"What the fuck, Jessica?"

"I've been in Eagle Rock for days, yet there's no Geersen here. No LAPD. Why?"

"I needed to be sure you really were Alicia Lavelle, and I needed to know how much you knew."

"Bullshit. You were using me as bait. You wanted me to lead you to the man who killed my mother."

Connor's eyes flitted nervously between her face and the gun.

"The killer is dead," he said. "All the evidence points to the man you knew as Tony Shaw being guilty."

"Bullshit," she said again. "What evidence? Just because a guy skips town, he has to be guilty?"

Connor said, "I know it's hard for you to believe the man you loved, the man who raised you as his daughter, could be capable of such a thing. But look at the facts, what we know for sure. There was no sign of forced entry. Rob Young had a key to the house. Eleanor had poured two glasses of wine, indicating she knew her killer. His boss, Ace Freeman, told police Rob Young was planning to go to Eleanor's house after his shift finished around midnight. Instead, he split town the night his girlfriend was murdered to go on a 'planned' trip no one, other than the McCools, knew anything about. You seriously believe he's innocent?"

"I knew Tony better than anyone. He wasn't a murderer."

"You don't know that for sure."

Jessica had heard enough. She pushed herself away from the desk and headed for the door. She reached for the doorknob and then paused. Turned back to Connor.

"These past few days, there were times when your truck wasn't parked in the lot," she said. "I assumed you were out chasing stories or interviewing folks for one of your articles. Where were you?"

"I was working on other cases."

"You weren't worried about me leaving town again while you were out on one of these jobs?"

Connor couldn't look her in the eye.

The realization of what he'd done hit Jessica like a wrecking ball.

"You asshole."

She threw open the door and marched toward her truck.

"Jessica . . ."

She heard Connor scurrying after her. He stood in the doorway and watched as she ran her hand along the underside of the Silverado. Under the front fender, then the rear. Her fingers closed around a small plastic square, and she ripped it free. A magnetic GPS tracker the length and width of a credit card and around an inch thick.

Jessica held it up for Connor to see. "You have got to be kidding me." She dropped the GPS tracker to the blacktop and showed him the gun.

Connor held his hands up. "Whoa, what're you doing?"

Jessica ignored him. She flipped the Glock around so she was holding it by its stubby barrel, crouched down, and used the grip to smash the tracker into a dozen splintered pieces. She went into her own room and picked up her bag and car keys. Then she pulled open the driver's side door of the truck, climbed behind the wheel, and started the engine.

Connor was still standing, motionless, in the doorway of his own room.

Jessica buzzed down the window. "Don't even think about following me this time."

29

JESSICA

A half hour later, Jessica was parked on Delrosa Drive. A small horse-shoe-shaped street located on the west side of Eagle Rock, it was mostly populated by single-story bungalows. Trees flopped languidly over each side of the street, forming a natural canopy that provided shade from the unrelenting sun, while the curved bends offered cover for the truck.

A surveillance job required patience and focus. It was the perfect way to alleviate the fury that had ripped through Jessica following the confrontation with Connor. She chewed on a takeout sandwich, sipped soda from a go-cup, and watched the property on the other side of the street fifty yards away.

After another thirty minutes, the anger had settled to a steady simmer.

The house was the color of wet cement and reminded Jessica of rainy days in New York. It was nothing fancy but not shabby either. Modest but well maintained. There was a tidy porch and a tiny strip of lawn and a driveway occupied by a silver sedan. Jessica hoped the car meant the occupant of the house was still at home and hadn't gone out for the day. She knew the son was away at college and the husband was long gone.

Jessica watched and waited. She stopped thinking about Matt Connor and started thinking about the letter from Tony.

Eventually, she reached into the glove compartment and pulled out the white envelope Pryce had given her. Turned it over in her hands a few times. It was light, suggesting its contents were no more than a sheet or two. But the words potentially contained within those pages weighed heavily on Jessica's mind.

Would it be more lies? A confession revealing a terrible truth? Jessica wasn't sure which would be worse.

"Oh, just open the damn thing," she muttered.

She slid a fingernail under the gummed seal and lifted up the corner of the flap and stopped.

Everything she had thought she'd known about her relationship with Tony had already changed forever. Whenever she thought of the complete and utter trust she had shown in a man who had turned out to be such an accomplished liar, she felt a toxic mix of anger, hurt, and humiliation. She knew that any further damage caused by this letter could be irreparable.

Still, she had to know. Jessica took a deep breath and lifted the seal farther.

Movement from the drab gray house caught her eye.

Jessica huffed out a sigh, a combination of relief and frustration, and stuffed the envelope back in the glove compartment.

Ninety-seven minutes after Jessica had pulled up at the curb, the screen door had opened. Now, a lumpy figure in a shapeless dress stepped onto the porch.

Jessica turned the key and started the engine. She expected Darla Kennedy to make her way straight to the sedan, but the woman set off on foot instead, heading in the opposite direction from where Jessica was parked, oblivious to the black truck tucked just out of view. After a few seconds, Jessica put the truck into drive and crawled along slowly, turning the bend just in time to see Darla take a left onto another residential street.

She followed the woman onto Addison Way. Darla's pace was no faster than a comfortable amble. Too slow to tail her by car. Jessica parked behind another truck, buzzed down the window, and leaned out, keeping the woman in her line of sight. She was heading west, in the direction of Eagle Rock Boulevard.

Before reaching the main thoroughfare, Darla disappeared into a small white building on the corner of Addison and Eagle Rock. Jessica eased back into the traffic and drove past the place, a small diner called Abby's, just as Darla heaved herself awkwardly into a booth by the window.

After finding a parking spot nearby, Jessica made her way back toward the diner. The exterior was whitewashed, with simple red signage. Clearly a no-frills joint, but it was busy. The kind of place where customers came for the food rather than the décor.

Diners had a choice between the round, backless stools lining the counter or red leatherette booths like the one Darla occupied. The woman was busy reading the menu. A thick paperback novel with yellowed pages sat on the table in front her. She didn't look like she was expecting company.

That was about to change.

"Hey, Darla."

Jessica was in the booth, sitting across from Darla, before the woman even realized what was happening. She lowered the menu, and her eyes widened, and her mouth formed a small O of surprise. "What the—"

Jessica cut her off. "You know who I am, right?"

"Yes, I remember who you are. You're a private investigator, and I have no interest in speaking to you. So, if you don't mind—"

"Look at me, Darla."

Darla picked up the menu again. "I'd like you to leave now." She pretended to read the brunch specials, but her lips betrayed the slightest hint of a tremor.

Jessica said, "I'm Alicia Lavelle."

"Okay, you need to leave right now." Darla slammed the menu on the table, her voice low and angry, her bangles jangling furiously. "Goddamn rubberneckers showing up in town back then was bad enough. But this? This is just sick. *You're* sick. Everyone knows that little girl is dead."

Darla looked around frantically, as though searching for a doorman or some local muscle, but this was a small diner in Eagle Rock, so there was none. Just a waitress, taking orders from old folks and families at the far end of the room. Probably a chef out back in the kitchen too. Jessica wasn't worried about the waitress or the chef. She was going nowhere.

She pulled her wallet from her bag and flipped it open to a photo tucked behind a rectangle of milky plastic. Jessica and Tony Shaw, taken around a year before he died. Another rare picture, just like the one at the art gallery in Williamsburg.

"If you won't look at my face, take a look at this photo."

Jessica threw the wallet in front of Darla, who gave the picture a cursory glance. Then she picked up the wallet slowly. She looked up at Jessica. Her face was the same color as the white Formica tabletop.

"This is Robbie."

Jessica nodded. "My father. Eleanor Lavelle was my mother."

Darla's gaze returned to the photo, then back to Jessica's face. She stared hard at her for what felt like a long time but was probably only a few seconds.

"Alicia?" Darla looked stunned. Her voice wasn't much louder than a whisper.

Jessica nodded again. "I only found out myself a few days ago."

The waitress appeared with a coffee pot and two mugs. "You guys both want coffee?"

"No," Darla said.

"Yes," Jessica said. "I think we could both do with one. With plenty of sugar."

Darla just nodded.

The waitress poured the drinks. "I'll come back in a few minutes and take your food orders."

"How is this even possible?" Darla asked, once the waitress was out of earshot.

"If you're finding all of this hard to take in, imagine how I felt." Jessica drank some of the coffee. It was good. "Less than a week ago, I was sitting in a diner a little like this one when I came across Alicia Lavelle's missing persons profile online. I knew immediately the kid in the photo was me, although I was sure it was a mistake at first. I'm a private investigator, so I came to Eagle Rock to try to get some answers."

Darla slowly stirred sugar into her coffee but made no move to drink it. "You're really a private investigator?"

"Yes, I am," Jessica said. "And I intend to find out who killed my mother."

Darla dropped the spoon on the table and put her hand over her mouth and closed her eyes. Fat tears spilled down her plump cheeks. "I'm so sorry."

"Sorry? Why?"

Darla opened her eyes and looked at Jessica. "Eleanor is dead because of me. It's all my fault."

30

JESSICA

The waitress was back at the booth. "Have you decided what you want to order yet?"

"Not now," Jessica said, without taking her eyes off Darla.

"Um, okay." The waitress disappeared out back to the kitchen.

"What do you mean Eleanor is dead because of you?" Jessica asked.

Darla wiped under each eye with her thumb, scraping away tears and mascara.

She said, "I might not have stuck that knife in her myself, but I might as well have. I was at Eleanor's place the night she died. Earlier in the evening, that is. I wasn't there when it happened. I wish I had been. Maybe I could have stopped it."

Jessica nodded. "I've read the witness statement you gave to the detectives who were investigating the murder. I also read Ace Freeman's statement. He claimed you were upset when you arrived at the bar that night. Seemed to think you and Eleanor had some sort of fight."

Darla was silent. She fidgeted with the bangles. Eventually, she said, "We did argue. We argued plenty of other times, too, of course. I mean, we weren't much older than kids. The difference is this time, we never got a chance to make up. The last words I spoke to Eleanor were said in anger, and I'll never forgive myself for that."

"What did you argue about?"

The woman sighed. "The evening started off well enough. Good fun. A typical Friday night. Drinking wine, smoking cigarettes, listening to music. Then Eleanor told me she was leaving."

"She was leaving Eagle Rock?"

Darla nodded. "Eagle Rock. LA. Maybe even the state. Said she was taking Alicia, and she wasn't going to tell Robbie. Was probably going to leave him a note. That's why I got so mad. Sure, I would have missed her when she'd gone, but to treat Robbie like that wasn't right. He loved that kid like she was his own."

Like she was his own.

Jessica was stunned. Was Darla telling her Tony wasn't her father? She needed a moment to compose herself before continuing with the questions.

"When was Eleanor planning on leaving?" she asked.

"I'm not sure," Darla said. "I'd guess a couple of weeks at most. Eleanor told me she was waiting for some money, and then she would be gone. Wouldn't even tell me where she was planning on heading."

"What money?"

"I don't know. From some guy, I think."

Jessica found the envelope with the photos from the murder house in her bag. The fifty grand was still in the Thrifty's bag, still burning a hole in her glove compartment, masquerading as deodorant sticks and shampoo.

Jessica handed over the envelope. "What do you know about these photos?"

Darla slid out the prints and flipped through each one of them. "Looks like Eleanor with a bunch of guys. No big deal. She never wanted for male attention and company."

"I already know she was blackmailing men, Darla. The men in those photos. I found money hidden at her house on Morrison. A lot of money."

Darla appeared genuinely shocked. "Eleanor told me she only did it once or twice when she was younger. To help pay the rent and buy food. Said it was better than turning tricks on street corners. I had no idea she was still involved with that kind of stuff."

"The money she was waiting for? Could it have been more blackmail cash?"

"I don't think so." Darla frowned. "What she did with those men, it was small time. I wouldn't even call it blackmail. Seems too big a word to me. She was scamming guys for a few extra bucks—that's all. To be honest, the life she'd had, I didn't really blame her.

"You know she grew up in a children's home? Don't get me wrong; she always said they treated her well there, especially the woman who ran the place, Miss Angeline. Closest thing Eleanor ever had to a mother. But she wanted a better life for herself as an adult than what she'd had as a kid. The way she was speaking, this money she was waiting for, it was going to set her up for life."

"Uh-huh," Jessica said. "So how exactly is Eleanor's death your fault? You said yourself you weren't even there."

Darla lowered her eyes, stared into the coffee cup. "Robbie was working a shift when I got to Ace's that night. I told him everything. All about Eleanor's plans to leave town and take Alicia with her. He was always a real quiet guy, a deep thinker I used to call him, so there was no screaming and shouting. But I could tell he was real mad. That kind of scary rage that bubbles just beneath the surface. I'd never seen him like that before. The next day, Eleanor is dead, and Alicia is gone—and so is Robbie."

"You really believe he killed her?"

Darla nodded. "Yes, I do. I think he snapped. Then he took Alicia so he could fool himself, and everyone else, that she was his kid."

Jessica swallowed hard. Even though she already knew what Darla's answer would be, she had to ask the question. "You really don't think there's any chance he was my real father?"

Darla picked up the wallet from the table and looked at the photo again. Then she handed it back to Jessica. "Eleanor always said he wasn't. I don't see any reason why she would have lied to me. I'm sorry, but this man isn't your father. He's a murderer."

Jessica touched a finger gently to Tony's face behind the cheap plastic. "I can't believe it."

Darla asked, "Where is he now?"

"He's dead."

"Did he pass a couple of years ago?"

"Yes," Jessica said, surprised. "How did you know?"

"A bunch of white roses were sent to Eleanor's graveside every year on the anniversary of her passing. No card from the sender. They were her favorite flowers. I always leave white roses too. A couple of years ago, the mystery flowers stopped. I always thought they were from him."

"White roses, huh?" Jessica laughed softly. "My favorite flower too." She closed the wallet and dropped it in her bag, then looked Darla straight in the eye. "Do you have any idea who my real father is?"

Darla shook her head and shifted uncomfortably in the cramped booth.

Jessica said, "Please, Darla, if you know anything at all, you need to tell me. I have a right to know."

The woman sighed. "I've said as much as I'm willing to say. But ask yourself one question, Jessica. How was Eleanor able to pay for the house on Morrison with no job and a kid to raise on her own?"

Five minutes later, Jessica was back in the truck, cell phone in hand, Connor's number on the screen. Her finger hovered over the green phone icon to make the call. She hated herself for needing his help. She hit the button.

It rang once before he answered. "Jessica. Are you okay? I was going to call but didn't know if—"

"I need the name of the company who owns the murder house."

"Does this mean you're talking to me again? You know, we could still work this case together."

"Just give me the damn name."

Silence. Then he said, "Hold on."

Jessica heard a dull thunk as the cell phone was dumped on a hard surface, followed by the faint rustle of papers in the background. Connor came back on the line. "I need to find the paperwork. I'll call you back."

"Don't bother. Just send a text."

Jessica killed the call before he could answer. Ten minutes passed, and she was starting to think she wasn't going to hear from him when her cell phone beeped.

The text read, They're called Sager Properties. Owner is a Don Sager.

Jessica tapped out a response: Where are their offices?

Connor replied with an address on Colorado Boulevard.

Jessica: Are they open on a Sunday?

Connor: No idea, I don't work there!

He ended the message with a smiley face emoji. Jessica wondered what she'd ever seen in a forty-year-old man who used emojis.

Jessica took Eagle Rock Boulevard north to Colorado and quickly found Sager Properties. It was a small, plain shop front. Not the gleaming, showy premises she would have expected of an LA Realtor. She noticed the lights were on, and a young woman was sitting behind a desk close to the front door. The place appeared to be open for business. Jessica drove farther along the street to find a parking spot. By the time she'd made her way back to Sager Properties, Connor was standing outside watching her approach.

"What did I tell you about following me?"

"I'm not following you—I'm helping you."

"I don't need your help."

"You did ten minutes ago when you asked for the address for this place. I thought I might be useful."

Connor grinned, and Jessica noticed his jaw was bruised where she'd hit him. She wished she had hit him harder.

She said, "Okay, but let me do the talking."

"You're the boss."

The girl behind the desk was several years younger than Jessica and about half the age of Connor. Pretty, slim, brunette. Her silver name tag identified her as Rachel. She glanced up from the copy of *Marie Claire* she'd been flicking through.

"Good afternoon, how can I help —" She did a double take when she noticed Connor's wounded jaw. "Good lord, what happened to your face? Are you okay?"

Connor jutted his thumb in Jessica's direction. "She beat me up."

Rachel laughed nervously, like she wasn't sure whether he was joking. "So, um, how can I help you?" she asked. "Are you guys looking to rent someplace?"

"We're not a couple," Jessica said sharply. "We're both private investigators looking for some information about one of your properties."

"Um, sure. Which one?"

The question was addressed to Jessica, but the girl couldn't take her eyes off Connor. She was clearly getting the sexy, wounded-hero vibe from him.

Jessica said, "A Craftsman cottage on Morrison Avenue, here in Eagle Rock. The place has been empty for the last twenty-five years. We need to know the name of the person who last rented the property and made the monthly payments."

Rachel showed no reaction to the address, and Jessica figured she was too young to understand the significance of the house or have any idea what had happened there.

"I'm sorry," Rachel said. "I don't have the authority to hand over clients' personal information. I'm just here to make bookings for viewings."

"Who does have the authority?" Jessica asked.

"My boss, Mr. Sager, but I'd rather not bother him on a weekend unless it's an emergency. You could try again tomorrow, but I'm not sure he would be willing to give out the information either."

"You do have access to the files, though?"

Rachel nodded.

"We really need the information as soon as possible," Jessica said. "It would be a big help if you could just let us have a very quick look at the paperwork."

Rachel shrugged. "Sorry, I can't help you."

Connor said, "How about you take a peek at the file and write the name down? We don't have to see anything official, and no one ever has to know you helped us out."

"I really shouldn't . . ." The young woman twirled a pen between her fingers. Looked up at Connor from under long eyelashes.

He said, "I'd really appreciate it, Rachel."

Jessica wasn't sure who was flirting hardest. She said, "I'll wait outside."

Out on the sidewalk, she lit a cigarette and waited for Connor. He reappeared a couple of minutes later, a pink Post-it Note in his hand, a triumphant look on his face.

Jessica dropped the cigarette, eyed the Post-it. "Any luck?"

"Getting Rachel's number? Sure."

Jessica rolled her eyes. "You're old enough to be her father."

"I'm joking," Connor said. He held up the slip of paper. "The name of the person who rented the house on Morrison and who made the monthly payments. You were right—it was someone else. Eleanor wasn't paying a cent to stay in that place."

Jessica's heartbeat quickened. She tried to grab the Post-it, but Connor held it out of her reach.

"Am I forgiven yet?" he asked.

"Yeah, whatever. Just give me the goddamn note."

He handed over the bright square of paper, and she stuffed it into her jeans pocket, then turned and set off along Colorado toward her truck.

"Where are you going?" Connor called after her.

Jessica ignored him. She wouldn't be surprised if he did have Rachel's number on another pink Post-it. Once back in the Silverado, she drove around the block and parked in a small residential street. She pulled the slip of paper from her pocket and stared at the name printed in Rachel's neat handwriting.

Those jigsaw pieces that had been missing from Eleanor Lavelle's life started to fall into place. For the first time since she'd arrived in Eagle Rock, Jessica felt like she was seeing the full picture.

The two words written on the piece of paper she held in her hand was the name of her real father; she was sure of it. Jessica picked up her cell phone from the charger on the dash.

It was time for a family reunion.

31

PRYCE

Medina was halfway out of his seat before he had even replaced the phone receiver and had one arm stuffed into his leather jacket by the time he'd finished speaking to Pryce across the desk.

"That was my buddy at QuikCar," he said. "His buddy at the Hollywood store thinks he has a match for the car from the CCTV. It's in their lot right now. I said we'd go check it out."

"Okay, let me just print off some stills."

Pryce pulled up the footage, took some screenshots, and sent them to the printing queue. He picked up the pages from the printer tray on the way out of the squad room. Adrenaline was starting to pop in his veins.

They emerged into humidity so stifling Pryce's shirt was stuck to his back by the time they wove their way past a dozen patrol cars and found his Dodge Charger parked close to the lot's exit. He had no idea how Medina could stand to wear heavy leather in this suffocating heat. They needed a good storm to break the hot spell.

Inside the car, Pryce cranked the AC up to the kind of level a city morgue worker would find cold, edged out onto Wilcox, and hopped onto Santa Monica Boulevard heading west. They cruised past low-rent studios and fast food strip malls and liquor stores and eventually found QuikCar's Hollywood premises next to a couple of burger joints.

The office was a single-story white building with a medium-size parking lot housing around a half dozen vehicles. There was no sign of a red Ford or any other red car. Pryce and Medina exchanged glances and shrugged.

The outdoor seating area of the restaurant right next door was filled with families making the most of a laid-back Sunday. There was loud chatter and babies crying and the clatter of metal cutlery being dropped onto plates. The distinct aroma of charred meat and fried onions and greasy french fries drifted on the warm breeze. Pryce could feel his cholesterol levels rising just sniffing the air.

Medina said, "If we don't have any luck with my buddy's buddy, at least dinner is figured out."

"If you say so."

Behind the counter of QuikCar, they found a fat guy in his early thirties sweating behind a desktop fan. He looked like he ate breakfast, lunch, and dinner at the restaurant next door seven days a week.

"Detectives?" he asked.

They nodded, and he wiped a hand on his work pants and offered it to Pryce and Medina. They all shook and introduced themselves. The guy behind the counter told them his name was Jimmy, even though it was right there on his plastic QuikCar name tag.

"I'm Ken's buddy," Medina said. "What you got for us, Jimmy? We couldn't help but notice there were no red cars in the lot outside. The Ford hasn't been rented since you spoke to Ken earlier, has it?"

"No, no, not at all. It's in our smaller lot out back. Follow me."

Jimmy ducked out from behind the counter and led them back out the front door and around the side of the building. A fire truck–red Ford Focus was squeezed between two silver Hondas, butt facing out.

"This is the staff lot," Jimmy explained. "I moved the Ford around here so you could give her the once-over without an audience from the folks dining at Crazy Burger next door."

Medina said, "Smart thinking, Jimmy."

Pryce took the folded printouts from his pants pocket. The digits on the license plate in front of them matched what they could see in the image, the barcode was in the same position, and Pryce could now see that what looked like a black smudge on the roof of the car in the footage was actually a roof rack.

"Popular with customers planning on surfing or cycling," Jimmy said, following Pryce's gaze. "You think this is the car you're looking for?"

"I think so," Pryce said, handing Medina the printed sheets of paper. "Vic?"

Medina did his own quick comparison of the Ford Focus in front of them with the car from the CCTV images and nodded in agreement. "As sure as I can be." He turned to Jimmy. "You able to pull up the rental agreement from last Saturday?"

Jimmy looked uncomfortable. He patted the hood of the fancier of the two Hondas. "My boss, Mr. Peterson, is here. Popped in for a couple of hours unexpectedly to catch up on some paperwork. I'll have to run it past him first."

Medina said, "Sure, no problem. Where can we find Mr. Peterson?"

Jimmy said, "He's in the back office. Follow me."

The three men retraced their steps back around the side of the building and through the front door. Jimmy ducked behind the counter again and knocked gently on a closed door. He waited a few seconds, smiling awkwardly at Pryce and Medina, before a muffled response came from the office beyond the door.

Jimmy slipped inside, closed the door behind him, and reemerged thirty seconds later with an even larger man. He was about fifty, with matted salt-and-pepper hair, a couple of double chins, and love handles that were fully testing the seams of his branded QuikCar polo shirt. If Crazy Burger gave out loyalty cards, the ones belonging to the car rental place's staff would be covered in stamps.

"Mr. Peterson? I'm Detective Pryce, and this is my partner, Detective Medina."

They both flashed their badges.

"Please, call me Stan." Peterson pumped both their hands enthusiastically. "I understand from Jimmy here you need my help with an investigation? How can I be of assistance, Detectives?"

Pryce explained how a car they were trying to trace, which was connected to a serious crime, was possibly parked in QuikCar's back lot, and they needed the details of the customer who'd rented the car last weekend as soon as possible.

Peterson asked, "Do you have a warrant?"

Pryce said, "Here's the thing, Mr. Peterson. *Stan.* We could get a warrant, and we *would* get a warrant, but it would mean getting hold of a judge and filling out paperwork and cutting through red tape. All of which takes time. And it's Sunday, and it's getting late, so the ball might not even get rolling until tomorrow morning."

"I completely understand, but—"

Pryce interrupted. "When I said we were investigating a serious crime, I was talking about a homicide. This car could lead us to the perpetrator before he attacks another young woman. Or we could waste time standing here talking all day?"

Peterson's eyes widened. "Is this to do with the college student found in the motel on La Brea?"

Pryce held Peterson's eye. "I can't go into details about the investigation, but your cooperation could be vitally important in helping us catch this guy."

"Christ, my daughter is at Cal State." Peterson ran a hand through his hair, thought hard for a moment. "Here at QuikCar, we take the privacy of our clients very seriously. We like to think we run a top-notch operation in Hollywood in particular. However, on this occasion, as we are talking about a matter of urgency, I'm prepared to bend the rules this once."

Pryce said, "Your cooperation is very much appreciated, Stan."

Peterson shook the mouse to wake up the computer and tapped some keys. He looked up from the screen at Pryce and Medina. "Oh, and if you are ever looking to rent a car, I'm sure we could offer a special deal for our friends in the police department."

Medina said, "We'll bear that in mind."

Peterson said, "The Ford Focus has been rented twice since last weekend, and all of our cars are thoroughly cleaned and waxed and polished to the highest standard after use, so I'm afraid your CSI team won't have much luck finding anything. We do a very thorough job with all of our vehicles. As I said, this is a top-notch operation."

"I don't doubt it for a minute, Stan," Medina said.

"Okay," Peterson said, reading the screen. "The customer you're interested in rented the car lunchtime on Saturday and returned the vehicle early evening the next day. A short-term rental." He turned to his colleague. "Jimmy, can you go fetch this file?"

"Of course, Mr. Peterson." Jimmy glanced at the screen, then walked over to a metal file cabinet, unlocked it with a small key from a jangling bunch produced from his pants pocket, and thumbed through a thick stack of files. He produced a slim green folder from the drawer. "Here we go."

Peterson snatched the folder from Jimmy's grasp and held it out to Pryce. Inside was a Xerox copy of both the rental agreement and the customer's driver's license.

The photo showed a glowering thirty-year-old man with a blond buzz cut and a cold dead-eyed stare.

32

PRYCE

Nate Daniels resided in Echo Park, according to the information filled out on the rental agreement. Pryce and Medina thanked Peterson and Jimmy for their help and jumped back into the Dodge Charger.

While Pryce drove east, in the general direction of Dodger Stadium, Medina made a call and received confirmation the address was accurate, that Daniels had no prior convictions, and that he had a vehicle registered in his name.

A black Subaru SUV.

Medina said, "I've ordered a BOLO on the Subaru in case our friend Mr. Daniels isn't at home. But if he already has a car of his own, why rent one?"

"Would you use your own car as the getaway from a murder scene?"

"Good point."

Daniels's apartment was on the second floor of a three-story cream cement block, with front doors leading straight onto narrow wraparound balconies. Two stairwells provided access to each floor at opposite ends of the building. It looked a little like a motel but without the free Wi-Fi and cable TV.

The sound of their footsteps echoed in the stairwell as Pryce and Medina made their way to the second level and found the apartment halfway along the balcony. The day had darkened suddenly, and a low rumble sounded in the distance before the sky lit up with a flash of white.

"Lightning," Medina said.

Pryce nodded. "Storm's coming."

They each withdrew a Beretta 92FS from their hip holsters and hugged the wall on either side of the door. Pryce's nerves were tuned tighter than a guitar string. He looked at Medina. His partner's jaw was set, his face tense. Pryce felt the familiar rush of adrenaline flood his veins.

Medina pounded on the door. "LAPD! Open up!"

They waited. There was no answer. They could hear the muffled sound of television sets burbling in other apartments. The smell of food being cooked wafted through open windows. There was no sign of life from inside apartment 210. Medina pounded again. The sound was hollow. A cheap door that wouldn't offer too much resistance.

It didn't.

Medina stepped back, braced himself against the balcony ledge, and aimed a heel at the lock, putting as much weight as possible behind the kick. The door and the frame splintered. The detectives made their way into a small dim hallway, both leading with their weapons.

Medina peeled off to the right, through a doorway into the living room. Pryce took the bedroom on the left. The furnishings were sparse. An unmade queen bed, dresser, and built-in closet. Most of the floor space was taken up by weights and a bench press machine. A typical bachelor apartment. Pryce crouched down and looked under the bed. He pulled open the closet doors and pushed aside hangers filled with suits and jeans and shirts. No Nate Daniels.

"Bedroom is clear!" he called.

"Living room is clear too!"

Pryce tried the bathroom next. The shower screen was still dappled with water. He reached down and touched a towel dumped on the tiled floor. It was damp. He heard a tap, tap, tap on the small frosted window and jumped. Then realized it was the sound of heavy rainfall outside.

"Bathroom is clear! We just missed him."

"Pryce," Medina called. "Take a look in here."

They met in the kitchen, where Medina silently pointed to a coffee mug on the table. Steam rose from the black liquid. Pryce crossed the small room and placed a hand against the coffee pot on the counter.

"Hot," he mouthed at Medina.

Daniels was still in the apartment.

They both raised their guns again and edged quietly toward the doorway. A crash came from the hallway, followed by another bang. The sound of wood on wood. Pryce and Medina burst out of the kitchen and saw the door to a small hallway closet was lying open and a mop and vacuum cleaner were upended on the floor. The busted front door was still shaking on its hinges where it had been thrown open against the wall as Daniels had made his noisy escape.

Pryce heard footsteps pounding on concrete outside the apartment and emerged onto the wraparound balcony just as a blond man disappeared down the stairwell. He raced after him, taking the stairs two at a time, switching the gun to his left hand so he could grasp the railings for support.

Outside, the rain was coming down hard. Pryce took in the empty street to his right. No sign of Daniels. He headed left and stuck his head around the side of the building, where he could just see through the heavy downpour a guy in dark clothing about halfway down a narrow alleyway that ran between the apartment block and the neighboring one.

Pryce gave chase, sprinting past local gang tags scrawled on the walls on either side, dodging trash cans that hadn't been emptied in days. His shirt and pants were plastered to his body, his loafers slipping and sliding on the slick asphalt. But he was still fast, and he was closing the gap.

Daniels glanced back, saw Pryce was gaining on him, and paused just long enough to throw a trash can into his path. Pryce cursed. He vaulted the metal cylinder, and the debris that spilled from it, and landed too heavily on his weaker knee. A sharp jolt of pain shot through his leg, but he gritted his teeth and pushed on, picking up speed again. No way was he letting this asshole get away.

Pryce saw Daniels take a left at the end of the alleyway, and he slowed, pressing himself against the building, breathing hard. His knee throbbed. He raised his weapon. He had no idea if Daniels was also armed. He cautiously looked around the side of the building and saw Daniels clambering up a ten-foot chain-link fence at the end of a smaller alley.

Lightning lit up the bruised sky above. Pryce walked briskly toward Daniels, the Beretta pointed at him in a two-handed grip. "Freeze!" he shouted. He blinked raindrops out of his eyes, kept two hands on the grip of the gun. "LAPD. Get down from that fence, and put your hands up."

Daniels had one leg over the top of the fence. He looked at Pryce, then down at the other side of the fence, as though weighing up the options.

"Don't even think about it, Daniels," Pryce yelled. "I will shoot, and I won't miss."

Daniels paused a beat, then slid back down the fence and landed on his haunches, his back to Pryce. He straightened up and slowly raised his arms, showing he was unarmed.

"It's cool, man," he shouted, looking over his shoulder. "Just don't shoot me."

Pryce approached the suspect, still holding the gun in one hand, the other reaching to unclip the cuffs from his holster. Too late, he saw Daniels spin around in a rapid, fluid movement, leg outstretched. The heel connected with Pryce's gun hand. The firearm was knocked from his grasp, and he saw it skid across the wet asphalt out of reach.

Daniels was on top of him all of a sudden, knocking Pryce to the ground. He felt a right hook glance across his jaw before catching the younger man with an uppercut to the gut. He heard Daniels take a sharp breath, but he was strong and quickly had Pryce pinned on his back against the sodden concrete, fist raised above him, ready to rain down more blows.

"I wouldn't do that if I were you, asshole."

Daniels froze, hand still in the air.

Pryce raised his head and saw Medina standing a few feet away, sheets of rain sliding off his leather jacket, his own Beretta pointed at Daniels's head. Pryce shoved the man off him and held him down with his knee until he was able to secure the cuffs on him this time.

He turned to Medina. "Nice of you to finally show up, partner."

Medina grinned. "You know me, Jase. Always like to make an entrance."

33

JESSICA

Jessica ended the call.

Her hands were shaking as badly as a junkie in need of a fix. She felt sick with nerves and excitement.

She had family.

She wasn't alone after all.

Jessica held down the button on the right side of the iPhone and powered it off. She didn't want Connor texting or calling. Tonight, she would break the news about who she really was to her own flesh and blood in person, and she wasn't going to allow a lying asshole to ruin the moment.

Goose bumps popped up along her arms. If she was right about her biological father, the implications were massive. There was going to be a lot to talk about. There would almost certainly be DNA tests. Big decisions would have to be made.

Jessica started the truck, pulled away from the curb, and made her way back onto Colorado. Black angry clouds were gathering overhead, blocking out the blue sky. Rain was on its way. Just as the thought manifested itself in her mind, she heard a crash of thunder, followed by a double fork of lightning splitting the somber sky. Fat drops of rain plopped onto the windshield, and Jessica flipped the switch for the wipers.

By the time she turned onto Eagle Rock Boulevard, the wipers were on the fastest speed, the raindrops now a downpour. Jessica leaned forward, trying to improve her visibility. The red taillights of the cars in front were blurry dots. She switched on the headlights. The wiper blades, which hadn't been used for months, groaned and squeaked and struggled to do their job against the torrent. All around her, sidewalks emptied as folks ducked into stores and bars for cover.

Once on York, Jessica continued on past the Blue Moon Inn until she saw hazy neon through the rain in the distance. Red and blue beer signs behind grilles pulled across windows. Despite the weather, the store's double doors were propped open. The red hand-painted sign above them read RALPH'S COUNTRY STORE.

Jessica parked and ran inside, her hair and clothes drenched despite the short distance between the truck and the convenience store. She headed straight for the booze refrigerators and considered the selection of beers and wine before making her way to the counter where the good stuff was kept.

A college kid looked up from his smartphone as she approached. "Crazy weather, huh?" He noticed she was empty handed. "Getcha anything?"

"A bottle of your best Scotch, please."

"We only have one kind, so I guess that would have to be the best."

He reached behind him to a top shelf and carefully lifted down a bottle of Johnnie Walker. Not Jessica's favorite brand, but it would do the job.

"Anything else?" he asked, slipping the whiskey into a brown paper bag.

"That's all, thanks." Jessica swiped her card across the pay machine.

The kid handed over the bag. "Special occasion?"

Jessica smiled. "I hope so."

◆ ◆ ◆

241

As she pulled up in front of her motel room, Jessica saw the space in front of room 6 was empty. No sign of Connor's green Ford pickup, no lights shining through the small window. Maybe he was on a date with Rachel, the rental property girl, already moving on quickly from Jessica. With a bit of luck, he'd left Eagle Rock altogether.

Jessica couldn't help but feel she'd had a lucky escape. Found out the truth before her heart had been well and truly trampled on, before she'd made an even bigger fool of herself over a man who clearly couldn't be trusted. God knows she'd had enough of them to last a lifetime.

Jessica flashed back to the kiss outside the Tahiti Club, the feel of Connor's hands on her body, the butterflies that had exploded in her belly. The fledgling hope that she had found a reason to finally stop running.

Her face burned.

She stepped out of the truck and stood for a moment, letting the heavy rain wash away the embarrassment. Then she picked up the bottle of whiskey and made her way to the motel room.

Once inside, she fastened the security chain in place. Dumped the baby Glock on the nightstand. The wet rubber soles of her sneakers squeaked against the hardwood floor as she made her way across the room to the bathroom. Her jeans and T-shirt clung to her. Droplets of water dripped from the ends of her hair.

Jessica kicked off the sneakers and peeled off the wet clothes and underwear, dumping the lot into a small messy pile. She turned on the shower, flipped the temperature setting up a few notches, and stood naked and shivering on the cold tiles as she waited for the water to heat. She glanced at her watch as she threw it on top of the bundle of discarded clothing. Just under an hour until showtime. She stepped into the shower stall.

Thirty-five minutes later, Jessica stood in front of the room's three-quarter-length mirror and scrutinized her appearance. She had deliberated for a good ten minutes over what to wear, finally selecting a black-and-white-plaid baby doll dress and black leather ankle boots. She blow-dried her hair and teased it into loose waves. Carefully applied eye makeup and a sweep of blush to her cheeks and a matte red lipstick blotted with tissue paper.

Then she sat on the chair next to the desk and twisted the cap off the bottle of Johnnie Walker and poured a generous measure into the stubby motel tumbler. The amber liquid almost reached the top. Jessica drank the lot in one gulp, breathed out hot whiskey fumes. She badly wanted a cigarette. The little plastic NO SMOKING sign on the desk and the smoke detector above her head told her it was a bad idea. She refilled the glass instead and wiped a smudge of red lipstick from the rim.

Rain hammered against the motel's small window. Jessica could hear the faint hiss of evening traffic on York. Her guest's car would soon be among those vehicles.

God, she was nervous. More nervous than she had ever been while waiting for a date to pick her up. Jessica's thoughts turned to Tony and the night he'd taken her to the Mexican restaurant. Nervously wiping salty frosting from his lips, just before a whole bunch of lies had come out of them.

She reached down to where she had thrown her bag on the floor, withdrew her wallet, and found the photo of Pamela Arnold behind a couple of crumpled twenty-dollar bills. She smoothed out the corners and stared at the woman and child. Jessica couldn't even begin to guess how many times she had looked at the photo, wishing she had known her mother properly. The shine from the print was long gone, dulled by Jessica's fingers tracing the features of the woman's face, unaware she had been longing for a lie the whole time.

Was her name really Pamela Arnold? Was she dead, like Tony's story suggested, or was she still alive? Was she sitting around the dinner table right now with her husband and daughter? Did the little girl in the photo carry around a similar picture from that fall day in the park in her own wallet, just as Jessica had done? Did the answers to any of these questions even matter?

Jessica realized they didn't. The woman was nothing to her. She ripped the time-tattered photo in half, then ripped it again and again. Let the tiny pieces flutter into the trash can under the desk.

She slipped the photo of herself and Tony from behind its plastic compartment. The one she had shown Darla Kennedy in the diner earlier. Their arms were around each other, Jessica laughing, Tony smiling awkwardly as usual, New York stretching out majestically behind them. It had been taken around three and a half years ago. Jessica remembered the moment like it was yesterday.

It had been a beautiful spring day. Warm, without being too hot, a slight breeze cooling the air, but definitely still T-shirt weather. The photo had happened while they were on the observation deck of the Rockefeller Center. A Scottish couple had approached them, brandishing a little point-and-shoot camera, asking if Jessica or Tony would mind taking their photo.

They had joked about Tony being a professional photographer and how the couple had lucked out with a great shot. Then Jessica had asked the couple if they would return the favor and take a quick picture of her and Tony on her iPhone. Later, she had printed off two copies at the local drugstore. One for her own wallet, one for Tony's.

Looking at the photo now, Jessica knew she couldn't discard Tony the same way she had Pamela Arnold. She returned the picture to the wallet.

If she was right about the identity of her biological father, the man couldn't possibly have killed Eleanor Lavelle. And Jessica could think of no one else who would have had the means or the motive other than Tony Shaw. She believed Darla Kennedy had called it right when she guessed Tony had snapped after being pushed too far by Eleanor.

Maybe he'd finally had enough of her. Maybe what had begun as a confrontation over her plans to leave town had ended badly. Jessica didn't doubt for a minute that Tony Shaw had spent the rest of his life regretting his actions that night.

His words came back to her now.

Not everything's black and white in this world, Jess. Sometimes good people make mistakes. Sometimes innocent folk are locked up for things they didn't do. And sometimes, the really bad ones never have to pay for what they've done.

Maybe the guilt had gnawed away at him so badly, the fear of being discovered had been so intense, it had all contributed to his premature death. Someone with an undiagnosed heart condition like his, Jessica figured there was only so much extreme stress the organ would be able to take before giving out completely in the end.

But despite the dark, violent secrets of his past, she knew Tony Shaw had been a good man deep down. Jessica had never once been scared of him, never had any reason to be. He had never raised a hand to her. She couldn't even recall a time when he had so much as raised his voice. She knew he had loved her like she was his own daughter. Just as she knew she would always love him. Their genetic makeup may have been totally different, but he would always be her dad. That would never change.

What *had* changed was that after two years of thinking she was completely and utterly alone in the world, Jessica now knew she wasn't. She didn't have to be on her own. Maybe she did have a reason to stand still, to stay in the City of Angels. A reason that had nothing to do with Matt Connor.

Her thoughts were interrupted by the rumble of an engine. The beam of a car's headlights swept across the dark rectangle of the window. Jessica heard the engine cut out, followed by the dull thunk of a car door slamming. Footsteps muffled by rainfall. A soft knock at the door.

She threw back what was left of the Scotch and stood. Smoothed down her dress and checked in the mirror to make sure there were no lipstick marks on her teeth. Wobbly legs carried her to the door, the boot heels echoing against the wooden floor.

Jessica looked through the peephole to confirm the person on the other side was who she was expecting. It was. She needed a couple of attempts before she was able to unhook the security chain.

She opened the door and smiled.

34

PRYCE

Nate Daniels was in the same interview room as Frank Sherman had been three days earlier. No windows. No AC. Just the persistent drumming of hard rain on a flat roof above his head.

He looked exactly like his DMV photo. Blond buzz cut, tan face, cold gray eyes. He wore a too-tight black T-shirt that clung to hard muscles. Not barrel chested, exactly, but definitely athletic. He leaned back in the chair so that it was balancing on the rear two legs and crossed his gym-honed arms across his chest. Nate Daniels looked remarkably relaxed for a man who had just been arrested in connection with a homicide.

Next to Daniels sat his lawyer. As far as looks went, the two men couldn't have been any more different. Mel Munro was small, rake thin, and mustachioed, and he wore the furtive expression of a weasel. His cheap navy pinstripe suit hung off his narrow shoulders like it would have hung off the hanger in the store. A battered briefcase was open on the table in front of him. He looked like a weasel, but he had the reputation of a rat.

Munro said, "Can we get this over and done with as quickly as possible, please, Detectives? I'd like to get back to enjoying my Sunday evening with Mrs. Munro. We are both devout churchgoers, and she is not comfortable with me working on the Sabbath."

"Happy to spend the overtime cash, though," Medina muttered.

Pryce informed Daniels and his lawyer that the interview was being recorded by the small camera mounted on the ceiling. He withdrew several printouts of CCTV screenshots from a file and showed Munro and Daniels the first printout, taken from the security footage from the Urban Heights complex, a dark-clad figure emerging from a motel room.

Pryce said, "The Dreamz Motel. Where Amy Ong was murdered a little over a week ago. Saturday night."

Munro laughed. "Is that what this is all about? The college student? From what I hear, you've already had one innocent man locked up for her murder. You're about to make it two. Are you losing your touch, Detective Pryce? Is the pressure getting to you? My client is innocent."

Daniels said, "Never heard of the bitch."

Munro shot him a look.

Pryce said, "Allow me to refresh your memory, Mr. Daniels." He took a photo of Amy Ong from the file, the one from the missing person posters, and placed it in front of Daniels.

The younger man grinned. "She was a looker, all right. I'm sure I'd remember if our paths had crossed."

Pryce felt like punching him.

He said, "This is the room where Amy Ong's body was found. The time stamp on the bottom of the image fits with the time the coroner estimates she died." Pryce tapped the dark figure. "And this, Mr. Daniels, is you."

Daniels snorted. "That ain't me."

Munro picked up the photo and studied it. "What you have here is a grainy image of a person who is completely unidentifiable. Now, if this is the best you've got, then you're wasting my time and Mr. Daniels's money."

Pryce said, "I'm not even close to being done, Mr. Munro."

He laid out the next three images: the figure in black heading past the office block of the Dreamz in the direction of La Brea, the same person on La Brea at the corner of Hawthorn, and finally, the perp climbing into a red car parked by the curb.

Pryce said, "These images provide us with a chronological sequence of events as backed up by the respective date and time stamps from the cameras." He looked at Munro. "Do you agree the person seen leaving Amy Ong's motel room is the same person who gets into the vehicle on Hawthorn Avenue?"

Munro made a big show of checking his watch. "If you say so, Detective Pryce."

Pryce nodded to Medina, who opened a file of his own. He produced Xerox copies of both the car rental agreement and Nate Daniels's driver's license.

Daniels was still leaning back in the chair. Still looking smug. Munro was looking impatient.

Medina said, "The CCTV footage indicates whoever was in Amy Ong's motel room around the time of her murder then used the car on Hawthorn Avenue to flee the scene. We've been able to trace the vehicle to a rental company called QuikCar on Santa Monica Boulevard."

He handed the copies of the rental agreement and driver's license to Munro, along with a shot of the Ford Focus from QuikCar's files.

Medina continued, "These documents show the car was rented by your client, Mr. Daniels, last Saturday."

Daniels's chair dropped back onto four legs with a bang against the tiled floor. He stared at his lawyer with wide eyes.

"I'm going to need a moment with my client," Munro snapped.

"Of course," Medina said.

Pryce used a small remote control to pause the video recording. Both detectives scraped back their chairs and left the room. They waited outside the door for a couple of minutes before it reopened, and Munro beckoned them back into the interview room.

Pryce restarted the tape.

Munro said, "My client confirms he rented the car, but he says he wasn't driving it Saturday night. The person on the tape isn't him."

Medina turned to Pryce. "I had a feeling our friend Mel was going to tell us just that. Funny, huh?"

"Not exactly original, though?" Pryce said. "I gotta say I'm disappointed. I would have expected better from you, Mr. Munro. Perhaps you're losing your touch."

Munro ignored the jibe. "You can clearly see Mr. Daniels has a more muscular build than the person on your security footage."

Pryce shrugged. "Difficult to tell, what with the loose dark clothing. I guess it would be up to a grand jury to decide if it's Mr. Daniels or not."

Munro said, "Mr. Daniels rented the car on behalf of his employer. He handed over both the vehicle and the keys shortly after completing the rental. He then collected the car the following day from his employer and returned it to the rental company immediately. He says such tasks are commonplace in his role as a personal assistant."

Medina snorted. "You don't look much like the secretarial type to me, Nate."

"I'm not office based. My duties are more practical."

Medina said, "You mean you're the hired muscle."

Munro said, "Detective Medina, that's quite enough."

Daniels said, "I mean I do things like rent cars and drop them at my boss's house like I'm told to, and I don't ask any questions."

There was a sharp rap on the door. A uniformed officer stuck his head into the room. "Apologies for interrupting," he said. "Detective Pryce, there's something you should see."

Pryce stepped out into the corridor and closed the door behind him. The satin nickel nameplate on the officer's breast pocket identified him as Joseph. The two silver chevrons on his sleeve told Pryce the man was an experienced officer. His hair was slick with rain, the uniform damp.

"What do you have for me, Officer Joseph?"

Joseph handed over a photo. "We found this in Nate Daniels's car. It was tucked behind the driver's side sun visor. We thought it might be important."

"Thank you, Officer. If you come across anything else, let me know immediately."

The uniform nodded and headed off down the corridor toward the exit. Pryce looked at the photo.

"Shit."

He pulled out his cell phone, scrolled through the contacts list until he found the number he was looking for. He hit the call button. It went straight to voice mail. He left a message and ended the call. He slammed a hand into the wall.

"*Shit.*"

Pryce returned to the interview room and threw the photo on the table in front of Daniels.

"What the hell were you doing with this photo in your car?"

Pryce dropped back into his chair and stared hard at Daniels, who matched his stare and said nothing. The only sound in the small, claustrophobic room was the relentless downpour battering the roof outside.

On the table in front of the four men was a photograph of Jessica Shaw. It was a head-and-shoulders shot with a neutral background and professional lighting. Probably a profile picture taken from the biography section of her website.

Pryce had taken a ride over to Eagle Rock the previous night, as planned. It had been late when he'd finally finished up at the office, and any hopes of salvaging date night with Angie had been long gone. He had called his wife and told her not to wait up. Then he had swung by the Blue Moon Inn to make sure Jessica had taken his advice and left town.

He didn't know what room she was staying in, but he knew what vehicle she drove. He had crawled slowly past the row of rooms and back again. It had been dark, and the only lighting provided by the motel was a blue neon light, but the beam of his car's headlights was bright enough to pick out a blue Toyota and a green Ford pickup truck. No black Chevy Silverado. Satisfied Jessica was long gone from LA, Pryce had gone home, drunk a beer, watched a movie, and slept soundly for the first time in days.

Now, the feeling of unease was back. His hand went to his pants pocket and his cell phone. He stopped himself from pulling it out and checking for missed calls in front of an audience. He knew he would have felt the vibration if she'd tried to return the call already.

Even if Jessica was safely miles away, he needed to know why Nate Daniels was cruising around Eagle Rock with her photo stuck to his sun visor. A guy who was being questioned over the murder of another young woman. Whatever his interest in Jessica Shaw was, Pryce didn't like it one bit.

He eyeballed Daniels. "I'm waiting for an answer."

Munro said, "What's going on, Detective Pryce? Do you mind explaining to us all what the relevance of this photograph is?"

Pryce could feel Medina looking at him. He knew Vic would have recognized the girl immediately, that he wouldn't be able to brush off his partner so easily this time. His eyes met Medina's briefly, and he gave an almost imperceptible shake of the head.

Let me handle this. We'll talk about it later.

To Munro, he said, "This photograph was found in Mr. Daniels's car."

"So?" challenged the lawyer. "I'll ask you again, Detective Pryce. Why is this photograph relevant to the case you've arrested my client in connection with? The woman in this photograph is clearly not the unfortunate Miss Ong."

Pryce ignored the lawyer and turned to Daniels. "Why did you have a photo of this woman in your car?"

Daniels shrugged. "It's not a crime having photos of pretty girls, is it? Why you getting so hot and bothered anyway? You hot for her or something?"

"Were you following her?"

He shrugged again. "So what if I was?"

Munro placed a hand on Daniels's arm, indicating he should stop talking. Daniels leaned over and whispered in the lawyer's ear.

Munro nodded.

"It was another job for my boss," Daniels said. "I was asked to keep tabs on someone in Eagle Rock for a few days. Turns out, this time it was a cute little blonde." He grinned. "Not exactly the toughest gig I've ever been given."

"What do you mean 'keep tabs'?"

"Exactly what I said. See where she went, who she spoke to, what she did. Then report back to the boss."

"Why were you told to tail her?" Pryce asked. "What's the significance of this woman?"

"I already told you. I don't get paid to ask questions."

"You said 'this time.' There were others?"

Daniels smiled. "Maybe."

"This boss of yours ever ask you to tail Amy Ong?"

Daniels's eyes flicked to the photo of the college student. He shook his head, but the smug smile faltered ever so slightly. "I already told you I never seen her before. I ain't got nothing to do with no murder."

"Did you kill Amy Ong last Saturday night?" Pryce asked.

"No."

"You're lying."

"Yeah? What time did she bite it?"

Daniels made a grab for the printouts with the date stamps. The smile returned, even bigger this time. He leaned over and whispered in Munro's ear again. The lawyer broke into a smile of his own.

Munro said, "It would appear my client has a cast-iron alibi for the time of the murder. Mr. Daniels was at the gym last Saturday night."

Medina said, "You seriously expect us to believe you were pumping iron on a Saturday night? What kind of loser spends a Saturday night at the gym?"

Daniels pulled up his T-shirt and jabbed a finger at his six-pack. "You wanna look like this? You have to put the work in. You should try it. Get rid of that middle-aged spread you got going on there, pal."

Medina said, "I think I'll stick to spending my Saturday nights in the company of beautiful women and vodka martinis rather than sweaty jocks grunting and groaning. But hey, whatever floats your boat, *pal*."

Munro consulted his watch again. "This is all very entertaining, but I would like to wrap things up now, if you don't mind. Mr. Daniels informs me the gym has a membership swipe-entry system and security cameras in the foyer and the gym area itself, so that should be enough verification of the alibi he has provided."

Medina said, "We'll need the name and address of the gym."

Daniels gave him the details.

"I'll go check it out right now."

Medina left the room.

Munro snapped shut the briefcase, indicating his work was done. Pryce realized the lawyer hadn't removed anything from the briefcase or added to it the whole time they'd been in the room. The guy was all show, and not very good at it.

"Not so fast," Pryce said. "I'm going to need some details about your boss, Mr. Daniels. About these odd jobs he has you doing for him. Otherwise, I'm charging you with aiding and abetting in a homicide. Alibi or no alibi. Believe me, you'll have plenty of time for push-ups and squats while locked up in a prison cell for the next ten years."

Daniels leaned back on the chair's two rear legs again and looked at Pryce for a long moment.

Finally, he nodded. "It's not him," he said. "It's her. My boss is a woman."

35

ELEANOR

OCTOBER 2, 1992

Eleanor touched the spot on her cheek where Darla had smacked her hard.

The redness had subsided, as had the sharp snap of pain, but she still felt stung. Not by the act itself but by Darla's need to lash out. Maybe Eleanor was a little bit impressed, too, she admitted to herself grudgingly. Frumpy, dumpy Darla, who would never speak up for herself, finally finding a backbone.

She had been right, of course. Darla was too good for Eleanor. Brad too.

Brad.

The poor guy had even had to change his name because of Eleanor.

She sipped from another full glass of wine and felt the heat in her cheeks as she thought of how he had tracked her down to Eagle Rock a few months earlier. Terrified and begging for her help after being beaten up outside a bar in Hollywood by two guys who had been caught up in their Tahiti Club scam years ago.

Or Eleanor's scam, to be precise. Brad always did just go along with whatever she wanted him to do, whether he was happy about it or not.

If Darla knew the truth, that his real name wasn't Rob Young, the reason why he'd adopted an alias, she would have hit Eleanor even harder.

Eleanor thought about her friend's advice, trying to work things out with Brad. Maybe it wasn't such a bad idea. She would still leave Eagle Rock, of course, but maybe he could go with them. Be a proper family. Eleanor, Brad, and Alicia, just like Darla said.

She drank some more wine, and a warm feeling spread inside her. Eleanor wasn't sure if it was the booze or the thought of a different future from the one she had imagined. One that included Brad.

She would tell him everything when he got back from the bar. About the money, the house, the truth about who Alicia's real father was. Then, once the check had cleared, they would head to Florida and start a new life together. Just the three of them.

Her thoughts were interrupted suddenly by a noise coming from the direction of the hallway. She strained to hear over the music. It sounded like a soft knock on the door. Brad had probably forgotten his key.

Eleanor got up from the couch and placed the wineglass on the coffee table. Swayed a little as she made her way across the room.

"Whoa." She laughed.

She reached the door and opened it, expecting to find Brad standing in front of her.

It wasn't Brad.

It was a stranger.

No, not a stranger, exactly.

Someone she had never met before but recognized from the photos in Lincoln's wallet. Back in the days when he was more than happy to splash the cash on Eleanor, before he needed a little more "persuading" after Alicia had come along. Eleanor bit back a smile. It looked like old Lincoln was going to be paying up one more time.

Big time.

She said, "I wondered when you'd show up. I guess you'd better come in."

Catherine Tavernier stepped into the hallway and closed the door behind her.

36
JESSICA

Jessica perched awkwardly on the edge of the bed and drummed her fingers nervously against her thighs. She watched as Catherine Tavernier propped a wet umbrella next to the door and made herself comfortable on the chair by the desk.

The woman crossed her long legs and leaned back. She appeared relaxed. She was dressed all in black. Sweatpants and a hooded top and sneakers. Black leather gloves. Her hair was pulled back in a neat chignon. She looked like she'd just come straight from a Pilates session or a yoga class. Apart from the gloves.

"Driving gloves," she said, following Jessica's gaze.

Catherine opened a plastic bag she'd brought with her and took out a bottle of wine, holding the 2013 zinfandel aloft like a prize. "I brought a little something for us to drink." She smiled. "Hope you don't mind."

Jessica smiled back. Her palms were starting to sweat, and she discreetly wiped them on the dress.

Catherine produced two fancy smoked-glass wine goblets. "I brought these too. I guessed a motel room might not be equipped with suitable glassware."

Jessica looked around her meager lodgings, feeling slightly embarrassed. "Yeah, it's not exactly the Beverly Wilshire, but it's not too bad, I guess."

Catherine laughed. "Oh, don't worry. I've seen much worse—I can assure you."

Jessica very much doubted it, but she smiled politely as Catherine popped the cork on the wine bottle and poured generously into the two glasses. As she handed one over, Jessica noticed the woman was still wearing the driving gloves.

Catherine said, "Another bottle from the Napa Valley. It's actually from a vineyard I bought some shares in last year. I do hope you like it."

She watched as Jessica took a sip of wine. It tasted awful.

"Please tell me you like it," Catherine said. "I'd hate to think I've wasted all that money on a bad grape. As you can imagine, Jessica, I'm very careful with my money."

"It's lovely," Jessica lied.

It reminded her of terrible, cheap booze at frat parties while she was at college. She took another, longer sip and longingly eyed the bottle of Johnnie Walker sitting next to Catherine's own wineglass, wishing she could pour herself another large measure of the far superior amber liquid. But she knew the woman really would be offended if Jessica switched to her own booze. She drank some more of the wine. It would at least help provide some much-needed Dutch courage for the conversation that was about to take place.

Jessica said, "As you know, Catherine, I've spent the last few days investigating what happened to Eleanor Lavelle and her daughter here in Eagle Rock twenty-five years ago. And I've, well, I've made some interesting discoveries."

Catherine Tavernier's immaculately groomed eyebrows arched slightly. "Really? How so?"

"You were right when you told me Eleanor was having an affair with a coworker at Tav-Con."

Jessica drained the wineglass.

Catherine sipped delicately from her own. A slightly amused smile played at the edges of her collagen-plumped lips. "I see," she said.

"There's really no easy way to say this," Jessica said. "Eleanor Lavelle was having an affair with Lincoln Tavernier. Your father."

As soon as she'd seen the name scribbled on the pink Post-it Note, Jessica had realized the familiar man in the photo with Eleanor outside the Tahiti Club was the same one in the wedding photo she had seen at Catherine's home in Pasadena.

Jessica stared at Catherine Tavernier now, expecting some kind of response. Shock, disbelief, surprise, anger, outrage. Something. The woman simply poured herself some more wine. "Top up?"

"No," Jessica said. "I'm good."

Catherine held up the bottle, wiggled it slightly. "Are you sure I can't tempt you with a little more?"

"I don't want any more wine. I'm not a big drinker."

Catherine Tavernier laughed. It was a hard sound that grated on Jessica's nerves.

"Oh, come on, Jessica," she said. "We both know that's a lie. If what my personal assistant tells me is true—and I've seen the photos, so I know it is true—you seem to spend quite a lot of your time drinking in that grubby little bar along the street. Like mother, like daughter, I suppose."

"What did you say?"

"I know exactly who you are and what you want," Catherine said. "And I can assure you it's not going to happen. Your whore of a mother didn't get a cent out of me, and neither will you."

"My mother? You knew?"

Jessica's head pounded. The room shifted and tilted all of a sudden, like she was on a small boat on a choppy sea. She felt like she was going to throw up. Perspiration dampened her skin.

Catherine said, "Give me some credit, Jessica. A PI from New York turns up out of the blue asking questions, and you don't think I'm going to check it out? Check *you* out?"

"You've been following me?"

"Not me personally, no. I'm a little too busy for such menial tasks. I did enjoy looking at the pictures, though. That's a *very* attractive friend you have, Jessica. Although *friend* probably isn't the right word. That was quite a show the two of you were putting on outside that strip bar in Hollywood last night."

"The black SUV. That was your guy."

"Oh, so you spotted him? Maybe you're not such a poor investigator after all."

"He was kind of hard to miss."

Catherine Tavernier smiled. "That's the thing with Nate: he's not the smartest. But he's very nice to look at—a *very* personal assistant, if you know what I mean—and he does what he's told. No questions asked. He's also very helpful when dealing with my little . . . problems."

"I'm not a problem. I'm your fucking sister."

"Half sister," Catherine snapped, the calm veneer slipping for the first time. "And even that's being generous. You were a dirty secret, a meal ticket, nothing more than a bargaining chip. You were a problem then, and you're a problem now."

Jessica tried to focus on the older woman. "You knew about me back then?"

"I've known a lot of things for a very long time," Tavernier said. "I just wonder how much you know? Did you know your mother was a dirty hooker who had sex with my father for money and then kept on screwing him again and again for cash? First, she wanted a job. Then a house. Then it was clothes, food, booze, drugs, a car. All paid for by my father in return for her silence. She knew exactly what she was doing when she got herself knocked up. The bitch must have felt like she'd won the lottery."

Catherine Tavernier shook her head in disgust.

She went on. "With people like her, though, it's never enough. She got greedy. When she found out my father was dying, that's when she really turned the screw. Told him she'd go public, claim half of everything he left behind. Ruin his name and make life hell for his family unless he wrote her a check for a million dollars. A million dollars! Eleanor Lavelle wasn't even worth ten bucks.

"Now, if there's something I really hate, Jessica, it's filthy whores who spread their legs and wreck families just to get their grubby hands on cash instead of going out and earning it decently and honestly like the rest of us."

Jessica's eyelids felt heavy, like each eyelash had a tiny weight attached to the end of it. "From what I've seen," she said, "all you've done is spend your daddy's cash to make a success of yourself. You're no better than Eleanor."

"I'm nothing like her," Catherine said. "Do you want to know how I found out about them? While my father was hooked up to tubes and machines in the hospital, just after the best doctors in California had broken the news to my mother and I that there was no hope for him. That's how I found out. How do you think that made me feel?

"When my father asked to speak to me in private, without my mother present, when he beckoned me close to him and used what strength he had left to pull the oxygen mask aside, I thought he was going to tell me he loved me, that he was proud of me. Instead, he told me about Eleanor Lavelle. How they'd met in some grubby strip bar, the paid-for trysts, how she'd quickly gone from prostitute to mistress. Then, he told me about you. And he told me to handle the problem. So I did."

"You got this Nate guy to kill my mother?"

Catherine looked confused. "Nate? He was barely out of diapers twenty-five years ago. In any case, if you want a job done well, do it yourself. Don't bother sending a man to do it."

"It was you." Jessica shook her head. "I can't believe I thought my father killed my mother."

"Oh, don't be ridiculous, Jessica," Catherine scoffed. "I thought you were supposed to be smart? Our father couldn't even make it to the bathroom on his own, never mind kill anyone."

"I was talking about the man who raised me. Tony Shaw. Rob Young. The man who was my father in every way that mattered."

"Rob Young? Are you serious? The guy was a pussy. Didn't have it in him to kill anyone. Weak and pathetic. You know he was there that night? Didn't even try to put up a fight. Just did as he was told. Took you from your bed and left town. Dumb too. Word of advice, Jessica: never leave sharp objects lying around with your fingerprints all over them."

"Why didn't you just kill me, too, if you thought I was such a problem?"

Catherine Tavernier looked surprised by the question. "Slaughter a child while she slept? I'm not a monster." She paused a beat. "But here's the thing, Jessica: you're not a child anymore."

"When did you find out who I was?" Jessica asked. "I only found out myself a few days ago."

Catherine said, "Within ten minutes of your phone call to my secretary. I told you, a PI from out of state turns up asking for me, I'm going to do some digging. The first hit was your own website. The second was a link to an article about Tony Shaw's photography exhibition attended by his proud daughter, Jessica. I recognized him immediately from the photo. Although, I have to say, he looked a lot happier in that art gallery than he did when he discovered your mother's dead body."

"You're sick."

Tavernier stared at her through narrowed eyes. "I think you're the one who's sick, Jessica. You know, you really don't look too good. Did the wine not agree with you?"

Jessica looked into the empty glass she still held loosely in her hand and saw a tiny smudge of white powder stuck to the bottom. The glass slipped from her grasp and shattered against the hard floor. "You drugged me?"

Each word, each syllable, was a massive effort.

Catherine shrugged again. "I didn't want to take any chances with you. The others? They were already full of booze and easy to take by surprise. I thought you'd be different. Street smart, alert, a decent match for me." She picked up the bottle of Scotch, a quart of it gone, and waved it at Jessica. "I guess I was wrong."

Catherine Tavernier set the whiskey on the table and pulled a knife from her pants pocket.

Jessica recognized the weapon as a Benchmade. She had carried one herself before swapping a blade for a firearm at Tony's suggestion. Her own knife had been a quality item, but this one was in a different league altogether. A high-end product. Five hundred dollars' worth of innovative design that could do untold damage in the wrong hands. Double-action, out-the-front automatic opening. Billet aluminum handle. A spear-point, plain-edged blade, length just shy of four inches, and glinting wickedly under the motel room's harsh light.

Not the kind of thing you'd find in the kitchen drawer. Or used by a bartender for cutting lemons and limes for drink garnishes.

The others.

Jessica wondered when Catherine Tavernier had upgraded to a more professional piece of equipment. Exactly how many others there had been.

"What did you think was going to happen tonight?" Catherine asked. "Did you really expect an emotional reunion? For me to throw my arms around you and welcome you to the family? To stand back while you wrecked the Tavernier name and took half of everything I've worked so hard for over the last twenty-five years? I don't fucking think so."

Jessica was positioned exactly halfway between the door and the nightstand. The door was unlocked. The security chain was unhooked. She edged ever so slightly in the direction of the door.

Catherine's gaze followed her. "Don't even bother. I wouldn't rate your chances of escaping through that door even if your bloodstream wasn't pumped full of sleeping pills."

Jessica feinted straight ahead, as though making a bid for the door, and she saw Catherine instinctively move in the same direction. Then she threw herself backward toward the nightstand instead. Jessica's legs collapsed beneath her as her fingers brushed the cold metal of the Glock, sending the gun spinning across the polished surface. Her shoulder crashed hard against the nightstand, knocking the gun onto the floor with a heavy thud. Pain shot through Jessica's shoulder and spread throughout the rest of her body as she stretched for the Glock.

Then the breath was knocked out of her lungs by the weight of Catherine Tavernier's body slamming into her own.

Jessica glimpsed a raised hand, saw the knife coming at her fast. She threw an arm across her chest, felt the blade rip through the flesh of the bicep. White-hot pain cut through the numb fog of the sleeping pills. Hot blood pulsed from the wound.

Catherine shifted her position on top of Jessica. Pinned her arms with both knees and leaned in close. Her face inches from Jessica's own. She pressed the cold knife against the soft, warm skin of her throat. Jessica could feel her pulse throb weakly beneath the blade. She gasped as the sharp point of the blade pierced the skin. Black clouds gathered at the edge of her vision. With what little strength she had left, she lifted her head and thrust it toward Catherine's face. Heard, rather than felt, the satisfying crack of forehead meeting nasal cartilage. The work of one of Beverly Hills' finest plastic surgeons ruined in an instant.

Catherine cursed and fell backward, releasing Jessica's arms, allowing air to flood her lungs. She sucked it in, then reached for the Glock again. Grappling fingers, warm and wet, closed around the grip. Before she could gain proper purchase, Catherine's hand was also around the gun, crushing the bones of her fingers.

She was too strong for Jessica.

Her eyes closed, the fight draining from her fast. Her grip on the gun loosened. She could no longer feel any pain in her arm or neck. Somewhere in the distance, Jessica thought she heard a bang and a crash, followed by the unmistakable crack of a gunshot. Too loud and too close.

Then there was nothing.

37

JESSICA

The storm had passed.

The sky was a cloudless, brilliant blue. The grass a lush green after two solid days of rainfall. The sun was bright enough to have folks reaching for their sunglasses again, but there was a definite crispness to the air.

Fall was finally here.

Laid gently across the foot of the headstone were a dozen white roses, tied with a white satin ribbon. Her favorite flower. There was no card, and there was no need for one. The flowers had been left earlier that morning by Darla Kennedy. Just as she had done on this date every year for the last quarter of a century. The grave marker wasn't the oldest in the memorial park, and it wasn't the newest either. After twenty-five years, the stone was tarnished and worn, its inscription no longer as sharp as it once had been.

Twenty-five years.

Eleanor Lavelle had now been dead for as many years as she had been alive.

Jessica gingerly knelt on the grass in front of the headstone. Her bones still ached, her muscles not yet back to full strength. She could feel the sharp sting of the arm and neck wounds, if she moved too quickly, despite the pain meds. The dampness of the grass soaked through the knees of her jeans as she placed a single white rose next to Darla's bouquet and gently ran her fingers across the name carved into the cold stone.

Eleanor Lavelle had been flawed, no doubt about it. She'd had a burning desire to kick back against a world she felt had treated her unfairly. Jessica knew the feeling all too well, but the truth was Eleanor Lavelle had been more lost than she had ever been.

Her mother had made decisions she would probably have looked back on with regret had she lived to see her fiftieth year. Even so, she was real. Eleanor Lavelle wasn't a picture-perfect photo of a stranger in a park. She was Jessica's mom. She was a million miles away from the tragic backstory Tony had tried to construct for her benefit, but after all the lies, the truth was good enough for Jessica.

She stood slowly and gazed around the vast memorial park. Wondered if Catherine Tavernier's final resting place would be here too. If anyone would mourn her.

Jessica hoped the answer to both of those questions would be no. The idea of the woman's rotting bones lying just yards from Eleanor for the rest of eternity just seemed wrong. The thought of anyone giving a damn about her was even harder to stomach.

A bullet in the head had been the least Catherine Tavernier had deserved.

Jessica strolled past other headstones on her way back to the gravel path. Some belonged to men, some belonged to women, and the saddest ones belonged to babies and children. Some of the dead were long gone and others more recently so. She wondered about their stories. Were they still mourned? Still loved? Did they have family who missed them every single day? Or did they have family out there who never even knew they'd existed? Jessica followed the path downhill a hundred yards until she reached the gates where her truck was parked.

Leaning against his own pickup truck was Matt Connor.

He straightened up when he saw her. Pushed himself off the truck and took off his shades. Those pretty green eyes were full of questions, and his smile was uncertain.

Jessica smiled. "Please tell me you're not still following me?"

"I wouldn't dream of it," Connor said. "I called the hospital earlier—they told me you'd discharged yourself. Figured I'd find you here, what with the date and all. I tried your cell phone, too, but it went straight to voice mail."

"Too many calls from journalists. You know, real ones. Thought it'd be best to disconnect for a while, just until the heat dies down and they move on to their next big story."

"They figured out who you are yet?"

"Nope. They still think I'm just some dumb PI who got too close to a killer. Looks like Darla Kennedy and Mack McCool aren't talking to anyone."

"What about the money, though?" he asked. "Tavernier's divorce wasn't finalized. You know her estranged husband could try to claim everything? If you need to go to court to fight him for it, the media will find out about you."

"I don't want the money."

Connor's eyes widened. "Are you serious? We're not talking a few bucks, Jessica— there's millions of dollars at stake here. It's your inheritance. You're entitled to every cent of it."

"I'm not interested," she said firmly. As soon as she said the words out loud, Jessica realized just how much she meant them. "As far as I'm concerned, Tony was my dad. Lincoln Tavernier means nothing to me, and neither does his money."

"What about the fifty grand?"

"I'll take care of it. Before I leave."

"So you *are* leaving?"

"Nothing keeping me here."

Connor stared at the blacktop, thrust his hands into his jeans pockets, and nodded. "I guess."

They stood there in silence for a few moments. Just the sound of the wind rustling through the trees and the flapping of hummingbird wings overhead.

Then Connor said, "I'm so sorry, Jessica."

"You were just doing your job."

He shook his head. "I'm sorry I wasn't there. When it all went down. I was so convinced Rob Young was our guy I didn't even realize how much danger you were in. I should have been there."

Connor had made a return visit to the Tahiti Club Sunday night, off the clock this time. Drinking double bourbons and enjoying the entertainment, while Catherine Tavernier was trying to slice Jessica's throat open. But she didn't blame him. She blamed herself. Jessica had been as blind to the truth as he had been. Even more so, in fact. After all, she was the one who had invited a killer into what was effectively her home.

Just like Eleanor had done twenty-five years earlier.

Jessica said, "Seriously, don't beat yourself up about it. You know if I was mad at you, I'd have hit you already, right?"

He grinned, then reached out his hand for her own and held on to it gently. "Will I see you again?"

Jessica looked down at their fingers laced together. Just like they'd been outside the strip bar. She untangled her hand from his and stood on tiptoes and kissed him softly on the cheek. "Take care of yourself, Connor. Maybe I'll see you around."

She climbed into the truck. She had Jason Pryce to thank for delivering the Silverado and her suitcase to the hospital. Jessica also had the detective to thank for having such a good aim with a Beretta 92FS. A couple of inches the other way and it could have been her brains splattered all over Hopper's retro wallpaper.

She backed out of the parking lot. Didn't look back at Connor.

Jessica had one more thing to take care of before she left the City of Angels for good.

38

PRYCE

Officially, Pryce was on paid administrative leave while the IAD investigated the shooting. But according to Grayling, it had been a good kill. She assured him the investigation would be nothing more than a box-checking exercise and should be completed within a matter of days.

Unofficially, Pryce needed to understand the reasons behind Catherine Tavernier's brutal slaughter of Amy Ong before waiting for his return to full duty to be rubber-stamped.

He crossed the lobby of the Bel Air hotel and headed for the lounge area. In the far corner sat a man on his own. Pryce hoped he would provide some of those answers, although David Fenton looked like he was trying to find some answers of his own at the bottom of the whiskey glass he was staring into.

Pryce glanced at his watch. It was just after three p.m., and Catherine Tavernier's recently estranged husband, and now widower, was already nursing a Scotch on the rocks. Pryce knew Fenton had been staying at the hotel since being thrown out of his Pasadena home by Catherine a few weeks ago, and most of his evenings since had been spent in the bar, no doubt mulling over the end of his marriage. The hotel's bar staff and CCTV had already confirmed Fenton had been right here the night Amy Ong was murdered. Now, after the events of the last few days, Fenton clearly wasn't even bothering to wait until happy hour to hit the liquor.

"Mr. Fenton? Detective Jason Pryce."

The man looked up from his drink. He was around the same age as Pryce and wore a polo shirt and chinos and a haunted expression. He rose from his seat and shook the hand Pryce offered him.

"Please take a seat, Detective. Can I order you a drink?"

"No, I'm good, thanks. Water is fine."

Pryce picked up a water decanter from the middle of the table and poured himself a drink. He looked around the elegant lounge area. There was a sleek black grand piano and a feature fireplace, neither of which was in use. Dark wood walls were adorned with black-and-white portraits of Cher, Tina Turner, Steve Jobs, and other big names who had probably resided at the hotel at some point. Patio doors led to a small lake, where swans glided by on the glassy surface.

"Nice place," Pryce said.

Fenton took in the room as though noticing it for the first time. "Yeah, it's okay, I guess."

Pryce guessed the most basic rooms probably started at around five hundred bucks a night, and he knew Fenton had been staying in a suite. For a partner in a law firm, maybe the place was simply "okay." To Pryce, it would mean being in Angie's good books for life if he treated his wife to a single night here.

He cleared his throat. "I explained briefly on the telephone why I wanted to meet with you today. It's important we get a proper under-standing of the events that led up to Amy Ong's homicide and the attempted murder of Jessica Shaw."

Fenton nodded, stared at the whiskey. "Where do you want me to start?"

"Was Amy Ong the first prostitute you met with?"

Fenton winced at the word *prostitute*, then shook his head. After a long pause, he finally met Pryce's eyes. "I know it sounds lame, Detective, but things hadn't been good between myself and Catherine for a long time. The first time it happened was on a business trip to

New York with a couple of other guys at my law firm. They'd arranged hookups with call girls before and didn't seem to think it was a big deal, so on that occasion, I went along with it as well."

"Then you started arranging these hookups on your own, while in LA?"

Fenton took a sip of whiskey and nodded. "Yes, although it wasn't really a regular thing. An occasional treat if I'd had a particularly stressful case at work or things had been really bad with Catherine. I found the girls online, usually met them someplace in Hollywood. Then Catherine found out. She'd suspected I was being unfaithful, but she hit the roof when she discovered I'd been seeing call girls. She warned me if I strayed again, the marriage would be over. This was a couple of years back."

Pryce nodded. "We believe your wife hired a man named Nate Daniels on a number of occasions to tail both you and the women you were seeing."

"I'd never even heard of this Nate Daniels guy until a couple of days ago," Fenton said bitterly. "I guess I wasn't the only one keeping secrets." He finished the whiskey and signaled to the bartender for another.

"What about Amy Ong?" Pryce asked. "When did you start seeing her?"

"Around four or five months ago. I hadn't hooked up with anyone since the night Catherine found out what was going on and went crazy. I'd really tried to give my marriage another shot, tried to make things work. Then, one night, after working late in my study, I opened a bottle of Scotch and clicked on one of the websites I used to use. That's when I saw the photo of Cindy. Sorry, Amy. She was so beautiful. I couldn't get her out of my mind. A couple of days later, I arranged to meet her."

"Then she got pregnant?"

"Unfortunately, yes. We hooked up a couple of times, and everything was great. The third time we met up, she broke the news. I couldn't believe it. Couldn't believe how dumb I'd been."

"How did you know the baby was yours?"

Fenton glanced up as the server placed another Scotch in front of him. Waited until the young man had retreated back to the bar before answering Pryce's question. Shame was written all over his face.

"The first time we had sex together, Cindy told me she always insisted on using protection with every client. No exceptions. She even brought her own condoms in case the guy wasn't carrying. But she reluctantly changed her mind when I offered her more than double. Five hundred bucks to ride bareback, so to speak. I assumed she was using birth control. I guess I assumed wrong."

"Amy wanted to keep the baby?"

"Not at first. We agreed a termination would be the best option for everyone involved. I gave her the cash, said I'd wait outside in the clinic's parking lot. You know, be there for her if she needed some support."

"What happened?"

"Cindy couldn't go through with the abortion. She was tearful, almost hysterical. We went for a coffee, and once she'd calmed down, she told me she'd thought of another option. She'd take a semester off college for 'personal reasons,' go away and have the baby, and put it up for adoption after it was born. But she needed me to provide the cash for an apartment and living costs until the baby arrived. It was a terrible plan. I mean, what if she demanded even more money to buy her silence? Or the kid tracked me down one day? Hell, what if Cindy decided to keep the baby?"

"What did you do?" Pryce asked.

"I told her to forget it, that her plan was a nonstarter. Then, and I'm ashamed to admit it now, I left her sitting there in the coffee shop. I had no intention of ever seeing her again. Or so I thought. The next day, she showed up at my place of work, yelling all sorts of stuff about taking responsibility for my actions. She must have gone through my wallet while I showered after sex and discovered my real name and the address of my law firm. I panicked and told Catherine everything. She said she'd take care of the problem. Then she told me to pack my bags. This was a few weeks ago."

A cold chill washed over Pryce. "And you had no idea what she meant by 'taking care of the problem'?" he asked.

Fenton's eyes widened. "God, no. Absolutely not. I assumed she would speak to the girl, persuade her to have the abortion. Catherine always was very persuasive."

"How did she know where to find Amy?"

Fenton took a long drink of whiskey before answering.

"I only knew her as Cindy, not by her real name, but I knew she was a student at Cal State. She'd told me she was studying criminal justice." He shrugged. "I think she'd been trying to impress me. I told Catherine what I knew and showed her Cindy's photo on the website listing." He held Pryce's gaze. "You have to believe me, Detective, when I tell you I had no idea what my wife had planned for that poor girl."

Pryce said, "The knife Catherine Tavernier used to attack the private investigator in Eagle Rock a couple of days ago is a match for the wounds that were inflicted upon Amy Ong. We also have Mr. Daniels's statement confessing to following both women on Catherine Tavernier's orders. What I need from you, Mr. Fenton, is as much information as you can recall about other prostitutes you have used in the past. Names, websites, hotels where you met. Anything at all."

Fenton looked shocked. "What? You don't seriously believe . . . ?"

In the statement she'd provided from her hospital bed that morning, Jessica had told how Catherine Tavernier had boasted about "the others" before attempting what would be her final attack. That she appeared to have a pathological hatred of women she believed seduced so-called family men to make easy money. And Pryce didn't believe for one second that after claiming Eleanor Lavelle as her first victim, Catherine Tavernier had waited twenty-five years to carry out another kill.

"We have reason to believe your wife may have killed other young women. Women you inadvertently led her to. Did you tell her about the other prostitutes you used?"

Fenton nodded. "Some of them. The ones I'd been seeing when she first found out about the call girls."

Pryce stood. "I'll be in touch for that list."

Then he walked out of the hotel, leaving David Fenton the way he had found him, staring into a glass filled with expensive whiskey that he hoped would do little to provide the man with any solace.

39

JESSICA

As she cruised down Los Feliz Boulevard toward Hollywood, Jessica realized she was excited at the thought of being back on the road again soon. She buzzed down the truck's window, leaned her elbow on the sill, and enjoyed the feel of the wind ruffling her hair. "L.A. Woman," by the Doors, blasted from the radio.

Jessica turned onto a narrow residential street and pulled up in front of a two-story redbrick building that took up the entire block. It stood proudly in well-kept grounds dotted with other smaller buildings. An American flag hung limply from a white flagpole stuck in the front lawn. As she walked up the path toward the front entrance, Jessica could hear the tinkly sound of kids' laughter from the backyard.

The reception area was light and bright and airy. Off to one side was a small waiting area with three seats for adults and an old rocking horse and a yellow plastic bucket overflowing with toys for younger visitors. Messy, splotchy paintings were scotch-taped to plain white walls. They were mostly tiny handprints in gooey primary paint colors or haphazard stick figures of families who were probably no longer together.

Jessica strode over to the reception counter, where a middle-aged woman was pouring coffee into a mug. She smiled sheepishly and set it down. "Sorry. You caught me on my coffee break. How can I help you?"

"I was hoping you might tell me how to get in touch with Miss Angeline?"

"I'm afraid you just missed her. She left about an hour ago."

"Miss Angeline still works here?"

"Oh, yes. Twice a week."

"I thought she'd be retired by now. She must be pretty old."

The woman laughed. "She's eighty-two and in better shape than the rest of us here at the children's home."

"Do you have an address or a number where I could contact her? I'm leaving town today."

The woman shook her head. "We can't give out information on our staff or residents. Is it something I could help with?"

"I have a package for Miss Angeline. Could I leave it here for her to pick up?"

"Of course."

Jessica pulled the Thrifty's bag from her purse and set it down on the counter.

The woman eyed it curiously. "Any message?"

Jessica thought for a moment. Then she said, "Tell her it's a gift from Eleanor Lavelle's daughter."

Jessica was in the middle of the Mojave Desert, about halfway between Barstow and Baker, when she remembered Tony's letter. Still stuffed in the glove compartment, still unread.

She pressed her foot harder on the gas and kept on going. Tried to focus on the breathtaking emptiness of the road stretching out in front of her, the vast expanse of arid brush on either side, the Joshua trees reaching up toward a cerulean sky. Tried not to think about what he might have written her. Thought about nothing else.

When Pryce had handed Jessica the envelope, she had thought the sight of Tony's handwriting, his words, would have been too hard to take. Later, she'd feared she might be faced with a confession. Tony, unburdening himself from beyond the grave by burdening Jessica with the knowledge he had killed her mother.

Now? She had no idea what he'd felt compelled to commit to paper, what Jessica needed to know, that he couldn't bring himself to tell her face to face when he was still alive.

When she did finally stop, it was the little needle hovering just above the *E* on the dash that forced her to pull off I-15 into Baker. Jessica filled the tank at a 76 gas station, then parked next door at the country store, where she bought a six-pack of Bud Light.

"Long journey ahead?" asked the sales assistant.

"Yeah," Jessica said.

"Where you going?"

"I haven't decided yet."

Jessica handed him some bills and shoved the change in her pocket. Outside, the world's tallest thermometer read seventy-two.

Jessica climbed behind the wheel of the Silverado but didn't start the engine. She popped the tab on a Bud Light and drained the can before crushing it and dumping it on the passenger seat. She retrieved the envelope from the glove compartment and ran a finger carefully under the gummed seal. Pulled out the letter.

It wasn't a letter.

It was a DNA test report.

Dated a little over ten years ago. There were a lot of numbers she didn't understand. There were three columns headed with a case number, the child's name, and the alleged father's name. The names were Jessica Shaw and Tony Shaw. The number at the bottom of the page she did understand. Probability of paternity: 99.9998 percent.

Jessica didn't know how he'd obtained her sample. She didn't care.

Tony Shaw.

Rob Young.

Brad Ferezy.

Only one name mattered.

Dad.

Back on I-15, Jessica drove another couple of miles, not knowing where she was heading to. She pulled onto the shoulder and got out of the truck. Stood in a dust cloud that had been kicked up by the big wheels and thought for a moment. Then she pulled a dime from her back pocket.

Heads for north, tails for south.

Jessica flipped the coin in the air and let it fall to the desert floor. Crouched down, picked it up, and wiped it clean of dust.

She looked at it and smiled.

Then she got back in the truck and drove.

ACKNOWLEDGMENTS

I wrote a story, but plenty of people played a part in helping to turn it into a book.

First of all, a massive thank-you to my brilliant agent, Phil Patterson, for believing in me and for being such a huge support throughout this journey so far. Thanks, also, to the rest of the team at Marjacq.

To the fantastic team at Thomas & Mercer, thanks for taking a chance on me and Jessica Shaw. Especially my editor, Jack Butler, for showing so much enthusiasm and belief right from the start.

I was lucky to have some awesome early readers who provided feedback and encouragement just when I needed it most. So thank you to Dan Stewart, Ian Patrick, Douglas Skelton, and Liz Barnsley.

An extra-special thank-you to Susi Holliday, not only for being an early reader but also for recommending me to the best agent I could have asked for and for offering advice and patiently answering all my daft questions.

To my mum, Scott, Alison, Ben, Sam, and Cody, thanks for your constant love and support. And a special mention for my dad, who gave up so much of his time to take me to all the libraries in Glasgow and fueled my love of reading. I know you would be so proud of this book.

Thanks also to the friends (especially Lorraine Hislop and Darren Reis) who put up with me talking about writing a book for years before

I finally got around to doing it. I told you I would! And thank you to my Californian cousin, Kirsty Fowler, for keeping me right on all things American.

Last but definitely not least, thank you to my readers. I hope you enjoyed reading *Thin Air* as much as I enjoyed writing it. Please keep in touch at www.lisagraywriter.com.

ABOUT THE AUTHOR

Lisa Gray has been writing professionally for years, serving as the chief Scottish soccer writer at the Press Association and the books editor at the *Daily Record Saturday Magazine*. Lisa currently works as a journalist for the *Daily Record* and *Sunday Mail*. This is her first crime novel. Learn more at www.lisagraywriter.com.